PRAISE FOR GOING HOME

"This is a story about courage and confronting danger. The segments outside Troy are thrilling in their descriptions of battles and camp life, and our hero's ruminations on how and why to continue fighting form the heart of both stories. Dan uncovers his own dharma, the life-path that fulfills his existence, as he meets epical challenges. This book can change your life."

—*Reader's review* (Judith K. Wilson)

Online Book Club, the reviewer wrote:
"I loved reading the book."

"It takes the reader through the gradual process of hatching a political career. The author, being a Buddhist, also includes his thoughts/reflections in every chapter of the book. The book has a poetic ending. I liked it.

"I must admit that the author's style of writing will leave the reader with many things to ponder, e.g., the story of the Greek war against Troy, which appears in italics in the book. . . . Some will wonder why and how the political part of the story and the historical Greek war against Troy converge in an author's mind and fit in one book. Well, the author's creativity tells it all.

"The author developed his characters and themes masterfully and thought-fully. I recommend it to everyone who believes that there is hope for a green economy in the USA and all over the world."

—*Review #22604*

"Macek (*A Rose from Charlie and Marie*, 2006) humorously chronicles Dan's unlikely rise from private obscurity . . . . Dan's quest isn't merely a political one—his ultimate goal is 'transcendence . . . .' [His] 'visions' are interspersed throughout the tale and manage to be both charming and . . . delightfully eccentric."

—*Kirkus Reviews*

GOING HOME

Dennis Frank Maček

High-Sierra Productions

This book is a work of fiction. The names, characters and events in this book are the products of the author's imagination or are used fictitiously. Any similarity to real persons living or dead is coincidental and not intended by the author.

Going Home: A Return to Golden Mycenae

High-Sierra Productions
Lincoln, Nebraska

ISBN (paperback): 9781642373813
eISBN: 9781642373806
Library of Congress Control Number: 2019931358

Printed in the United States of America

CHAPTER 1

Reno, Nevada, USA Post-Obama Presidency

Even now—I'm glad to be anywhere. My long existence hasn't always been due to my management. Nor has it always been celebrated. People who know me well have called me a crazy old man to my face. I retort that I'm not very old. They probably understand that I consider their remark a compliment.

You—you to whom I tell this story—might note that I have never claimed to be especially "well" in any respect, and often I have been considered fractious (my wife uses "cranky"). And that's fine. Secretly I take some pride in my vagaries and surly moods because I've earned the right to have them. They help people who deal with me sharpen their self-awareness.

I must have been feeling good before my brother telephoned me that Wednesday because I decided to answer the phone when "Caller I-D" named Harry Hachek. He would call us mid-morning only if he wanted a favor. Then he would bitch about something. I had just finished drinking my morning coffee and I picked up the receiver. With 20-20 hindsight, I can say that if I hadn't done that, I would be a lot better off.

"Dan here," I said. "Whada ya want?"

He just wanted to know where I'd bought my three-stage, heavy-duty ladder and how much I'd paid. And—had I heard that Shell Oil was full-out drilling in the Arctic Ocean off the coast of Alaska since they had found a rich oil deposit and their permit was renewed.

"For God's sake! What we need is more damned oil," Hal almost shouted. "Next thing you know they'll be drilling off shore in Iowa!"

For a second I had to feature what he meant. "I guess that hasn't happened yet," I said. "Or has it?" (I actually began fearing the worst.)

His response explicitly compared certain human bodily functions to the collective mentality of the U. S. Congress, with barbs for the Executive Branch and even the Supreme Court. "I tell you, we've got to take *directed*, drastic action against the greed-heads," Hal added. "It'll be *really drastic* if the government just uses good sense and a little vision."

From our talks before this I knew he was implying that we—everybody—won't transition off using fossil fuels by drilling for more, let alone in pristine waters.

My kid brother (by a few years) had a solid point. He usually did. We called him "Hal" after the mainspring computer in *2001*, the time-trip movie. Harry—*Hal*—didn't mind being considered a "geek." He did have a slight testosterone problem, though, which meant having too much of it.

"So how is Astrid these days?" I said, referring to Hal's living partner.

"Oh, she's fine."

"*I know* she's 'fine,'" I said understatedly. There was no limit to favors I would have done for Astrid.

"I think she wants us to marry," Hal said.

"How about you?"

"Marriage would mean hatching kids. Almost necessarily. I like kids. So I don't want to bring any more of 'em into the world. Not the way it is; especially not the way it's shaping up. [Beat.] If you ask me, making more kids live in this world might actually be considered criminal!"

"Fair point," I said (shrug). "And the world is full of criminals at work."

Came a vocable of disgust that segued into, "Of *course*."

I said: "Y' know . . . you should put your social-media skills to work and drive that point home. We've got *way too many* kids, way too many *people* using up the planet. We're on track for two-point-six billion more, I think by 2050. [Beat.] Can you imagine nine-and-a-half billion people clawing into what'll be left of Mother Earth?"

"I won't be here. You neither."

"We *might* be . . . . Maybe we can chuck a few billion new souls into the Grand Canyon.—I wonder if a lot of Catholics wouldn't mind long-term desert living."

Beat. Said Hal: "Hey, why don't *you* do what you said I should do on social media? You know—put out the word! Create a vast wave of followers in India."

That gave me pause. I took an easy out: "I'm not tech-savvy enough."

"Well, I'm busy. *Astrid*, remember? Look, you're more articulate than me. You know all kinds of stuff. Your life is nicely settled; it gives you space. I'm in no position to save the world. Maybe *you* can help restore reality in the minds of some people. It's a commodity that seems to be grossly overlooked. At least in *this* country."

"Hey, I'm busy, too. You might have forgotten: *I've done* my life's work. *I've paid* my share of dues. So leave me alone. I'm busy."

Beat. "I can help you," Hal said. "It's what I do."

CHAPTER 2

Frontal Assault

Beginning later that day I realized that my personality template had been subtly altered. On a moment-to-moment basis I started viewing quotidian affairs through a different prism: What could—and would—I *do* to stem global-climate change? What should *I do* to block deeper national debt? How can *I* help preclude American soldiers' going door-to-door again in the Middle East? What should be done regarding unauthorized immigration to the U. S.—and what is supposed to be my role? What do *I do* about . . . . Et cetera, et cetera.

My focusing on how to resolve specific issues started to become a habit of mind; consciously I refrained from swimming in a stew of discontent as Hal did (and, yes, I often had). My transformation didn't take firm hold right away, but it didn't take long.

The street past our house runs up a gentle grade for a long block and ends at a naked foothill. Once a day, most days, I'd habitually stride up to the street terminus, turn around, and gaze southerly at a panoramic view of a large part of the city of Reno, with the Truckee Meadows beyond it spreading east-west to the great wall of the Carson Range in the Sierra Nevada. The sight would cause a caffeine addict to contemplate eternal verities, or at least to meditate.

Without forethought, for about a week I found myself at the end of my street maybe a few times a day instead of just once. Early-spring warmth helped draw me out. From my singular vantage point I would stare out as far as I could, then wait. I never knew how long.

Without fail, when I did that, topography and terrain would appear as almost, well . . . Biblical, as though the Levant or Asia Minor had ramified all the way to beneath my feet. Even now I prefer to regard the landscape as *Aegean*—like what I'd behold on the Peloponnesian Peninsula gazing inland from the sea.

If one discounts Reno streets and sprawl (and ignores the high-rise buildings), by looking out at the Meadows from heights in the north part of town a person can imagine seeing outlines of a totally different place—and time. In my experience, though, I rarely need imagination. This I explain here:

Sometimes I swear I glimpse a patch of Aegean Sea beyond arid hills and sun-dappled strand. I am on serious business in the land; all that I see there is part of my home. Familiar immediate sensations, my feet strapped in sandals, heavy leather pulling down on my shoulders, pleasant fatigue in my forearms and hands, everything feels different from what I have known in this life. When I am there, in that land beside sapphire-blue water, air and soil feel good; the country feels right.

But never in my life have I traveled "there." The closest I had ever gotten was on a trip to Prague and Salzburg and Budapest. I have never even been to Italy, let alone Greece.

You see, until now I had told only one living human about my experiencing the lands of the Aegean. Over the past three or four decades—since I was a young man struggling to make my way in the world—during random moments of tranquility (say, while waking from a nap or mowing a lawn) I would feel intimations of that different place—and different time. My mind's eye might glimpse boundless ocean water as though from an open boat, or feel physical sensations totally foreign, or spot landscape images I couldn't identify. These were like seeds scattered over my years, while people would routinely ask what in the world Dan Hachek has been smoking.

One morning about a month before the happenings I have recounted here, I began to realize that the intimations of different times and places that I'd experienced over so many years had subtly morphed into *visions* that I could recall in toto. They were similar to random trailers used to preview a movie. But I could not control when to have them, nor could I block them if I chose. They simply happened. At first this caused me frissons of satisfaction I can't account for even now.

But being a realistic person I had to regard my "visions"—random and occasional—as just dreams. When a dramatic episode set in the distant past would play out in my head, it would recede as dreams do. After this happened perhaps a half-dozen times over a few days, I decided to try to elide my visions of the Aegean to see if I could do that; they *must be* dreams, and dreams you can wake up from and forget. So I tried blocking or preempting and forgetting them. Soon the visions recurred more often, maybe two or three times daily, usually during moments of peace, sometimes before I'd completely awaken from a sound sleep. And they would hover about me.

Moreover, when I am *there*—astride in that semi-arid country by the sea—I learn that developments have arisen in the land; I am involved in hard matters and arduous preparations. I know that we—myself and comrades whose faces always appear shadowed—will depart on a perilous enterprise, for us a matter of honor and urgency. After about two weeks of my undergoing intense, often gut-wrenching, seemingly unconnected bits of drama, I knew that I was not experiencing "dreams."

Roll of drums to signal retreat is not necessary. Our own shouts make clear: pull back at once! From his chariot amidst us Agamemnon himself spits out words of defeat, raw frustration. My driver cuts to our left and I fight to raise my tower shield to fend missiles well aimed.

We had caught the Trojan column scuttling home on the plain, but a company of their chariots and mounted archers lay in wait for us and nearly cut off our return route in line with the south wall of their cursed city. Only the gods would know our fate if they had succeeded.

Rapid retreat truly galls us. Sun and dust—and, yes, fear like that of hunted beasts—take a toll. Dispirited, we reach our encampment. No sanctuary here, we have but a fortified point from which to return directly to our ships. We crave fresh water.

*   *   *

See what I mean? Now you can understand why I felt beleaguered. For several days I wondered whether to be alarmed. But soon I projected seeing vistas that might animate me to live more vibrantly. Indeed my new "problem" *opened me* to live more intensely (sometimes *too* intensely), and it gave me an inspired perspective on the present. Surely my outré experiences could have been detrimental to Dan Hachek's mental health, but I never claimed to be "well" anyway.

At the behest of prudence I decided that I'd better consult the insights of Dr. Julia Tamara Underwood (no hyphen) Hachek. My wife. First, though, I had to divine how to best tell her that I'd been having Aegean adventures, the nature of which I understood about as well as I apprehended the essence of "dark energy."

By now you might wonder how I could be married to an accomplished M.D., have fathered the hero of my life, Jay, an orthopedic surgeon, and have a very smart brother—while I myself had been lucky to survive on Earth as long as I had. The key of course is to have good genes (much to my credit) and *a lot* of unexpected, advantageous breaks. Then to *use* the good fortune. Everybody knows this. What *nobody* knows is *why*. Ultimately.

Throughout my adult life I've been striving to grasp the *ultimate why*. Even now I am doing that—maybe *especially* now.

You could say I've been striving for "enlightenment," whatever that actually means (which I aim to find out). Aside from my good looks, I think Julie and Jay and Hal love me for my constantly *trying* to do "enlightened" things—which might be why I've tried doing enlightened things.

Of course I have had a lot of prime help.

In my formative years I went to nun-run schools, so I've never shaken off (or wish to shake off) a mantle of mysticism. Everywhere—in everyone—I detect spirituality. This strikes me as one reason that we can only guess what being *human* actually means. Still, we had better have *some idea* about that because when we don't act according to our nature we're in deep trouble. Nothing I say here is profound, but I think I was already in college before I got a handle on most of it. Reality always poses a problem for me.

Most of my life I have fancied calling myself a Buddhist-deist-Christian-existentialist. We learned to come up with neat things like this when I was a very young man.

Actually my self-designation is not superficial: From what I've read and heard, the universe has no edge or center; the "Big Bang" was just a recent episode of probably many Bangs; *nothing* comes from nothing, and nothing much larger than your typical amoeba organizes *itself*. Recently some astrophysicist declared that 20 billion (*billion*, with a "B") planets are potentially inhabitable in just our galaxy. The *Source* of all that cosmos around the cosmos around us we can't possibly offend or please let alone comprehend. But we *are* graced with telling details. My—let's say *our*—perceptions of spirituality should tell us something.

A gleaming hint of supra-reality that we're part of is that our Earth is so unique and *organized*. That's hard to compute as an accident. Yet probably (*most* probably) nothing that is happening in this world will amount to a hill of beans (an image I love) 200,000 years from now. Still, we partake of divinity, we *can do* things that are utterly divine; so we'd better make the most of our Selves while we're here. Reality is so simple and difficult.

For the record, I went to Marquette University up in Milwaukee and did hard time at the Universities of Arizona and Texas. Somewhere along the way I decided to become a literary artist—my natural bent—so I turned away from a likely career in teaching or journalism (or some really cool field like hydrology or meteorology). Maybe a bad mistake. I wound up learning how air conditioning works (how to heat and cool), and how to fix and install the equipment, then segued into building my own HVAC business so we could eat better. I had to learn a lot about many things. End of story? Not at all.

My very best friend and the absolute center of my being for the last thirty-plus years is Doc Julie, my wife. (At delightfully unexpected times she has said to me, "You know you're the heart of my life, Danny." And whenever she would say that I knew *my* life was peaking.) Julie is a *uber*-doctor with expertise in many arts, one of which had been raising my hero, our grown son Jay, and the darling girl we lost when she was barely two—our biggest catastrophe.

Karma goes a long way with me. *Good* karma. After more than thirty years of putting out my energy and soul (and putting out, and putting out), finally I'd gotten poised to stride onto my personal plateau and live *nirvana* on Earth with dearest Julie. Our retirement plans radiated burnished gold. I say "poised"—past tense—because of what happened before I could take my first step.

CHAPTER 3

Frontal Assault (Part B)

Basically, I became outraged. Not choking, red-faced furious; just thoroughly angry. Current popular parlance would put me as pissed off—*big-time*, as we'd say, because my anger had been pent up. This occurred one Thursday evening as I watched *The PBS News Hour*.

Bad enough that some U. S. Senators (and a bunch of House members) kept insisting that the U. S. get entangled--and mired—in Middle-East conflicts all over again (as if we hadn't been taking all kinds of costly measures against the Islamic State and Taliban, et al). Bad enough that our fabled "leaders" wanted to cut the budget precisely in sectors where the U. S. should be *investing*. (Human capital doesn't just happen to develop by itself; the same being true for large-scale climate-safe technology and renovated highways and bridges).

But somehow a claque of enlightened U. S. senators and a whole caucus of reps not only announced they were set against two proposed very-sensible measures to arrest global-climate change, they publicly insisted such measures were outright unnecessary. This went atop a current pile of other highly responsible Congressional work.

Later that evening, Doc Julie began to broach the prospect of retiring from her hospital position and our promptly moving to the south of Spain. (Or was it France?) Since weeks before this, I had been decrying the acceleration of my psychic demise—for good reason.

Otherwise I considered my role peripheral in political matters. I voted diligently. But too often those pesky words *karma* and (especially) *dharma* would spring to mind. My unconscious insisted I'd better do *something*—beyond expecting that somebody would.

First I cooked curry for supper before Julie returned from work. As soon as I could I Emailed Harry and sent carbons to Julie and Jay.

"If you ask me, only congressional action can relieve our overheated and trashed-out planet **effectively**," I wrote. "The U.S. does **not** have to go deeper into debt to get the job done right. Right? Not if we spend smarter; not if we *profit* from investments in **whatever it takes** for the country to **rely entirely** on renewable sources of energy. (This wouldn't require using 'rocket science'!) We just have to get Congress to act accordingly (and in the process maybe block policies that splatter dead people all over Iraq and Afghanistan and Pakistan and Mexico and Colombia and probably some other places)."

This is where I Hoovered out some hard words that need not be reported here except for my remarks about—guess what bunch—providing "comfort and support to sickies who want to harm people with military-style ordnance designed solely to kill a lot of people fast." [The word *collusion* or *collude* didn't occur to me until later at night after I hit 'SEND.']

Dinner took priority, so at about 10:00 pm I finished my Email to Hal (and Jay and Julie) by concluding, "You should know we can bypass congressional gridlock by generating **a third party**, the proverbial 'third rail,' that'll aim to get things done. It would only take, maybe, 24 members in the House to get Congress moving. –Beats me what you'd call that party."

Round about midnight Harry wrote back: "Let's do it!" During breakfast that morning Julie remarked that I'd presented some "interesting ideas" in her Email.

"Overall, I'd say the stuff you've written could be considered *cogent*," she said.

"I would *hope so!*" I said with my signature wit.

Fresh water is in short supply but we drink what we have and try to wash ourselves. Few words are spoken at first. Looking back on the day we see that our foray past the east wall had been ill-advised.

"So much depends on you," I say to Agamemnon (and we know that to be less than true, for everything depends on him), "why did you go there to be with us?" He must have understood the dangers of our action that day.

Agamemnon's grizzled beard drips water in the harsh sunlight. His gray-green eyes turn toward home as he considers his words.

"I do what I must," he says.

* * *

Later that day my son Jay stopped by (briefly) and surprised me by agreeing with putatively everything I proposed in my Email to Hal and him and Julie. Jay is also an *uber*-doctor, but unlike his mother who's an internist, he's an orthopedic surgeon, steeped in his specialty. Politically he is a closet Libertarian. For him "reform" means mainly one thing.

"Hey, what you're propounding sounds right on, D. If you get the word out to enough people, and to the right people, that would be a great service," Jay said before he left.

Coming from Jay that was heartening, but I instructed myself to be realistic as well as pragmatic. If I—and a bunch of reasonable, far-sighted, sensitive and sensible people—somehow managed to build the ideal nation, would that carry any beneficial impact on generations to come, let alone over eons ahead? It would! At least it might. But my question slips around primary considerations. It disregards human nature—in the here and now. Thus it disregards the *dharma*. We must do what we must do.

Like most men my age the role of sage suits me. I must have crossed a point of balance because after Jay's visit I found myself resolving to *get on message*. To whom? I didn't know.

First I wrote. In longhand, on yellow legal paper. I wrote that we—of the USA—need Congress to take actual *conservative* measures to preserve what we have and regain what we've lost or had stolen from us. Nothing really profound. We need reform. "*Conservative*" reform. Initiating that—and *fighting for it*—would be the work of a whole new movement. Call it the "Lead Pony-Caucus," or something like that. For sure, I could be counted on to help support such a movement. Maybe my ego drove me to put this into an Email that I fired it off to my usual targets. Then I started preparing trout and rice for dinner before Julie would come home from work.

Of course once I got into my cooking work, the damned telephone rang. Of course the caller was Harry and I happened to be near the phone so I answered it. Hal said he was fixing to call me to possibly learn the starting time of a special city-council meeting that evening. A moment ago he happened to spot the Email I'd just sent him.

We talked for about six minutes, as one topic led to another and I wound up telling him the biggest danger confronting the United States and all civilization is not international terrorism or nuclear insanity or world-wide cyber warfare or even the U. S. government: it's carbon dioxide augmented by other gases. "Plainly *that is* the most inevitable and overwhelming danger on Earth," I said. "Think about it."

Beat. Beat. "Actually, I knew that."

"You'd think it's not immediate or pressing," I said. So far we haven't seen a real plan coming out of Washington. One of our primary national goals is *supposed to be* transitioning to a climate-safe economy. A 'green' economy. Everything, everybody—*off petroleum.* [Beat.] Also coal."

Harry said, "I thought you're planning to propose, y' know, `*conservative* reform.'"

"I am. I want us to conserve, y' know. —But sometimes I gotta wonder why."

Hal let my last remark slip by. He had been privy to the occasion about 40 years before, when I apprised an old Slovak immigrant of what I was learning at the university and what I planned to accomplish in the world beyond personal gains. The *Gestalt* looked possible and maybe likely. "*Goot,*" said the fellow. "Tzounds goot."—Nodding, pulling stogie from his mouth.—But ven you do all dzis, *tzen* vhat?" Several times since then, I or Hal explicitly drew on that minor event as a major element in our maturation process.

"Well," said Harry, "you're going to have to do *some* thing. Looks like it has to be political. Let me know what's going to happen, man. I'll figure out how to get you started."

"You know—you're evil."

"Hello to Miss Julie."

CUNNING

Fear, sweat, dust almost choke us. I cease to hear my chariot bells. Our drum bearers roll out my shouted command— orderly retreat! Hold formations. (We will not flee like startled sheep. I pray.)

Once again the Trojan dogs have pounced on our assault companies. Now they try to capture us with their chariots driving at my east flank as infantry and archers prepare to block our escape to the hills, our sole haven. To my eyes the hills appear achingly distant.

Before I can order a thrust to the south we hear Achaean drum rolls in that direction. Abruptly the ranks of enemy infantry and archers arrayed before us part. The soldiers break for safety inside their wall. Agamemnon himself leads the chariot charge that frees us, and we turn on the dogs tearing at our flank.

My blood still runs high as I approach Agamemnon's chariot now stopped beside a hill. The day is closing into gold. We will disband soon for our encampment. My king and I are grateful to our soldiers coming forth to bring us barley beer.

"A hard day for you, eh, Amphilochus," says Agamemnon, his manner hearty. "Good thing I learned of your plight in time."

"We thank the gods for your arrival," I respond, for in truth our situation looked dim. My o-ka lost three chariots this day. Loss of one charioteer and driver usually means we lose six or eight other soldiers as well. Today's numbers are high, and we were not in battle. It was but a large skirmish.

I say, "Many Greeks died this day."

Agamemnon nods. He gazes toward fortified villages and encampments and hilltop strongholds hard by the walls of Ilios. "All of Troy is acropolis," he says.

*   *   *

Probably Julie and I could not count on dying together in our sleep. Otherwise our best chance for a successful end would be an airliner in which we'd be traveling (sipping cognac on our way home from Tuscany or Paris) exploding mid-air.

Positing that, occasionally I would rub against the grain of normal sentiment (including my own), by saying that if Julie and I couldn't die together, *she* should go first. For good reason. I would not have wanted her taking care of me should I linger before dying and then she ends up being alone (at least for a while). Of course were *I* to be left without her, I'd simply have taken care of business and figured out the best way to join her. Let me go on record (especially now) by declaring that you can't die or be killed. The body can be destroyed, but the essence of you is immaterial and transcendent. Killing your essential-real Self would be like trying to shoot holes in the wind.

Beyond a doubt Doc Julie, as I sometimes referred to her, has a brain as big as her heart—about the size of a semi-trailer. Of course the rest of her I would never have disdained. She didn't actually *need* my ministrations but she got them anyway. Usually I cooked a mean dinner (as I'd done with the trout and fixings) and put out a dazzling array of libations for her to delight in having to choose.

Several hours after I'd sent off my latest Email (which she had yet to read), when Julie arrived home we sat together briefly so she could put her work day behind her before dinner. I played my usual prank of lining up a bottle each of Maker's Mark, Bushmills, Hennessey, a pricey Napa or Sonoma pinot noir, and a cold microbrew. Take your pick, Ma'am. Which she did—with gusto.

Dramatically I swept my open right hand over the array of bottles while I declared: "Here's solid, compelling reason for any drinking man to get *rabid* about fighting global-climate change." I turned my head slightly to make eye contact and said: "These products are fruits of the Earth. They're all in jeopardy! At the rate we're going we could lose 'em all."

Julie absolutely understood. While she sipped at a shot of M-M I outlined the content of the Email I'd sent earlier to her and Hal and Jay, with Hal's response to it.

My conclusion seemed foregone: "I'm going to have to do something kind of radical. Looks like it might be, uh, political. —Although *of course*, yeah, I know; I'm anything but a politician."

"Well that remains to be seen," Julie said absently, savoring her bourbon. For a moment she studied the cosmos, then turned her dark, penetrating eyes on me.

"How's your fiddling coming along?" she said.

"Haven't picked it up for a few days."

"You haven't been doin' it long enough to lay off and not lose your chops."

"I know it."

"I don't suppose you're doing any writing."

"That's true. Just political notes for myself. —Be sure to check your Email."

For a few heartbeats I considered the tenor of Julie's remarks. I declaimed: "Ah, the *writing* life! The *musician's* life, high-brow *and* low-brow . . . . The life of the lab scientist . . . and the philosopher and the scholar . . . . It's all just fine—so long as there's food on the table and drinkable water, and medical and dental care, and beer in the fridge, and the lights stay on." I did not say this to the cosmos or to Julie. I simply said it.

To her credit, I thought, Julie replied that we loved "living our dream" as people liked to gush. But sometimes a person has to set that aside and do more than his *"share."*

Later over dinner, I brought up that maxim about a butterfly in the Amazon rainforest fluttering its wings and ultimately causing actual effects in Nebraska and Nevada.

"So maybe I can be like the equivalent of a noisy butter-fly—right *here*," I said.

Beat. Beat. "Probably I saw this coming," said Julie. "You might as well try to get yourself heard. Maybe that'll do some good. That might do *you* some good."

I declared that I didn't want to be "political." Anything I might broadcast to the world would either be good sense or insight derived from experience. Period. And I could tell she was fine with that.

The next day—during dinnertime of course—Jay came to our house and waxed almost enthusiastic about the prospect of his old dad taking a public stand on thorny, maybe explosive issues.

"Like what issues?" I said.

"Oh, you know, climate change, wasteful defense and intel-ligence spending. The U. S. needs some kind of reform move-ment; we've been *failing* in our fiscal and moral responsibilities."

"What makes you say this—aside from my Emails. Do you know something I don't?"

"Uncle Harrison told me to check you out on the Web so I did. You oughta do likewise."

I thought I'd damned well "oughta."

"What's this about a "public stand?" I asked.

According to Jay, Harry had said I wanted publicity for getting my points across. I replied that I didn't know how *public* I wanted to *be*.

"Hey, you used to use a word we don't hear anymore," said Jay. "*Welch.* Like welch on a debt or a responsibility. Well, y' know, don't welch."

I nodded. Damned kid had a fair point. He also had the advantage of abilities from his mother's side. I liked that his height was more "medium" than mine and his frame sturdier. He could heft and swing his off-road chopper much like a weapon.

Before he left Jay reminded me to look up what Hal had posted on the Web for me. (I told him I shuddered to think.) Then he urged me to "definitely go public. Mom would be proud." Oh, yes, and *he* would be proud.

I said, "I'll see what I can do."

"By all means," said Jay. "Y' know, this could even be huge."

"Nothing is *huge*, really. Except the cosmos. And cosmic law."

That caused little shrugs from Jay and Julie across the room. They knew how I think.

CHAPTER 5

ENTER THE CHAMPIONS

Of all my comrades' faces on that cursed plain spreading from the Bay of Troia only one shows itself free of shadow—that of my king. He says we have always known each other, a truth. I think I helped him learn to read—and use—script of the Minoans and perhaps of the Hittites. He made me captain of all chariot forces at Ilios, but I wished to be home in the Argolid. Shrouds of glory hold no charm for me.

Three days before we debarked on Trojan soil I declared that our champions in lone combat could settle our grievances with Pariamu's kingdom in the known way. Surely Troy has champions to set against ours. On our side are the gods and two of the greatest warriors of all time. We have other champions as well. Any match would be uneven—for the Trojans. We would be wise to take the path I advised, thus to return home soon. Agamemnon's silence toward this counsel meant our course—our destiny—forges in a current beyond human knowing.

Now as we fight Trojans and their Hittite allies I hear Agamemnon's truth when he says (often), "We can never again live alongside these Trojans," or when he says (often), "Long ago we learned a basic lesson—Troy is never to be trusted except to use treachery." Thus I know one thing more: Were Achilles of Phthiotis or Diomedes, Prince of the Argives, to best a Trojan champion, agreement on the issue at stake would be of no more value than a small hill of sand.

As the size of our enterprise at Ilios looms higher and spreads wider, I look for no portents (as does Agamemnon) but for a glimmer, perhaps only a shadow, of a large plan shaping my own little life. Thus I might divine my place in this conflict and take favorable action. I feel the plan put into my life is clearly before me at all times, but beyond my powers to see and grasp it.

"Do you think the gods have a plan for the life of each of us?" I say to my king.

He answers, "We have a destiny. Every man, every woman, even beasts."

"Perhaps within the life of each man the gods lay a plan as well," I say.

I regroup my thoughts and continue: "Do you not sometimes think there is a direction in how you live? It is unrevealed to you—but still you follow it."

Agamemnon shrugs. We stand together in silver sunlight reflected on nearby sea. While in thought we raise off our helmets. I feel dampness rise from my hair. Agamemnon's face shines as a new olive, with a great curved nose and broad cheekbones, teeth *able to tear leather. I think his hair and beard hold more patches of white than mine.*

He nods before he speaks and gazes at the sea toward Mycenae. He knows I know he has twice consulted the seer in the shrine to the Earth-Mother goddess at Delphi (and vows to again).

"To see such a plan is of no use," he says. "For what we see always lies in the past. Even if we look into the future—when the gods grant vision at Delphi—we can never understand why the gods plan for us what they want."

Still, I think seeing the directions and signs in a human's life can be of value, perhaps great value, and I tell him that. Now his eyes beam into my soul.

"We can only give our best efforts," he says. "You know—for you have said—we must act in accordance with how the gods design us, each of us. We can do no more, nor shall we accept doing less."

With this I agree, but I am unsettled. "We might fail to do as we are directed," I say, "if we do not heed the plan within our lives."

"We might."

"For some people this is a cruel twist by the gods," I declare. "Not so cruel as a Trojan dagger, or the sword of Achilles."

*   *   *

Sure enough: I did what Jay advised and found that I was the subject of a "page" on the Internet. Actually, my words— just basic tenets—were the subject. Thanks to Hal and his buddy, who worked with Hal as a Web-master, I was able to gaze upon an eye-fetching layout that trumpeted the birth of the "Conservative-Reform Movement." Even I could appreciate the tasteful design, with the little doo-dad icons and subtle colors and pictures of sky and water and nubile women. Later I learned that Jay and Julie were impressed with it, too, so I was doubly pleased.

Otherwise I gave the phenomenon almost no attention. Even though I had "retired," Julie was doing too many of our household chores. We had investments to cultivate. I knew that sooner or later we'd have to decide whether we should tour Umbria and Liguria or hang out in Tuscany our first time in Italy. I had actually *given up* my weekly fly fishing. Too damned busy.

That was why, having gone public (so to speak), I needed to keep extraneous matters in balance. So late the following Sunday morning I telephoned Hal. When he answered he sounded maybe hung-over but lucid. Despite all my attempts at otherwise, Hal had somehow managed to defend his ignorance of how I think. I planned to sound doubly clear and ultra-emphatic.

"Y' know," I said, "Julie and Jay and I love my Web page, so what the hell am I supposed to do with it now that I've got it?"

"Well, you use it."

"*Use it?!* 'Use it' how?"

"Leave that to me. Just tell me what you want me to say."

"I don't want to *say* anything that I haven't said already."

"You wanna make an impact . . . you gotta make your points known. [extended untoward bodily noise] Excuse me! . . . So write me precisely the main things you want to say—every day."

"What're you trying to get me to do, Harry? —*Blog*? Write letters to editors? Get on Facebook? Make a fool of myself?"

"You won't make a fool of yourself. All of the above. *Make that impact!*"

"I'll see what I can do."

"Well if you're gonna do something, *do* it. But you know that. Life is a journey; how many times have you and I said that. —Astrid,too, come to think of it.— It ain't worth taking if you don't give it hell. You know that, too."

"I thought Life is a fountain." [No response.] "Look, whatever I might do or *we* might do won't make a rat's ass bit of difference in about twenty years, let alone two-three hundred years."

Beat. "It might make a difference *now*."

Complete success in Hal's proposal might not surpass the importance of a thin water vapor hanging over Uranus. I knew that from the start. But his vision had a credible ring to it.

So I told him I couldn't agree more and showed him my own spin: "Put all humankind's importance into a lump and it wouldn't amount to a mote in the eye of eternity," I said, "but, hell, we've gotta *live* here; so do our kids." ("Here" meant Earth.)

"Ain't that so. —Gotta go! *Do* what you think you oughtta do."

So much for my pushing off "tangential matters." But subliminally I got a dose of my own reality therapy. In my mind's ear I could hear myself telling Hal or Julie, "Given our national debts and pollution levels, *and our damned fears,* it's a good bet we've lost our national sanity. Overseas they must think we're crazy or utterly benighted. But we just keep diggin' ourselves in deeper and deeper!"

And I could hear Hal say, "Ain't that so."

Almost immediately my life changed under my feet. Hal wanted me to vent my ideas (and expose my psyche) in political "chat rooms" on the Web. I wrote out a list of issues the U.S. and state governments must confront; he posted them under my name. Jay wanted me to "unburden my brain" by blogging, which I made some efforts to do. Julie urged me to draft and send letters regarding key issues to magazine editors ranging from the AARP magazine to *Playboy.* (Thank goodness for Email.) Something always came up for me to do. Daring to attend afternoon movie matinees downtown became *verboten.* Still, this was a game of badminton compared to the treadmill marathons I'd be running down the road.

One day I took a telephone call from a university student named Scott Upton.

"I've read on your Web page that our political life has been hijacked and you want it back," he said. "You got our attention by advocating 'conservative-reform principles.' At least that's what you say. We're glad you're here in Reno."

Turned out that he wanted me to meet with—perhaps address—the group he represented, Campus Conservatives of Northern Nevada. I declined. Within a few days I received four more telephone calls of the same order (two of them from California). The callers were members of groups so far on the fringe they made the Campus Conservatives appear mainstream. Half-mindlessly I telephoned Upton and asked to attend the next CCNN meeting.

(I did attend, and even spoke briefly against the Yucca Flats nuclear-waste dump and the annual federal budget deficit— and I was politely disregarded. Those fellows had their agenda, which I appreciated, but their priorities were oblique to mine. Which means they were mistaken. This made me resolve to get out my word better.)

Meanwhile I actually did some "blogging." It was gratifying, it felt good, but it sure devoured time. Since I'd begun writing letters to editors, the two endeavors complemented each other.

My "message" was simple: arrest global-climate change by government (led by the feds) *partnering with* clean-energy industries to transform the national economy to a climate-safe one, and balance the federal budget by leveling the military and intelligence budgets to parity with other Western nations. A good start would be to sell off obsolete military hardware (to fund national education initiatives) and stringently prohibit buying any more until the weapons we've got are paid for. Not exactly nuclear science. Unintended consequences we'd deal with in turn.

HOLY BUZZ

While trying to avoid reading newspapers during those halcyon days I noticed that our Congressman, a good guy (his wife might aver) but capable of embarrassing the whole state, was about to host a meeting of local Republicans, ostensibly to set some issues straight but also to raise cash. The venue and time were convenient, so I attended, without my checkbook.

The man had plenty to preach to the choir and he delivered it. And delivered it. Eventually my brain drifted into a different reality. I came awake when I caught words to the effect that our country was leading the world in environmental protection, followed by applause as the speech ended. As I came fully conscious I felt anger rising up in me and taking over. That puppet was selling the same bill of goods shilled by a recent federal administration and its NGO's (certain construction and energy mega-corporations) whose record of acting antithetically to ecological stewardship was clearly seamless.

Someone asked the Congressman a congenial question and got an innocuous reply. That gave me the slightest opening.

I stood up and said loudly: "Sir, I'm Dan Hachek from northwest Reno. You can't be *serious* about what you just said! The U.S. didn't even sign the Kyoto Accord. The fossil-fuel industries have been getting *all kinds* of regulatory breaks, barely to mention at least eight billion dollars a year in subsidies. The fire-smoke that goes into the air from those explosions we've caused in Iraq and Afghanistan—what do you suppose happens to it?"

All the oxygen seemed to get sucked from the auditorium. The Congressman fixed on me blankly. He uttered some inanity; then a functionary spirited him away. For a long moment I was the only person standing; eyes were on me from every angle. Then everyone else rose to leave or gather in groups. I heard dark mutterings but nobody approached me. If even a cop put a hand on me I was ready to break noses.

Shockingly a hand nudged my left elbow. I barely turned and saw an attractive blonde woman beside me, a television-news cameraman just behind her. Channel Two News! The young woman simply asked me two or three questions, thanked me, and went off. To my surprise I was approached by two other TV-news personnel and a newspaper reporter. All questions were brief and easy, my answers anything but profound. I wished they would have let me say more. After I'd had time to reflect, I especially wished that.

Seeing glimpses of myself on local TV news was admittedly pleasing. I thought I appeared earnest, dynamic, conceivably intelligent; they showed my good looks. Hearing my name in the media was sheer pleasure, except for one instance when my addressing the Congressman was inexplicably called heckling. Harry was fully pleased by all this. So was Jay. Julie just smiled noncommittally when I told her about what had happened. After she saw a tiny clip of it on TV news she said, "I should have known you'd get into trouble if we left you alone too long."

Probably I received all kinds of Emails from people who know my address, but I'd gone back to my post-retirement habit of rarely checking Email. I did answer a few telephone calls regarding my recent escapade, and not all were amusing. One caller, a young man, left a cryptic message in my voice mail: it urged me to visit an address in the Virginia-Range foothills (near town) that coming Sunday evening. Then a young woman's voice supplanted the man's, saying I should be prepared to "speak to about thirty people." If I wanted to bring a plate of cold seafood or a vegetarian dish, that would be fine.

I was surprised when I made attending that occasion a priority, and more so when Julie said she'd go with me. We were still in early May so I wore a blue-gray tweed sport jacket with a black tee-shirt and black denims and black cowboy boots. Julie put on a black blazer and slacks and a lot of silver. With her black hair she looked great. Somehow black also suits my ruddy complexion and blue eyes. For us, deciding what shade of black to wear was often a problem. Our destination turned out to be a house that was modest for the neighborhood although it rose three levels.

On the lower level (like a basement, but above the ground), in a large open room, was placed a small podium with a lectern. Behind the lectern a welter of nondescript banners and flags festooned the wall. We'd arrived there at exactly 7:30; a young man and a very young woman accepted our bowl of Julie's brown-rice-and-mango salad and looked at each other tentatively. The pair of youngsters overtly assayed Julie.

The fellow said, "We don't usually have guests at our meetings who aren't invited."

The woman nodded concurrence.

I said, "Doctor Julie here *is invited*. She's my wife."

Downstairs we all went to hear bits of obscure business moderated from the podium by a tall, willowy young man. Most of the forty or so people in attendance appeared quite young and intense, also physically fit. A few old hippies were there along with a handful of forty-somethings who wore braided hair, even braided beards. The air was redolent of incense although sets of windows were open.

In fairly short order I was introduced as "a friend of the environment" and "the man who recently put egg all over the face of our enlightened Congressman." I heard polite applause as I took the podium. My message was "the necessity for conservative-reform," so I went right into it beginning with how the huge federal debt, compounded by out-of-control budget deficits, was undermining every priority and program the United States fosters. In almost no time I saw eyes glaze over. To emphasize a point I happened to turn to my right and clearly saw words on one of the banners. They read, "EARTH FIRST!"

Oops! I had to discard my planned discourse; these people had a different agenda, which I empathized with. (I did manage—once—to point out that environmental protection "is connected to virtually all the other current issues, so we need to take a political approach that's *holistic*," a notion I tried to elucidate.)

Mainly I gave a reasoned pep-talk. Then I urged them to do—in vague terms—just what they were doing. (That's basically how I raised Jay and counseled his buddies.) Thus I covered my rear and my front. Twice I glanced at Julie and felt satisfied that she appeared interested in everything I said. After about five minutes I concluded by making the analogy between Washington and Troy: we were like those heroic Greeks who refused to allow Trojan gangs and pirates to commandeer their way of life. "Nowadays our mandate—our *mission*—is to deny that gang in Washington the rewards of exploitation they think they deserve," I said. "*Gaia* demands that we stop 'em cold! We *dare not* fail!"

I wasn't surprised to hear hearty applause as I left the podium. So I returned and thanked them and pumped my arms in the air to dramatize our solidarity. Julie looked as astonished as I felt incredulous about what I'd just done.

In a little while we all went upstairs to nosh on delicious snacks. Conversation had barely begun when all of a sudden grossly loud racket erupted immediately outside the house; heavy thuds on the doors partly obscured the source of noise to be blaring sirens. Julie and I opened the front door to step out for a look and were promptly arrested by a contingent of law-enforcement types.

Everybody at the meeting was arrested. We soon learned that some vicious pranks committed on the edge of Reno that afternoon were considered acts of "eco-terrorism," so guess who was sure to be guilty. Julie and I never found out whether Earth First! members were responsible for the wanton destruction. Days after we posted bail we were still too busy stinking up officials responsible for the stupid mass arrest. Guilt by association, of course, is pure crap.

Ah, but this forced me to turn crap into gold, although I hadn't wished for it. Now I overtly embodied a "cause"—which had actually motivated me to speak at the meeting. Circumstances enabled me and prodded me to make sure people heard about it. Media buzz is a good thing—usually.

CHAPTER 7

CRISIS POINT

Even now I can hear Julie's voice calling me "a politician" after my speech to our local Earth First! chapter. ("I didn't know you were such a politician!" she remarked after we'd gotten home from the county jail.) A few days later I heard *this* spoken to me in my kitchen: "You oughta consider starting your own political party. —You know, an actual party that *stands for* something you can nail down."

This was said by my neighbor Bully Kendall, a CPA of about my age, still a working stiff, a good guy from Texas.

I regarded him wordlessly. He resumed:

"Look at the way Ross Perot kicked butt. America owes him a debt for engendering budgetary and fiscal responsibility. Even though we've since blown it."

"Surely you jest," I said. "To register a political party, do you know how many signatures I'd have to get from non-party-affiliated voters? In Nevada that's almost impossible."

"No, it's possible. There's lots of young people out there who are eligible but haven't voted. There's more comin' up. People can change their affiliation, by the way—if someone gives 'em reason to. Remember when there wasn't a Green Party? Getting a brand-new political organization off the ground mainly requires a lot of ego . . . and big *cojones*, probably."

"That's why you're talking to the wrong fella," I said. "My ego's long been satisfied; I'm just not willing to put myself out there as a target for all kinds of nuts—figurative or otherwise. Even for a good cause."

Bully sat wordless. I laid out a postscript: "I've done *plenty* of neat things in my time; I don't want to do any more. [Beat.] Shrouds of glory hold no charm for me."

Bully looked at me oddly. Then he said, "Really, you should give it some thought. America needs a good dose of reality therapy."

I said, "Okay, I'll think about it. [Beat.] Not for me."

"Hello to Doc Julie for me," Bully said, rising to leave. "How's Jared doin'?"

"Jay is doing great if he doesn't overwork."

After Bully left I took a mindless drive on a road that gave me a vista of the Truckee Meadows from a fair height. I didn't expect—and didn't have—one of my Aegean experiences. I simply enjoyed high-desert beauty stippled with innumerable plots of Reno rooftops and studded with tree tops. Rugged landscape blocked the downtown and casino districts from my sight. Somehow in my mind's ear, I heard the words *dharma* and "design" uttered a few times each.

Off and on the rest of that day I wondered whether a plan, a design, might be intrinsic to anybody's life, specifically to mine. If so, is it discernible? Without thinking about it directly, I decided I'd try to apprehend whether the major experiences I've had during my decades on Earth point to a likely objective. Julie would help me. Does a *pattern* appear in all that?

I hoped so. Then I'd have a clear *reason* for making decisions about what I might do in the future—outside the plans Julie and I had already made for ourselves. Nobody with vision should have to go thrusting headlong into darkness while seeing plot points only in retrospect.

With a frisson I can't explain I answered the telephone while I was sipping morning coffee, and a deep-voiced stranger addressed me and disclosed his name: Mitchell Freeman. Perhaps I've read his newspaper column, he offered (modestly).

Of course I'd read his newspaper column countless times; it's been an elementary feature of life in northern Nevada for decades. The writing is facile and usually amusing. Mitch could be self-deprecating while he bludgeons almost everything that moves on the political right (although I do not recall his soundly whacking our junior U.S. Senator, who's a Republican). His cudgel of choice: laughter at perpetrators of public stupidity or intentional meanness. Most of them appeared on the national stage (plenty of easy targets), but some perpetrators could be viewed in bathroom mirrors in Reno and Carson City.

"I've read your blogs," Mitch Freeman informed me. "And I've been known to watch television and read the newspaper."

From me a lame riposte.

"If you ask me," said Mitch, "if you're serious about the need for 'conservative reform,' as you call it, we should get together *soon,* like tomorrow. Maybe I can be of assistance, although I can't guarantee it's gonna be valuable. [Beat.] I'll do my best to bring along someone you'd probably want to meet."

That sounded intriguing and I said so. We decided to meet at 2:00 the next day at a brew pub called "The Peak." After we rang off I called Hal and told him about this.

Hal sounded mildly surprised. Then he remarked, "Y' know that guy's 'liberalism' stands out like what you'd see on a unicorn."

"Yeah, I know. But his heart's in the right place. And he's funny."

Then I induced Hal to go with me the next day.

"If you don't mind," he said, "I'll bring a buddy of mine. Someone you need to know."

The next day, I think a Thursday, I would have asked Julie to accompany me to meet Mitch and whomever, but she was up to her hairline in work. When I entered the busy brew pub downtown near the river, I could identify Mitch Freeman straightaway (a beefy, kindly looking fellow) from his appearances on local TV spots; usually he'd decry Reno traffic and drivers. Now he sat with a scrawny, hard-bitten, youngish-looking man in a suit who (in actuality) was almost the same age as Mitch and me.

"I'm Dan Hachek," I said to the two men when I reached their table.

Smiles. Handshakes. Mitch introduced the other fellow as Jimmy Kestrel.

I sat with them and, seeing no beer or food on the table, looked around for a waitperson. Aside from its neon art, the place was designed for efficiency and crowds. It wasn't yet crowded.

"Your name sounds familiar," I told Kestrel. "Are you from Sacramento?"

Turned out he was a California political consultant and fund-raiser; I wouldn't know him from that. He'd been in the news as a principal organizer of Gay-Pride Day in California and a civil-rights spokesman.

"Of course! I knew that," I said. "I'd forgotten it, but I knew it."

A waitress and my brother and his buddy arrived simultaneously. After things got settled I was introduced to Frankie Lopez, also known as Pancho, a husky Latino who had a ring in his left ear lobe. He and Hal often worked together as Web *Meisters.*

"Good to finally meet Hal's more-handsome brother," Pancho told me.

I liked him instantly. He and Hal were there to slake their thirst, Pancho said, and maybe offer technical assistance. Mostly they kept quiet during the following half hour while Mitch and I did most of the talking. Sometimes Jimmy offered commentary.

Mitch casually asked me a few questions about myself and told me a little about himself, such as he couldn't be labeled a non-patriot if only because he'd put in two full tours as a combat medic in Vietnam, which I knew about.

In return I mentioned that forty-plus years ago I'd sporadically worked on the ground as a contractor "in that part of the world" while hostilities were still going on (long after Mitch had rotated out) for maybe a combined total of two weeks. I couldn't divulge what kind of work I'd done. I chose not to mention injuries I'd incurred or that I'd gone there when my first marriage broke up. I did aver that the experiences might have caused me a desire to write something—a novel, a play, a series of poems—that would "illuminate certain aspects of reality with truth we can live with," although I never have.

"So why the hell haven't you?" Jimmy asked.

"I could never decide . . . well, first I didn't know enough, when I was in my thirties . . . then I couldn't determine *what* aspects of life I should try to illuminate. Almost all the stuff I've read, or seen in movies or on stage—it all seems so *trivial*, you know? Why contribute more of that? I can't say I'd do much better."

After some prodding I narrated a sketchy résumé of my attempts to get educated along with my trade and business experiences (exclusive of investing, which is a list of boring details). I talked briefly about my family life and aspirations. I omitted mention of my Aegean experiences.

"Evidently you're a man of diversified interests and a rich, varied background," Mitch commented. Jimmy and Pancho nodded affirmatively.

"I suppose so," I said, "but I can't brag much. Except for the halo effect I get from my wife and my son—I call him Doctor Jay."

We drank good beer. Someone raised the subject of "conservative reform." I declared that the concept is anything but "political." Its cornerstone is simply the common good—evidently an alien concept these days.

"Conservative" means "conserve," I said, "which mandates taking effective action against the opposite, and then solving problems that result."

I went on to say that this would entail setting priorities designed to meet the common good, like smarter defense and intelligence spending, and rebuilding our roads and bridges and power grid. "Not exactly profound stuff . . . ."

Nods, sips; apparent concurrence all round.

Since I still had an opening, I managed to say that primary to *everything* is the U. S. taking the lead in arresting—even reversing—global warming and getting us off petroleum and coal; urgent necessities that are anything but "political."

What kind of car did I drive? A hybrid. My former company's trucks were all four-cylinder. We sold and installed a lot of R-13 air conditioners. My wife's and my diet has been mostly vegetarian (we love our salmon and trout). We've had but two children, an important fact.

"Well," Mitch declared, "you give 'conservative' a special twist. I am *not* a conservative, as you know, but I can be with you."

Jimmy offered something about how I could be the "poster boy" for a "movement long overdue"—to which Harry nodded.

"Well, the facts are *in*," I said, a little embarrassed. "All I'm doin' is saying we've gotta put the planet back in balance. If we keep disrupting ocean currents, for instance, we're going to get more 'Katrinas'; warm ocean waters fuel hurricanes, as everyone knows. If we don't pay down the national debt we'll be strangling our lives—and our kids' lives—because, you know, we gotta pay out so much interest. Forget that debt-to-GNP ratio; our kids *don't need* to be paying tons of interest. —I could go on and on."

Harry demurred about a couple things I'd said, so Mitch called him "Candide." I had to declare that Harry was a defender of the commonweal and the devil-dog foe of carbon dioxide, which wasn't quite true.

Time was slipping away. Mitch unfurled his message: he—utilizing expertise offered by Jimmy Kestrel—would help in every way he could to promote a conservative-reform movement. My job: generate the movement. Perhaps implement it by forming a bona-fide political party replete with officers and platform. Hal interposed that he and Frankie Lopez would also champion my cause, although in ways less public.

Finally, I had to say this to Mitch and Jimmy: "I suppose you're willing to step up and help from the goodness of your heart."

"Yes, no," said Mitch. "I'm always going to be the muck-raking liberal I'm accused of; I won't turn my back on causes I care about deeply. But I—mainly that means my wife and kids—have to *live in* this world. It's the only place you can find good pizza. With the planet—along with the country's finances—going to hell, your 'movement' could help turn things around. *If* we get it chugging forward, in the open, as an actual political party."

I was sure that I saw one of the black-clad young wait-persons pause beside Mitch's chair to listen.

"This is crazy!" I said. "I can't say hey, first thing next morning I'll start up a political party. I'm gonna have to give it give it serious thought! Like *how* do I *do* it."

"Not to put on pressure, but according to everybody's news, time's a-wastin'," said Jimmy.

"Of course not to put on the pressure!" said Mitch. "By the way, when the prophets go silent, the people perish."

Mirthless laughs and smiles.

"Listen," I said (*without* being unduly modest): "I'm not even a—what do they call it?—simulacrum of a shaker and mover, let alone a freakin' prophet. Goodness!"

"The man's soul hints of garlic," said Jimmy.

"What's wrong with *that*?" said Harry.

Mitch smiled and looked at me levelly. "If you decline to do what we've been discussing," he said, "and you do something else, what will you strive for? What valid alternatives would you pursue? I mean, besides great sex and a reliable source of prunes."

I responded, "Living." (Brief pause.) "That is all I have to say."

Summarily we exchanged Email addresses and telephone numbers so we could stay in touch. I think I knew the matter was far from closed.

When Julie arrived home after a difficult day at the hospital (a phenomenon that often made us wonder how, for example, a hedge-fund maven could be so nonessential, like a societal appendix, while some people who do actual work also have to balance life and fend off death for other people), I waited over a half hour for the proper moment to tell her of my misadventures that day.

"Mitchell Freeman, the newspaper guy, thinks I should run for King of the USA," I blurted. Then I outlined my experience at the brew pub.

Julie was charmed. "What kind of guy *is* Mitch Freeman?" she asked, truly interested. I filled in the picture as best I could. By the time I finished she was pondering a clutch of issues, such as whether the world had gone mad.

"It all really happened," I said, hastening to explain that I would have preferred she'd been there with me.

"That's what I mean about your getting into trouble when you're left alone," Julie said, not being entirely facetious.

I mentioned that I'd driven Harry home from the pub (so I hadn't been alone much that day); on the way he expressed enthusiasm for the notion of my originating a political party.

Julie had her own take: "Danny, look at it this way: the *efforts* we make to set things right, and maybe the *results* we get from making those efforts—that's not nothing, y' know. You might be causing real effects in the very heart of eternity. [Beat.] It's possible!"

That put me in a quandary: "Look," I said, "I'm afraid of sacrificing my *and your* priorities. They're also 'not nothing.'"

Julie said, "Now consider this: If we count you and Jay and me, and Hal and his buddy—what's his name, Panchito?—and Mitch Freeman and his buddy, Kestrel—I gotta wonder if that's really his name—you've got a party of seven without even trying. You might be doing something right!"

"Sounds more like a *Gang of Seven*."

A few moments passed while I got us coffee. Something piquant crossed my mind; I tried to let it go but it felt true. I turned to Julie; she looked receptive to anything I'd say.

"Sometimes I feel like a stranger in a strange land," I said. "Setting aside all the stuff we've been talking about, I keep getting a distinct sense that I'm in temporary exile—starting before I can remember. Maybe this is what everyone experiences; I don't know. Exile from where, for what reason? Who knows. Even when everything we've got here is right, I can't help feeling we really belong somewhere else. I'm not referring to a different *place*, now."

"What *are* you referring to?"

"I don't really know. All I know is 'home' is transient."

"I can't say I've experienced the same . . . uh, *sense* . . . you have," Julie said. "Maybe I have. I'm willing to bet, though, we *humans belong on* this planet. We didn't just evolve here by accident, y' know. For this human, that's 'home' enough."

I was about to say I wouldn't disagree with that, although our inferences were still essentially guesses. But I dropped the whole matter because damned if I could explain what I'd meant by "not referring to a different *place*," even though it felt deeply right to have said that.

At last we have made good camp on a headland edging their plain. From here we gaze across land spread before Ilios, a wind-driven, wretched plain, which for Ilios provides a wide border to the Bay of Troia, and upon which, from their walls, they can observe even the movements of a rat.

For us, comforts are few and the night carries chill. I hunker near a fire with fellow captains of Agamemnon's expedition and we pray (each man in his silence) to be spared from attack this night, for our defenses yet lack stoutness.

I break the stillness to say, "Truly, do we hate Trojans?" For already we have seen many die alongside our young men, almost all of them but grown boys. Agamemnon keeps his own counsel nearby in the darkness, as does Achilles.

We reach agreement: we do not hate Trojans, but we must destroy Ilios. This is simple necessity.

Agamemnon comes forward, having heard perhaps all we said.

"You cannot love them," he says, grinning in firelight. "But for Trojans, we would be thriving in Hellas."

Agamemnon regards us thoughtfully. He speaks with care:

"Hittites, those many clans here in the service of Ilios, are cousins to us, but Trojans are our brothers. Their language we understand and they understand ours. Our gods are also their gods, I think. Where we differ matters little.

"But for this one thing we cannot abide: they block us and squeeze us. They choke Achaean genius and our very lives—and the lives of our children. The destiny of Mycenae and all Greeks demands that we endure these hardships until we prevail. Pariamu—that old, stupid king we call Priam—knows this.

Trojans deserve to be destroyed, along with their cursed city. I think this is the will of the gods."

Agamemnon's words lend me comfort, although I feel something else is coming. He regards me with a thin smile and adds: "We know also—this war makes for necessary business. Builders of ships and masters of bronze and weapons thrive because of us. As do many others. Fellow Danaoi, my fate is to make business! No god will deny this."

I nod and return the smile. Nor might I deny the truth of what he says.

*   *   *

CHAPTER 8

STRATEGY

"If you ask me," Mitch Freeman said at my eyes, "the first thing you need—all right, the first thing *we* need to do—is crystallize a platform."

I heard concurrence around our table. We had gathered at the "Hacienda," a neighborhood bar-restaurant on the edge of Old Northwest Reno. Our aim was to resolve feasibility issues around starting a recognizable, viable political party, and then clear out before the happy-hour trade arrived. Hal was there, as was Pancho—for some reason I had taken to calling him "Panchito"—and a well-heeled associate of Jimmy Kestrel named Ira Blumenthal, and a quiet, blonde, earnest-looking young woman named Alyssa Bender, who Mitch informed us was an intern at the newspaper.

"Sounds right to me," I responded to Mitch. "It won't take me long to come up with a list of planks. Mainly we want to arrest global warming and balance the budget."

Ira spoke up: "Don't you want a transition, you know, like to a "green economy"?

"*Sub rosa,*" I said, overtly placing my hands behind me.

Ira said: "That's fine. Maybe someone at Mitch's office can draft a concise, punchy document. It should state your platform in a way that's . . . *compelling.*"

Mitch said he had access to services of another intern who holds a master's in political science. Hal said he and Pancho would post the document on my Google Web page, enter parts of it in likely chat rooms, and set me up with a special cutting-edged Web site if I would pay for a TypePad program.

"I'm good for a hundred or two," I said, and Pancho and I summarily set the date for a "technical meeting" at Hal's house.

Ira lived and worked in Carson City. He knew how to register a "minor" political party with our Secretary of State. "You're gonna need a slate of officers," he apprised me, along with saying that he knew a thing or two about running petition drives and fund raising. And his services never came cheap.

"Just a minute!" I said to all. "Say we post a platform and decide to form a bona-fide political party. Who's going to run it?" I had just envisioned a *welter* of exigencies eclipsing Julie's and my intermediate plans, perhaps our long-term plans as well.

Nobody responded. Beat. Beat. Beat.

"Looks like you're The Man," Mitch informed me.

Harry nodded affirmation. Ira and Pancho displayed the mien of presuming an obvious reality.

"Well, you know, I'm kind of busy," I said.

"Well, if you don't take the reins," Mitch said, "if you decline to do it, what would you do instead? I mean, what else do you seek or want?"

We'd been here before. This time I was prepared: "I suppose I want the same things everybody wants: a happy life with family and friends. After I've ensured the same for my wife and my son as far as I can. Beyond that . . . the cliché is 'follow my bliss.'"

I paused and scanned faces [beat, quick beat] before anyone piped up I resumed: "Uh, that's for openers. I bet everyone here wants about the same things. But *beyond that*, what I'm *really* after—what I'm really trying to achieve—is what you might call 'transcendence.' It's been my goal for about forty years."

I glanced about and got the impression I was understood. Of course that might have been caused by the beer. "This is all I have to say."

Mitch said, "Okay."

Said Ira, "And you've been working on it."

"When I'm not hassled too much."

Mitch said, "And how do you plan to achieve your . . . uh, *'transcendence'*?"

"That's what I'm still working on. To some degree I might have achieved it. But I still don't think so."

Harry declared, "You could be accomplishing exactly what you're after by contributing to society. To the whole country! Set your hand to making life better for everyone—yourself and Julie and me included. I bet you've thought of that or else we wouldn't be here."

A little gap of silence. Mitch's stentorian voice intoned, "What this republic absolutely needs is a political party *beyond* political parties. I'm talking transcendent goals. Transcendent values! Somebody's got to start one. Looks like . . . you're The Man."

I didn't bother to turn and see whom that was directed at.

We still had to finalize logistics entailed in conceiving a political body. Ira took concise command, as did Pancho. Hal essentially concurred with their proposals. Alyssa sat absorbed.

At some juncture Mitch interposed: "Now none of this has anything to do with attempting to gain 'power,' a term I use guardedly. We're all clear on this, aren't we: We're *not after* 'power.' Right?"

Mitch went on to assert that our basic purpose in starting up a new political party was to wield enough influence to cause critical changes. Could we—I and the new party in process—generate influence where it counts most, like in reversing global warming and restoring our national sanity? Of course we could!

Alyssa asked me to disclose the top three or four planks of the platform I would propound. I said sure, given our overall objective. ("We've all heard of 'the common good'?")

After barely a pause I rattled off about six proposals: Stop and reverse global warming *and* its opposite, so-called "sun dimming"; this we do by weaning ourselves off fossil fuels. That we do by *using* the technology *already out there* for relying on renewable energy. Eventually balance the federal budget and start paying down the national debt; we can start by putting defense expenditures on parity with other nations. I mentioned that China's recent military buildup raised the level of their defense spending to about one-fourth the size of ours.

"A really cool thing I'd *like to* propose," I said, "would be transforming our military establishment into a lean skills-training machine capable of defending half the universe. (By the way, is there a Pentagon—anything halfway resembling the U. S. Pentagon—anywhere else on Earth?) Ditto using the 'War on Terror.' We should take advantage of it by training up people in *a spectrum* of occupational skills."

Before anyone could demur I added, "That'll be for another day. There's a whole range of issues I don't want to deal with unless I were running for President, which of course I'm not."

Alyssa had dutifully noted the points that I'd trucked out. "I like your progressive planks," she said, jabbing her pen onto a page of notepaper.

"Ah, an undergraduate," I said to her, quoting Ronald Reagan's rejoinder to a female student's insult when he was governor of California. "They're *conservative* planks, dear." Later I learned I was wrong on one point.

Hal and Pancho and Ira asked me if I didn't approve of campaign-finance reform, and referenda on temporary tax increases (as had been done in California), and replacing the Electoral College with direct voting.

"Hold on!" I said. "I'm taking notes"—which I was, but for another day.

We still had a little time for more iced tea or coffee—or let's say beer for someone who's a mature retiree—so we relaxed.

Alyssa and Mitch casually raised the issue of illegal immigration, a long-term hot-button topic. I averred that I didn't know how *any* political-party plank could address it.

"I'd like to be a sage on the subject but I'm not," I said. "I've heard that lately they've got some kind of gonzo economic problem in Mexico. Whatever it is, it seems to be getting alarmingly worse. I know that people go through hell to come here. Little kids are dying in the desert." I was about to add that nothing we've ever done has squelched illegal immigration, so we need to get really creative.

Ira pulled me up short. "You need to keep mum on polarizing issues," he admonished. "And we all know 'political correctness' sucks. We still have to accede to it."

"Good thing I'm not a politician," I murmured.

"Maybe not," Mitch retorted, "but you're going to wind up being a 'political animal.' It's inevitable. Trust me."

Ira asserted that wielding the right kind of influence where it counts forestalls having to resort to partisan politics. He and Jimmy Kestrel did that for an array of clients, often working in tandem to pull the same strings in Sacramento and Carson City.

A momentary lull in table chatter occurred just as Alyssa declared, "We've gotta be careful not to squeeze the joy out of what we're doing! Part of the political process is supposed to be *fun*—high-level. That's why we're calling this a 'political *party*'!"

That fetched our attention. We soon learned that bright-eyed Alyssa had experienced a short career as a high-school teacher and was involved—with several mostly young people—in starting up an alternative newspaper in the Truckee Meadows. (No undergraduate she.)

"As my older sister used to say, 'it's not worth it if it ain't fun,'" Alyssa averred. "That's why I quit high-school teaching. That's why I like working with Mitch. In fact that's why I'm here!"

I winked at her, and I think Mitch did likewise. Pancho, beholding her dreamily, inquired: "Your sister *used to* say that?"

"She doesn't anymore. Too busy *not* having fun. She runs a PR firm in Carson."

"What firm is that?" Ira asked Alyssa, plainly keenly interested.

"It's under her name: Maya Catchings, Purveyor of Evil Relations or whatever."

Ira's expressions went mercurial. I saw astonishment, dismay, amusement, and something imponderable. "*Wow,*" he said. "Maya's your sister?"

"My older sister. Much-older sister. I'll make it a point to tell her about what's going on here. She can be a valuable ally once she's in your corner."

Ira regarded Alyssa with full-bore earnest. "Never mention my name to her," he said. "Repeat: never, *ever* mention my name to her."

I know now that I should have registered that colloquy but it didn't seem important.

CHAPTER 9

GETTIN' STRONG

Seeing my name on the computer screen and then seeing it in newsprint—as Chairman of the Conservative-Reform Party—always gave me a frisson of pleasure, although I preferred the rare instances of hearing it on the news.

Those things were as *nada* compared to the blizzard of Emails I received, barely to mention at least two-dozen telephone calls and a clutch of letters. Evidently Hal and Pancho outdid themselves putting my message into cyberspace. I checked my two Web sites conscientiously and found that Hal had done a good job of framing blogs attributed to me. I did have a few quibbles about things I allegedly said, and I insisted they be amended, which they were.

The cool thing was seeing flattering photos of me, family photos that Harry kept, on my TypePad site. (Soon he and Pancho would incorporate audio elements.) I had to borrow those same photos from Harry so I could give copies to two alternative newspapers in Reno that offered to give me coverage. The local Spanish-language weekly newspaper sent over a photographer, whom Julie invited to stay for dinner with us.

But I had yet to register the Conservative-Reform party with our Secretary of State. We had a Chairman, all right (me), an ad hoc Vice-Chairman (Harrison), and a Secretary (Pancho), but no Treasurer. What's more, Mitch's intern was taking his time framing the party platform, and Ira hadn't finished drafting the bylaws required for registration. My political party was news before it existed, a fact Jimmy Kestrel labeled "instructional."

I asked my neighbor Bully Kendall to be Treasurer or sit on the executive committee and he said no. "I'll vote for you if you run for public office," he said, "but you'll have to promise not to raise taxes." I knew I was in for a hard row.

Ira Blumenthal said he would advise me on tactical matters, but he shunned public association with any political group. Jimmy Kestrel said about the same thing (anyway he resided in California). Julie's and my array of friends could have helped me out, but none came forward and I would have had to prevail upon them; not a good thing. Once again I didn't know what to do. About a week had passed.

Just like a downslope zephyr, Jimmy Kestrel telephoned me. "Well, your party's about to become a registered entity in Nevada," he said. "Better plan your next move."

I declared that impossible; we hadn't even named a treasurer, or an executive committee. Our bylaws were still unwritten.

"Ira tells me that's been taken care of," Jimmy said. "Your Treasurer's name is Daigan Kawakami."

"Who in the hell is Daigan Kawakami?"

"Oh, he's a good friend of Ira. Me, too. You can trust him with your life—or your wife. He said he believes in your Cause."

"My *Cause*?"

"Mitch's intern at the newspaper polished up the bylaws Ira wrote. You should see them."

I just nodded.

"You're good to go—as soon as you sign a few papers they'll be sending you, probably next week," Jimmy said. "Let me know what I can do."

I responded that someone should tell me what *I* should do.

Jimmy uttered banal assurances and we rang off. An instant later the phone rang again: a woman well-wisher named Janice, maybe a Mormon (a persuasion of people I often perceive correctly), calling from Fernley, a bedroom community east of Reno. She spoke to me as though we knew each other so I gathered she was a customer of my old company.

"We *need* the kind of reform you're talking about," she said. "The country's been drifting for *decades*. Now we're being driven completely off course! Maybe you—and your new political organization—can do something about it. My family and I would be truly grateful if you did."

In the most sincere tones I could muster I thanked her for calling and said that, yes, we needed conservative reform, so long as it took dead aim at solving critical problems and wasn't just defensive. Without elaboration I added: "otherwise we jeopardize our stewardship"—a line Julie liked hearing. When the lady and I signed off I decided that I would rent an office for the Party's headquarters—if I could find a feasible (*i.e.*, cheap) space nearby—which I did.

*   *   *

The place smelled of varnish and old carpet. My chair creaked when I leaned back to plant my feet on the battered wooden desk that we'd moved here from my garage. I was wearing a blue-tweed vest with a white dress shirt and red-blue tie; we had found my old gray fedora in the garage and it was perfect for the occasion. There was an opened pint of Scotch in a desk drawer that I slid shut. I lacked the .38 colt, but I packed my cell phone in a holster behind my hip. I felt like the protagonist in a Dashiell Hammet novel waiting for "her" to come through the doorway. A sharp double rap outside, and the door swung open exposing me to the world.

She floated into my office like a funeral wreath flung off a dock at Lake Tahoe.

"Lookin' for me?" I said.

I could have been friendlier but I was busy trying to figure out what she wanted before she opened her mouth. This one looked like she didn't need help. Anybody built like that could take care of herself any time she wanted.

"I'm looking for Dan Hachek," she purred, "and I think that's you. You look like the picture on your blog page."

That brought me back to reality, and, yes, *she* was actually standing in front of me. I jettisoned my chair back and sprang to my feet. We extended hands and shook them over my desk. She stood a head taller than I and had a firm grip. Her hair was a natural honey blonde, shoulder length. Those shoulders looked like a pro skier's.

"At your service," I said.

"My name is Maya Catchings," said the lady. "You know my sister Alyssa."

"Wow!" I said (stunned by all that womanhood). "Alyssa told me she has a sister, but I didn't dream . . . I'd be meeting you this soon. What brings you by?"

"I'm in public relations; I own a firm in Carson City. I happened to be in Reno today, and Alyssa—she's my slightly younger sister—urged me to look you up. I'm thinking that I can help you out *and*, of course, make contacts for myself. We should be able to finesse *all kinds* of events that'll make splashes for both of us."

"Do you know anything about the political party we're launching?"

"Not really. Only what Alyssa has told me. It doesn't make much difference at the outset. I'm a quick study."

"Ah. You'd better know I can only afford to pay you a token."

"I accept tokens. And I'm betting later on you'll be able to pay me close to my usual fee. We'll start out by raising a campaign chest."

"Great! How do we do that?"

"I'm not an expert down that line. People like Jimmy Kestrel and some unnameable political flaks down in Carson are the experts. We'll put 'em on task after more people get to know you better."

Again I said "great" and asked how we'd do it.

"Well," Maya said, "for openers we get you some speaking engagements. While I'm at it I'll make sure the media know what you're about. Then we try to score some high-profile endorsements that'll go a long way. But I'll need printed propaganda as well as the electronic stuff. I'm gonna have to make contacts."

I told her that I'd draft a declaration about the party's genesis and platform, but it might take a little time.

"The day after tomorrow will be fine," she said and handed me her business card. "See you down in Carson. We'll do lunch."

Maya Catchings proceeded to leave but stopped at the door and turned to look at me as I gazed at her black twill skirt stretched taut over round nates. "This can really be exciting!" she said, blue eyes crinkling with her smile.

That same day Bully Kendall asked me to visit his house after dinner to meet one of his associates, so I did. The fellow was already there and Bully was mixing drinks in his kitchen when I arrived. I declined a cocktail because I had too much work to do (thanks to Miss Maya), and I was introduced to Kip Whitbread, a professor of accounting at the University of Nevada. With his warm smile and calm demeanor, I perceived this man as a pleasant contrast to our extroverted host.

Right off, Whitbread said he mostly agreed with my "politics" as he understood them. Then he suggested that we pointedly exclude any talk of religion this evening for the sake of effective discourse.

Immediately Bully said, "*You* attend church, don't you Dan?"

"Not if I can help it," I said. "Although I have been known to darken the doorstep of the Reno Buddhist Church."

That piqued Kip's interest and he asked me a few questions about it.

"Interesting," he declared when I'd answered as best I could. Bully appeared mildly curious but said nothing.

We went to sit in the living room. I sipped Pepsi from an oversized glass; Kip and Bully savored their drinks. Soon we addressed the nature and need for "conservative reform." (I would not call it "*my* conservative reform.")

After I defined my take on the concept, Kip asked if I wasn't advocating a primarily "*green*" political movement. Bully declared that it sounded "pretty damned progressive at base."

"Heavens, no," I said. "The 'green' emphasis on arresting and reversing climate change is just a matter of gross necessity. Call it global survival, like having to win a war. Once we've got it in place, when everybody's on board, I mean all hands at the oars, it'll become essentially good business.

"The 'progressive' measures I've been proposing, well, they stem from a philosophy—of conservation and preservation rooted in the U.S. Constitution. It's called striving for the common good—I'd say for divine purposes."

Nobody reprised my last statement. We talked about congressional dysfunction. That led to clearing the air about the usual brands of political ideology currently brewing nation-wide. I allowed that my brand of "reform" was no elixir, but as we turned it over and assayed it a few times it sure sounded like one to me. By my lights, I was advocating almost pure pragmatism.

The centerpiece of the "movement" would be a *comprehensive* program to eliminate use of fossil fuels spearheaded by the federal government *in partnership with* all industries that innovate and manufacture the tools for getting and using renewable energy. The ultimate objective: *transition* the U. S. economy to a climate-friendly one; this would almost necessarily entail full employment well into the future. Providing hands-on vocational training to all comers would be mandated by the feds in collaboration with the states. *This* is how the U. S. should lead the world; not the way we're leading now, as the biggest, most successful debtor nation that's ever been. I took most of two minutes to say this.

I never got to mention (although I wished I had) that taken together, my proposed *collaboration* between government and industries to transform the U. S. economy by arresting global-climate change (as far as we can) mirrored almost exactly the U. S. and Allied efforts to win World War II. (Hitler's gang deployed the same *modus operandi* but stretched it too thin.) And I failed to remark that while we sat sipping drinks and talking, World War III raged right outside Bully Kendall's window. The world's climate is under attack by greenhouse-gas emissions and the planet faces catastrophe. We—all creatures on Earth—are in a war, and the world is losing. That *had to* stop. This last point I did manage to imply.

When I finished my disquisition Bully and Kip looked at me baldly. I gulped the rest of my cola and asked for more, and did Bully have any fresh lime handy? This was to give them space. But I must have felt amped up because I heard myself saying: "Is it—is my program—wholesome to our purposes?"

A momentary dead zone ensued.

Finally Kip said, "Well, your *casus belli* has currency; it's definitely gaining traction in the world. Your core issue—dealing with greenhouse gases—makes the burden of proof fall on the other guys, where it belongs. After all, the facts *are in.*"

"I can only take partial credit," I said.

"Now you need to pull in critical mass."

"Precisely! That's why I'm doing what I'm doing."

After a beat, Kip offered: "I think we might start with that old 'War-on-Whatever' modality. In this case, The War on Carbon. Then another 'war' against federal and state regulations that hamper the main war effort. Maybe another 'war' against second- or third-rate occupational training . . . ."

We sat on that for a moment. Bully offered sketchy remarks about environmental preservation being good business (that is, imminently). "The tricky part is getting written *permission* from Mobile-Exxon, Halliburton, Root and Brown, and their well-meaning allies."

"You're talking about slapping some of the hands that feed you!" Kip admonished him.

Bully rejoined, "I can't always be *overhead!*"

["Accountant humor." Not necessarily an oxymoron.]

Rueful chortles by the accountants.

Kip said he knew someone who could be helpful: "There's an associate of mine, an emeritus professor in two departments, who I think believes in basically the same things you propound. His name is Mickey Caldwell. He swings some weight downtown and with the Ledg."

"That's good," I said.

"Oh, it's better than you think."

Bully put in: "I met Caldwell once, at a Chamber affair. My wife's in love with him."

I meant to have that clarified but Kip interposed: "Ah—that's what I mean. Mickey doesn't *look like* a lady-killer, but women respond to him as though he exudes pheromones or something. I think it's his voice they love, also his demeanor. I'm sure he can help get your cause wider support, presuming you choose to advance it."

"I need all the help I can get," I said. "And then some."

Bully said, "He needs all the help he can get."

Kip told us that he would see Mickey Caldwell the next day and tell him about my "movement" if he didn't already know and about having met me.

"He'll be in touch with you I'm sure. Write out your Email address."

As we began to disband Kip said he was enthused about "conservative reform as a *political* enterprise because it kind of . . . infiltrates something that's megalithic, even dominant."

"You're speaking of what, may I ask?" Bully said.

"We'll call it the anal-retentive, everything's-all-right-because-it's-ours mentality," Kip replied. "You know what I mean. Ever hear of 'red' states? This fellow here [gesturing my way] is trying to slip something into the heart of Godzilla in order to shrink huge problems inside the beast. —We might say he's building a kind of Trojan Horse. If you get my drift."

"*Interesting,*" I commented.

"So long as it's economically viable," Bully asserted, a point I took to heart.

As we walked back through the kitchen I declared I had some hard work pending because of my "new boss," one Maya Catchings. The name passed right over Kip, but Bully repeated it with an exclamation mark. This prompted me to ask him what he knew about her.

"She's got a heavy-hitting PR firm down in Carson," Bully said. "I've done some work for her, though not recently. Actually I worked for Catchings and her former associate, a fellow named Blumenthal or Blumenfeld."

That put a hook in me. When I asked him to tell me about the "former" association he'd cited, Bully said there was "bad blood" between them. He could only add that they had never gone public about their falling-out. By now I intended to learn every *who-did-and-what.*

CHAPTER 10

CUNNING (PART B)

Speaking as ad hoc Vice-Chairman of the brand-new Conservative-Reform Party, my brother was emphatic about the notion that I needed to project a higher profile both for myself and the Party. My having been contacted by Maya Catchings and the counsel she offered piqued his enthusiasm. We spoke by telephone a short time after I'd left Bully's.

"Man, you ought 'a see what she looks like," I said, intending to cap off talking about Maya and her firm.

"Tell me more," Harry said, so I described Maya's physical assets as best I could, the most prominent (I thought) being her powerful and, yes, ample size.

"Oh, *man,*" said Harry. "How would you like to dive right into all that—and let her crush you to death!"

I pondered the image for a second, then added that Maya's rear end (in a tight skirt) owned a drastic roundness I considered remarkable.

"Man, I'm looking forward to seeing that," Harry responded. "I'll probably try to sink my teeth into it and let her drag me to death!"

Ol' Harrison had always taken pride in being tunnel-visioned.

"Well, look who's the feisty one after a hard day!" Julie remarked from her pillow after I'd nestled my head into its favorite place on the planet: between—but partaking of—her right and left breasts. We were spent and sated and happy. It was all I could do to reach a sheet and pull it over us.

After several moments respite I averred that lately I'd been feeling energized. But, upon looking into things deeply, I told Julie, I intuited that maybe I'd been unconsciously aware of setting some kind of catastrophe in motion—one that I *should see* coming. So perhaps I was scrambling to grab as many good moments as I could before it hit.

Cul-de-sac. Julie waited for me to explain.

Soon I said: "Events seem to be spinning every which way around me, and I caused 'em. But I'm rocked by the extent that I can't control what's happening. And I don't know where it's all going."

She asked what events those were, although she knew of some. I told her how the Maya Catchings' P-R firm was gearing to set me up with god-knows what kind of commitments, and soon I'd be meeting a Mickey Caldwell, who'd likely pluck suggestions out of the blue for me to implement, and how I'd been engulfed by commitments that were already impinging on my life—and therefore on Julie's well-being—and how this enterprise offered no visible horizon.

"Well, you sure are the bedeviled one," she remarked after a moment.

"Do y' think I'm beyond help? I seem to be cruisin' for a bruisin'."

"Fine," said Julie. "Let it happen. And go *with* it. See where it takes you—where it takes *us.* —How many times have we been through this before?— At the moment, everything seems to be right and true; you're in a good place."

"You can say *that* again."

I nuzzled her to the left and right. Soon I rolled back onto my own space and we let ourselves sink into deepening softness. I felt sure that I would not shake my intuition of some pending catastrophe. Were that to meet me, though, I would buck it. Or ride over it.

Agamemnon broods near his captains' dwindling fire. Light rain had fallen. Now we have but this chill night. Supplies to sustain us are meager, and ships from Argos remain yet away. Our sole comfort is the vile-black-sticky stuff that we set to flame in a hollow handle and suck the smoke into our hearts.

Our enterprise has grown quickly but not blossomed. And Ilios grows yet stronger. Almost daily we see clusters of fresh arrivals from different lands come to bolster Priam's acropolis. This day our horsemen reported a column of new infantry marching to join the city's defense; we think them sent by the Hittite king far away who, says Agamemnon, believes our numbers to be far greater. With few allies, our Greek force encircles Troy but our strength is porous. In no way do we find that cursed state assailable, unless by the gods.

From securing my chariot horses I return to our fire and find my place among five other captains. Agamemnon hardly pays me his mind. Our long history together tells me this will soon change.

"We have the means for victory," our king declares. "Plainly we do not use them correctly, for Ilios stands and grows while we falter. Yet we have the means . . . . I know this to be so because the gods are with us."

Surely none of us thinks to dispute this. We nod slowly, gaze at the fire, say nothing.

Says Agamemnon, "Amphilochus, you tell me a purpose threads through your life but you are yet unable to read it. You say my life takes a direction I cannot see, yet I follow it. So goes this affair here, to level Troy!

"We—all of us—must strive to uncover what the gods hold for us within our purpose. Then we must declare it among us. Thus we might know how to grasp victory."

Agamemnon rises to stand and speaks again: "When I learn clearly what we must yet do, we will do it well. This I promise."

The king of men strides off into darkness. He will return shortly. Our heads nodding slowly, we fix our eyes now on glowing embers, wrap ourselves in our mantles, wish for home.

Soon Agamemnon returns to his place among us, and to my own surprise I push myself up to my knees and declare: "We have the intelligence and the courage and we are clever enough to prevail here! If we could find a way to place soldiers inside the walls of Ilios to our benefit, that will be our path to victory."

My psyche surges upward as our king rises to his feet and seizing on my words he declares: "Thus from this very moment, we shall exercise our Achaean cunning. Somehow we will accomplish—make real—the goal set by Amphilochus. We must find a way to do that."

*　　*　　*

And in time so we did, with the help of some gold and a bronze helmet too small for Achilles.

Maya called my office the next morning and cancelled our pending lunch date, which I admit was a disappointment but also a relief. Then she announced: "Well, you're in luck. —This has to come from living right.— Sunday afternoon, downtown Reno—in that big performance plaza next to Harrah's that gives onto Sierra Street—there's going to be a showcase called `Alternate Political Parties of Nevada.' They call it a `conference,' but it's really going to be schmooze-fest for fringe parties; and guess who's going to be part of it. You should be getting your invitation today or tomorrow."

She declared this event a good opportunity for my political party to get public exposure, which was prerequisite to expanding our membership and raising donations. Of course I said I felt heartened. My job as party chairman suddenly became more viable; I might be able to accomplish something away from my desk and computer.

Maya added: "There'll be at least four other parties on the docket besides yours; some of them have been around for a while. There's the Nevada Independent Conservative Party, which is still unregistered; I think it's a group of post-campus right-wingers. There's some kind of 'progressive coalition' the exact name of which and their program I could never get a fix on, although I'm sure they're underfunded. Then there's the Green Party, which swings a little clout, and the Independent American Party, which has got a track record of sorts, and there's the Libertarians, who probably won't bother to show because everybody knows where they stand. And now there's you."

Of course I murmured appreciation.

Weather for Sunday looked to be good but breezy, Maya related. The affair would include music (by two local jazz-rock groups), refreshments (quite minimal), and an emcee from Sacramento who packed some talent. I should have a good experience.

After my logistical questions, such as what time the fun would begin, I learned the conference was sponsored by the main newspaper in town (which explained why I hadn't heard of the event before this) and a few local businesses. All fine, I told Maya. I would make ready to champion my Cause.

The invitation came by both kinds of mail. During the next few days I gave my imminent public appearance plenty of thought and discussed it with Julie, who had other commitments for Sunday and wouldn't be there with me. Expecting Julie to be absent caused me a sense of relief. Subconsciously I chose not to mention the event to Doctor Jay. Harry, though, would be up at Tahoe so he wouldn't be there either, and this

I thought misfortunate. I had some long meditations gazing over the Truckee Meadows during the next few days but no Aegean events. Mainly I marveled at all the trees I could see and the fact that a pretty, mostly clean river cut through the valley. The sky had never looked as blue.

All of a sudden it was Sunday, and time to read the morning newspaper and take Julie out for an early lunch before she went off to meet friends and do a workout. For my first public appearance I decided to wear my usual denim jeans and boots and sport jacket, but since the occasion was special I opted for a pastel-blue dress shirt (sans necktie) instead of my black T-shirt. Lately I'd been pumping iron and stretching, so I felt dynamic, fit. Somehow I was having a "good-hair day," which gave me another boost.

By 1:45 in the afternoon I was downtown and parked and primed to deliver a reasoned, impassioned (as they say) exposition. When I arrived at the casino plaza I was surprised by the turnout, probably over four dozen with more arriving. I went to the speakers' platform, which was backed by a yellow canvas partition, and checked in with organizers, two of whom, a man and woman, took me "backstage" to wait my turn. The emcee, who hadn't yet been told of me, came on at 2:05 and called speakers up from the crowd.

*　　*　　*

They sat me alone at a wooden picnic table behind the canvas backdrop. I helped myself to a jug of bottled water and dug corn chips into a bowl of fresh bean dip topped with salsa and guacamole, which tasted good and dampered the fluttering in my gut. Then I found myself in the company of two attractive, blonde, daughter-aged women, one of whom looked familiar. They moved in to sit at the table with me and said they were taking a respite from their job. I realized that I'd seen one of them on local television news. Turned out the other one worked for the daily newspaper.

"I'll be speaking last," I told them. "My name is Hachek."

One of the blondes said she thought she'd heard of me. The other nodded affirmatively, as though to imply likewise. I arose to shake each one's hand before they sat down. Happily my cowboy boots had good heels, so I was about their height. They regarded me with interest, as was their job. Offhandedly, the one named Shelby asked me whether I "seriously believe" what I would say in my speech.

"I'll get plenty serious when someone gives me a raise," I responded.

"Remember," said the other equally pretty woman, "this is northern Nevada. Anything you say can—*and will be*—held against you."

Rueful chortles.

"Seriously," she added, "make sure people know you as a pure conservative, and always, I repeat, *always* be sure to declare you'll fight any kind of tax increase no matter *what*—regardless of all consequences or crises."

"She must be a big spender from California," I said with a wink to Shelby.

"Note! *Central* California, very hardscrabble," the second woman allowed.

I resolved to integrate her advice whenever I had to, if I could.

We sipped from water bottles while I indulged in a casual meditation. I felt confident about the speech I would give; I only needed to clear my mind. After a few moments I heard one of the women remark to the other (and maybe to me) that events like this conveyed so little substance. We all shrugged. Still, I thought this occasion might help me make an impact with good effects.

Since verbal space was available I decided to prime myself for speechifying. "Blood simple," I declared in case they'd care to hear me, "we've got some gonzo problems we *know* we've got to fix." I didn't bother to see if I had fetched their attention.

I went on, "We know the killer droughts we've had here in the West are the direct result of water warming up in the North Pacific. A lot of things have gotta change—quickly. We *can't* just try to stay the course we've been on since World War Two. We can't even live and work the way we did as recently as 2001. If we don't stop heating the atmosphere right away, we'll be cooking up the perfect storm for disaster. And I don't mean just here in the West in the USA.

"Really, it can't be *too* difficult. We just need more creativity. Look at how the ozone layer has been repaired, mostly. Tell me we don't have the technology to fix *any* problem that's physical, even like denying terrorists space on the Internet. If *we* can't, maybe the Chinese can."

The women looked at me expectedly, as though to say: Okay, let's have something we can put in our pockets and take home. I thought, all right; I was game.

"So," I said, "we've got to *immediately* deploy technology that's available to eliminate having to burn coal—and phase in new stuff as we get it. The new stuff is *almost out there* just *waiting* to be discovered and deployed. The cool technology that's available now is getting cheaper to use every year—at least it's getting less expensive. We don't have to rely on nuclear power the way they do in France, or did in Germany. Anyway that's courting disaster."

"Yeah, hold on there," one of the female voices declared. "Since when is getting and using energy a *political* problem? I know you're a politician; you might be playing in the wrong game, though."

Both of my hands pushed at my chest as though I'd been shot. "I wish I weren't in politics, dear!" I thought I'd remind them of what Pope Francis said about global-climate change to influence political "leaders" world-wide, but I didn't get the chance.

One of the blonde lovelies remarked that science and technology are "inspired pretty much the way art is made. Even the way we apply most kinds of technology *is actually* artful."

Shelby, the other blonde, and I voiced our appreciation for that.

A brief dead zone ensued. I felt my mind pulling me elsewhere.

"But sometimes you've gotta wonder," I injected, "*why bother* doing all this? I mean, we try to do great, good things, but *for what.* [Beat.] Hey, sorry; don't mind me! Sometimes I can't help but wonder. I mean, why even bother to *survive?*"

I gazed into a pair of bright, lovely faces. Predictably they nodded—to show me they were listening carefully. But neither rose to the swinging bar, and this old existentialist-Buddhist knew I'd been whited out. I thought, all right. I don't just *ask* the central questions. Not being a wussie, I give answers. But evidently not here and now. So, well, that's their loss.

In a minute I redeemed myself by asking my two companions how each stayed in such fine physical shape and they gave me an earful. Nothing unexpected, but telling me pleased them.

(Again my mind got pulled elsewhere. Notions barely relevant to the moment popped up in my head. I could almost hear Julie declaring that we couldn't evolve into humans solely due to random chemical combinations with hydrogen (even though a brilliant scientist named Crick maintains otherwise). That means we're part of reality beyond anything we can remotely comprehend or dream, so we'd better act as the transcendent beings that we are.)

I noticed my young, blonde companions casting about for distractions. Amplified voices on the other side of the canvas were remarkably easy to ignore. And for the barest second, I felt sure that I was being observed by parties not visible to me (or anybody present), which caused me a sense of validation, profound comfort.

Surprisingly, the woman *not* named Shelby pointed an expensive-looking cigar at me.

"Here," she said as she put it in my hand. "Make believe you're the king of Cah-lee-*for*-neeyah," as though to mimic a Teutonic accent.

"Thanks," I said, flattered (in a way).

Actually, in my mind's eye I caught images of Fidel Castro using cigars as props. I unwrapped mine straightaway, performed required dental circumcision, and extracted a pad of matches from my sport coat. The two women sipped from their water bottles and looked on while I lit up mightily, then elegantly blew smoke into what had been relatively unpolluted air.

Americans are suckers for personal image. I struck a few poses with my new accoutrement to see what the effect would be and got soft little laughs in return. I confess I reminded myself of Robert E. Lee on the streets of Richmond after the Civil War. An historical account says that on horseback he would stop to flirt with young female admirers (although he was faultlessly faithful to his wife), and while he was doing that he manfully restrained his horse as it balked and snorted and bridled—because he was covertly jabbing the beast with his spurs. Now I wished my brother could see me.

Barely a minute after I'd stoked up my cigar, of course one of the organizers of the event came back of the partition to announce: "You're up next, Dan."

She waited and wrinkled her nose at the acrid-burnt-tobacco smell. I stood, knocked the ash tip off my cigar, and turned to gaze briefly into the eyes of two blonde media members, expecting they would also go out front.

"About time t' rock `n' roll," I said to bright smiles.

So much for the foreplay. Just before I slipped around the canvas on the speakers' platform I did a quick *namaste* toward the audience that I was about to address. "*In Gassho*," I said reflexively, indifferent to whether the women nearby were privy to this.

One of them called out, "Try to ignore the TV cameras!"

CHAPTER 11

HAPPINESS

I strode onto the platform and took the podium and gazed at maybe three-dozen people still gathered in the plaza languorously sitting on folding chairs or standing about, many clutching bottles of water or cans of soda. I reckoned most of them were partisans of the organizations represented by the previous four speakers, with a few curious souls and street people sprinkled in. No partisans there for me.

Before he gestured at me to speak, the emcee introduced the Conservative-Reform Party by reading aloud from a white sheet of paper several verbose sentences about its recent founding and me.

We wait for mid-morning heat to shimmer over sand and rocks on that desolate plain before us. As we expected, beyond the swift-flowing Xanthos more and more smoke rises from many campfires as they cook to eat and brew their drink. Trojan soldiers and all their allies—surely purchased by shallow promises—or else fear of treachery—must endure this day as we do. Perhaps they fortify themselves to attack us this very morning.

Agamemnon believes the Trojans wish to overwhelm us before we can lay proper siege. This may be so. But we know we cannot sustain a long war here.

Stealthily I lead my personal o-ka onto the swelling of plain. Another o-ka I hold behind us, staying near, for help if we need it. My intent is double: find better river fords, test their new battle order. My plan is to cover much ground, hit only when necessary.

This will not be an empty exercise, for we need safe paths to strike their cursed acropolis at points we think best. At the same time we must choke off their sustenance and block them from help. We must do all this before they divine how to overwhelm us.

My driver moves our chariot down to marshy ground turned dry, and we hew to a line of thin brush to hide our movement as far as we can, with the rest of my o-ka following closely. Then we ride on open ground.

"Fast now!" I say, and the reins fly and the great flanks before me flex into hard motion. Bells on my chariot sound merrily—and mightily—as we surge forward. In one hand I grasp the spear man's loop, my arm sinews rising. To hold my balance I clutch the archer's rail by pressing it with the back of one thigh and front of the other. Muscles in my legs tense and bulge. Pleased, I glance down at my greaves, so well designed. My chariot tops a sandy rise and I bend forward a little searching out enemy presence.

With my free hand I touch the hafts on my swords. Spear and bow are in order, at the ready. No enemy can slay me except by chance. A thought comes to me that I have known at times such as this, and it causes a surge within me: I think I am happy.

*   *   *

"I'm Dan Hachek," I said manfully into the microphone. There was a smattering of polite applause while I tried to look the audience in their collective eye. Then I declared that I didn't want any votes in the fall election because I wasn't running for anything. However, everyone had better pay attention to *the party* I represented.

Some people began to melt away. I thought, well, *of course.* So I called out to them—and to everyone there—"Hey, you all! I'm as pissed off at our politicians, at our government, as you are. But I know what to do about it."

That captured some attention.

"What'd *you know* that's so important?!" a man's voice called out.

"The same thing *you* know, the same thing *everyone* knows: We've got to be smarter than we've been. Mainly we've gotta stop being stupid! The planet is going to hell and our national debt is over the moon. You know it, I know it."

I heard a different man's voice: "Tell it, Danny!"

That almost gave me pause. Only Julie and my mother-in-law called me Danny. The fellow's voice sounded friendly, trusting. I thought, oh-*kay* . . . .

During the next four or five minutes I basically delivered what I'd told the two women backstage. Of course I said it differently and let myself get carried away a little bit. At first

I had to tell myself to gesture with my arms to emphasize a point now and then. By the time I finished I had to tell myself to ease up on the arm waving.

I used a lot of parallel grammatical structures; I used the word "obscene" probably three times. (A national debt over 21 *trillion*? Pentagon getting over 700 billion *in one year*? Student debt at 1.3 trillion and counting?) I might have used the words "delusory" and "irresponsible" and "pathological" regarding how our congress dealt with—or didn't deal with—cutting green-house-gas emissions.

That last point provided my main thrust, and I reprised it a few times because it demanded federal-government solutions *in partnership with* the so-called free market. The endgame, of course, would be a transformed (so-called "green") economy. "We can't do without that. It's absolutely mandatory!" I said. "Heaven help us if we fail."

I didn't mention the necessity for a new and different national power grid but I wished I had because constructing it would generate a river of jobs and help rebuild the middle class. "Conservative-Reform" stood for this, too. Nor did I mention that arresting global-climate change was not a *political* issue, but sure as the sky it required political solutions. At some point I realized I should have prepared for this better.

National issues are all connected in a web, I told my meager audience, and the Conservative-Reform Party could only deal with some of them. Mainly we aimed to provide leadership toward *sustainability*—environmental and economic. Consequently the U. S. *should not be* the world's police force. We *can't* be. Congress needs to understand that we're no longer "the richest country in the world" because, to quote myself, "We're freakin' broke!" And we can't be giving away money to other countries, no matter what.

For barely an instant I clearly saw my old comrades observing me from nearby. The face only of King Agamemnon appeared distinct as he showed me keen interest.

Ahhhh! That's when I actually felt my neck swell and deltoids thicken and chest expand. In my head and heart some kind of valve opened to release a fountain of conviction that I wished were a storm.

But my time was almost up. I felt like delivering a stemwinder, or get some practice delivering one, so I gave it a shot.

For a second I thought to invoke what the federal government was doing *right* in Twenty-First-Century USA, but the instances were too embarrassingly few. Inexperience again taught me to prepare a lot better.

Instead I chose to cite the many *good things* in American life. ("*Who makes* the best air conditioners and heavy-duty machinery and medical equipment in the *world*? Who makes the best computers and cars and movies in the world? Who makes the best *music*?! All right, who's got the best doctors and nurses and teachers and city libraries in the world? The same country that's got the best universities and supermarkets and shopping malls on Earth: *We do*! The USA!")

That got me some "Amen's"

When I tried to make eye contact with the audience as a whole and declare—"Everybody *consider this*: what all the rest of the world produces that *benefits mankind* . . . is mostly just frosting on the cake, or stuffing in the turkey, or dill butter on the trout!"—that's when I knew I'd gotten carried away.

(By then I felt relief that Julie wasn't there to see me lose myself in public.)

The hard part was coming up with a couple sentences to solidify my point about the Conservative-Reform Party being crucial to the health of the U-S-of-A, and I can't say that I succeeded. So when I finished I sure was surprised—gratified—by patches of hearty applause. An emphatically loud source was one of the attractive young women I had talked with earlier (the one other than the one who'd given me the cigar). I definitely wished Harry were there. Maybe it would have been all right if Julie and Jay had been there, too.

After the emcee finished his *shtick* I got a chance to meet and talk with a number of earnest souls. About five of us even walked together to "The Peak," the nearby brew pub, where somebody paid for my round and somebody else ordered plates of nachos, which I couldn't disdain. After another gift-round of good, fresh brew and hearty conversation, I went home weighing more and whistling.

Of course media coverage of the event was maybe less than superficial, barely to mention off the mark regarding my speech: "Dan Hachek, chairperson of the new Conservative Reform Party, invoked Higher Powers to curtail greenhouse gases and restore fiscal and political integrity in our national government." I actually read this on Monday morning. But on television news that Sunday evening I did get a few seconds of exposure (at least on two stations), and what I saw and heard seemed fairly cogent. I could confidently say that I had generated a little name recognition for the Party. Henceforth I would acknowledge that, yes, *I had a "Cause."* Welching would not be an option.

CHAPTER 12

SMALL PARTY

"Well, some good news," Maya Catchings announced abruptly, "is the endorsement we got from the archbishop yesterday. Anybody see it in the newspaper? It's quite emphatic."

This was true. The Conservative-Reform Party had received unexpected advocacy from the local Roman-Catholic archbishop in a printed newspaper interview. Some of us around the big glass table nodded affirmatively.

"The archbishop is definitely cool," Harry declared, "although I can't say I've read what he said in the papers."

Next we got blessed by vocal tones that sounded bathed in molasses and bourbon declaring: "The Church hierarchy is commendably well informed"—uttered by a late-middle-aged white man wearing a bowtie and sport coat but otherwise best described as nondescript.

We—Maya, Jimmy Kestrel, Hal, Pancho, Alyssa, Kip, myself, and another man whom I didn't know—regarded this speaker benignly.

"Sir!" I addressed him. "I'm Dan Hachek. We shook hands when I arrived but I didn't hear your name."

"Mickey Caldwell," the fellow said. —A little nod or bow— "At your service."

"*Encantado*," I responded, puckishly charmed.

Kip introduced the other new person in the group (who I thought looked familiar) as Wilson Kocourek, "a concerned citizen of many arts," a lawyer-businessman well known in town. A big fellow, to me he evoked an older Bully Kendall.

We had just gathered this evening at Kip Whitbread's house in one of the upscale west-side suburbs. Our aim was to strategize a high-profile campaign to make more impact quicker. Doing that entailed, once again, clarifying the Party's message (Harry called it "the new party line"). Even though I was the one who had called this meeting, I chose to let things develop as they would.

Jimmy declared, "Well, our mission is our message, as Dan says. So we have to get the message out. For the time being, that's enough to do."

Maya offered that broadcasting a party's message entailed two endeavors: "We've got to get speaking engagements for Dan, we've got to raise money. They go hand-in-hand; one feeds the other. *Everyone* can help in both areas." She promptly gave us examples of how we could all pitch in.

Jimmy added a fillip: "Maybe we'll actually pay Maya some of her fees."

Kip took the helm: "Okay, now what can we say that'll grab minds—what do we broadcast to people who don't vote yet but might? How do we *transform* public thinking to gain critical mass?"

"A *transformational enterprise*—that's good," Wilson said.

I held back for a beat, then interposed that the *basis* for everything the Party would do is to advance the common good, the general welfare. We, our fetus of a party, needed to emphasize this—very publicly—because that principle had been *wrung out of* political discourse in recent years. In so many words I added that 'common good' is *a basic necessity* for *everyone* because we humans have divine attributes, so we've got the responsibility to live up to them. Government's job is to enable us—*all* of us—to do that. "Hence," I said, "'conservative reform.'"

"All *right*"—from Harry. From Mickey: pipe-tobacco-sweet vocables of approval.

Not to be outdone, Kip and Wilson each uttered reinforcing abstractions. I especially liked the parts about our form of government having been founded to "empower us" to "best exercise our natures." (But neither man offered to say why.) In the meantime Harry studied his shoe and Alyssa and Pancho found ways to explore Saturn.

(After the meeting I corralled those three and expounded that maybe I'm odd, but as far as I can see we all *need* philosophy. Without it, I said, "there's hardly reason to do anything except breathe." I expected a noncommittal response but they seemed to regard what I'd said as axiomatic. If anything sustains hope, there it is.)

Reaching consensus on which of the Party's themes we'd nail to the door turned out to be surprisingly easy because for us the mandates were clear: government, led by the feds, must partner with industry to wean the U. S. off fossil fuels; federal budgets must be balanced in the foreseeable future and implement a feasible plan for paying off the national debt in our current lifetimes. Et cetera, et cetera, et cetera. Nothing unreasonable, all of it good sense. But we might have overused the cliché "political will."

Conversation ebbed. The process we'd undergone this evening had taken longer than I'd expected; it felt bone-sapping. (My goodness.)

As kind of a post-script Mickey declared: "We should note that *infrastructure* includes airports and water systems and wastewater plants and our rail system. Also dams. It's not just roads and bridges."

Alyssa piped up: "You mean it doesn't include PBS?" Glitter of her eyes and a wry smile told us she'd meant this tongue-in-cheek. Still Kip offered: "We can be sure that *quadrupling* federal-government funding for PBS and NPR would barely scratch the hood on the federal budget!"

Time to break off. We wrapped by quickly expressing the consensus that we lacked insight to how the government should deal with illegal immigration (a real hot-button issue), so we wouldn't mention it within a party statement of purpose. ("*What is* 'comprehensive immigration reform' anyway?" someone interposed rhetorically. Nobody knew.)

Thus I didn't broach, however tentatively, my proposal that the country legalize—and of course regulate—so-called narcotics. Good thing I didn't. The proposal blatantly expels reality and reason because implementing it would merely save bunches of lives, barely to mention billions on enforcement. It would never fly.

Kip had taken notes on a laptop. He said he'd post our mandates on the Party's Web page and submit them to *Reddit*. Desultory affirmative nods. For a moment we sat or stood wordlessly. As though on signal "smart phones" came up all around.

I happened to glance at Harry and notice him looking, briefly but intently, across the table to search Maya's face. Maya registered this, and a pall crossed her countenance. Did I spot disdain there?

Wilson spoke up: "There's a kind of symmetrical beauty to our agenda. Achieving any one of our stated objectives hinges on accomplishing all the others."

"Analogous to an object of art," Mickey intoned.

"This is really exciting!" said Alyssa. (*Not* tongue-in-cheek.) She stood up, backed away from the rest of us and raised her *iPad*. Everyone had to look toward her and smile.

Briefly I wondered if we were enthralled by naïveté, but some Western-European countries and China and Japan and (dare we mention) California were already implementing some measures that we'd been propounding.

Seemingly apropos of nothing, Alyssa did herself proud (in my playbook) by abruptly, firmly declaring: "When we stand for the U. S. *making the transition* to a climate-safe economy as our *core principle*—it's like we're inventing a metaphorical hub of a bicycle wheel, with all of the spokes radiating from it. The grand transition isn't just a centerpiece. It's *the hub* for all the spokes! It keeps 'em together and moves 'em forward."

"Bravo!" I said, and I wasn't alone.

Unhappily, an anonymous loud voice called Alyssa's hub "the new lodestar," and another voice declared "it should create a *river* of jobs," then from various directions came a thicket of intentionally mixed metaphors. I might have been guilty of one or two.

Regardless. Our mission was clear: proclaim our Conservative-Reform message. Where? Everywhere; everywhere across the land. Maya was in charge.

Before we tried again to adjourn, Maya verbally observed that we had to raise Party membership, for only about a dozen names were actually registered. Someone pointed out that attracting people to a political party surely necessitated fronting candidates for political office. That implicitly raised issues we would confront in a week or two. (Dan Hachek having resolved to keep absolutely clear of running for anything.) In the interim, Party members should voice opinions about current events and issues on the basis of *why we'd formed* this new party. But no one—Maya and Hal included—could speak on behalf of the chairman, me.

Wilson offered three ideas for publicizing the Party on the Web. I was not charmed, so I deferred to Pancho and Hal.

"We've got that covered," Pancho said in response. Hal nodded affirmatively. (It occurred to me they both made cratefuls of cash by programming things for businesses and designing stuff for the Web, activities they regarded much like a hobby.)

Alyssa proposed putting a video about the C-R Party on *YouTube* and some other Internet site to attract membership and donations. Pancho and Hal said they had the video equipment and a perfect place to use it. Wilson said he'd like to work up a script for me to deliver—with Alyssa's input. I thought this sounded very cool. We set a tentative date for bringing it to fruition.

"Don't clutter up your calendar much," Maya advised me. "Before you plan something, let me know. It's called prudence." She added: "I'm trying to set you up with speeches, I hope interviews. Plan A. Remember?"

"Right." For some reason I was bemused wondering what in the world Ira Blumenthal was doing. I couldn't afford his services, of course, but I hoped to see more of him; I needed his savvy and considered him a friend. I didn't convey this to Maya. She was busy rooting in a folder for a paper that she finally extracted and showed to me: a flyer advertising an imminent face-off in east Clark County among major-party candidates for state office. Elections were months away; this event was essentially an interest-stimulator, something to put on the calendar. It didn't look like it was for me.

"I'll bet I can get you a speaker's slot at this," Maya said. "It'll get you good exposure; I'm sure of that. What do you think about going to Vegas in four days?"

My initial thought was hell, no. I'd had enough of Las Vegas many times over. But Doc Julie could use a break; she might actually enjoy going there. I decided to broach it to her that evening, and I told Maya that I'd put my answer on her office voice-mail.

"Best not to pass up any opportunities for getting publicity," was her response.

CHAPTER 13

GETTIN' STRONGER

Of course during the week of my speaking engagement in east Las Vegas Julie couldn't take a couple days off. *Of course* Maya was successful getting me included on the roster of speakers for the event. The theme of my slot: "An Alternative Party's Middle Way—Implications for Nevada." It struck me as an interesting challenge.

In a few days Julie would be attending a workshop at a hospital in Sacramento; I wouldn't be deserting her at home. Harry actually expressed enthusiasm for a trip to Sin City when I broached his going with me. So I accepted the opportunity to speak, and Harry and I took a commuter flight to Las Vegas and got a good rate on separate rooms at a hotel-casino owned by a pair of muscular brothers. (Harry insisted on his own room; for what purpose—I declined to ask.) We managed a good time during two nights we spent there, verifying the maxim that superior persons turn adversity to advantage.

But early-evening heat puts anyone to disadvantage in Las Vegas in summer. The event *would* have to be an outdoor affair. I'd hydrated plenty (wishing for crisp pale ale) before taking a seat on the speakers' platform following an intermission. For a half hour we listened to a Democrat and a Republican trade obscurities dealing with local issues. The audience—somewhere between two and three hundred—had been having a pleasant but unremarkable time. When I finally got up to speak I needed a bathroom and a shot of adrenalin. In two minutes I'd introduced the Party (rather tepidly), then unvolitionally my presentation bounded up an incline and went airborne.

"You can't miss the parallels!" I fairly shouted as I tried to make a point and inject some juice in the proceedings. "If we say to hell with climate change here in Nevada, they'll say that's fine in Washington; if they say in D.C. that it's okay to heat up the planet—profits and salaries *mustn't* be lost—we go right along with it here. Send the National Guard to fight for governments overseas? Perfectly okay; we are the world's cops. Don't worry about the budget! Don't worry about our national debt. We give the world leadership! And all around the world they gotta think we're crazy, just bonkers-nuts.

"Well, at least here in Nevada we do worry about the budget! Which means we scrimp on everything that's precious to us, and the federal government doesn't help us worth squat—like sufficiently funding education initiatives. Then Washington won't take the lead in developing—or deploying— clean-power technologies, so of course we don't, either. But it's okay if *California* does heavy lifting!"

By this juncture I thought I'd said most of what I'd intended, so I indulged myself by dipping into a thought that led me to say: "Do you know why you can't reasonably take a walking tour of the Pentagon? —Have you ever been there?— It's too big! You know, you'd have real difficulty walking the halls and checking out all the rooms in the U.S. embassy in Baghdad. You know why? Same reason; too big. Now don't try to believe all that stuff is essential! And guess who's gonna have to pay for it: our kids and grandkids! Maybe their kids, too."

When I paused to look into nearby (predominately white) faces, I could see they were taking me seriously. Implicitly my major theme was that Nevada—*the whole country*—needs, absolutely needs, "conservative reform." At the outset of my speech I'd outlined what the Conservative-Reform Party stood for, with some specifics. Now I couldn't resist railing against recent federal-government failures and how they played out in Clark County and Carson City. ("Have you noticed the price of prescription drugs lately? How 'bout gas? You know, some of us might depend on those things!") I didn't bother to point out the travesty of a national nuclear-waste dump at Yucca Mountain near Las Vegas; that was too easy a target.

Now, my bladder over-full and my temperature over-heated, I had to hammer home my last point: that politicians— and people generally—have to change the way we do business, and it all begins at home, right now. The Conservative-Reform Party stands for that kind of change.

I said exactly that but I tried to infuse it with enthusiasm. When I finished I did a *namaste* (taking care not to overdo it) and returned to my seat.

I definitely heard some applause, and quite a few people approached me on the grounds later and expressed concurrence or affinity. That was good, but only after I had found a lavatory. When I did, I saw that my pastel-blue dress shirt was soaked through in obvious spots; I almost tore off my necktie (worn for no good reason I could think of) and ripped the top buttons off my shirt.

"Hey, hey, that was sort of good," my brother said when I met him back outside. "Too bad you're not running for Congress or something."

"Sure, I can just see myself *compounding* disaster in the hallowed halls of Congress."

"You can probably do that as well as anybody there."

"A fair point."

The time was right for Harry to buy me a beer.

*   *   *

Unusual occurrences made of whole cloth seem to come in clusters. When I called up Maya the next morning to apprise her of how I thought my speech had gone (along with whether I'd received any TV coverage, which to my knowledge I hadn't), I capped my report with a comment about how I'd lately come to look remarkably like . . . "a politician."

"Well, from what I can see, maybe you *are* one," Maya rejoined. "That's *honorable*. So go with it!"

What could I say? I did ask whether she had any more speaking events lined up for me, and she said she did; I should contact her, *sans* failure, in two days.

After Julie and I returned home from our separate trips and cleared the baggage, I recounted, in passing, what Harry and Maya had said about my being a closet politician. Just as I suspected, Julie not only agreed with that, she considered it axiomatic. But she surprised me by waxing emphatic.

I had to grant that everything I'd done since I'd gone public was consonant with my conscience, with no down-side other than the small change I paid for the privilege of self-fulfillment. (Plus I got ego strokes I didn't need.) But from the very outset of this fine adventure I suspected that one day I would get overwhelmed by my urge to crusade, which would surely be to Julie's and my detriment.

And of course I was right about that.

*   *   *

Two days later I contacted Maya to learn about all sorts of pending events at which I could raise the Party's profile (if that's what I seriously, really, wanted to do). Subconsciously I started upgrading the décor in my office, beginning with my commissioning the manufacture of two classy metal signs designating the office as Party headquarters. To be on the safe side, I rented a large postal box (should Party mail swell with donations), and I opened a Party checking account at a nearby Wells Fargo in the event we waged some kind of campaign. Once I even considered renting a satellite office in Carson City.

Maya expected me to receive and respond to a lot of information. With almost no forethought I bought the latest Dell computer for Party headquarters, also a small brown refrigerator to go in the corner there. Since the place was still my own office, I hung pictures of Julie and Jay and me on one wall. On the opposite wall I mounted large portraits of Thomas Jefferson, Benjamin Franklin, and Claude Williams.

Claude Williams? Sometimes people would ask. (His portrait—that of a debonair, vibrant, aged black man jovially cradling a fiddle—I'd labeled with his name and the dates of his well-spent life, 1908-2005.) Usually I just replied that he was "one of my heroes." In fact he might have been the finest jazz fiddler who'd ever lived. As Julie avers, nowhere on his discs do we hear a bar "that he just phones in." He might have done his finest recorded work after he turned eighty. Everyone needs inspiration like that.

As Maya was busy finding speaking engagements for me, and when delivering the Conservative-Reform message collided with my life at home, I got extra motivation from two of Mitch Freeman's columns (maybe prompted by dear Alyssa).

In one column Mitch called me "an earnest fellow with sound ideas." Good; I accepted that. In a column the following week, though, he actually declared that the Conservative-Reform Party agenda was "difficult to confute with any validity." Everyone, he said, "would be well advised to pay it close attention." I was so pleased with that I telephoned him at his office. I couldn't *thank* him, of course, but I could tell him that I agreed with his take on the Party and his encomium was "not too shabby."

I hope he felt gratified.

LONG ODDS

Our reasoning told us this expedition—to sail for three days (providing fair seas), then forge onto hostile land and destroy a stronghold of mighty resources—could be disastrous. Now on many days we know this to be so. United by promises of Agamemnon—sometimes by his threats—Achaean and Danaan fighting men and ships are soon to outnumber those of Ilios. But as we begin to choke off commerce with Ilios and prepare to encircle its walls, Trojan might swells before us.

Warriors from many tribes of the Hittite empire come to protect the walls we wish to level. We have learned names of strange enemies: Carians, Paionians, Leleges, Pelasgians, Lycians, Mysians, and others. Chariots and soldiers of Lydia and even Phrygia, a land that once nourished roots of my king's Atreid family, join the Trojan battle order. Our daring plan of conquest changes: we struggle not to be overwhelmed.

Late this day we attack their west flank of encampments to cut supply routes. We find a strange surprise: my o-kas are beset by proud horsemen who speak a language we know to be Helladic. These are Greeks! They charge my chariots, a headstrong mistake. Yet they cause us painful casualties. I see what must be done and order retreat, for our mission is not possible against many Hittite horsemen—now these as well.

In retreat we fight to survive amid wind and dust. Surprise and difficulty make me forget fear. Strong gusts from the gods spare my driver from horsemen's arrows I cannot fend. Again this happens, then at close quarters I miss my throw. We must fly for bare safety and breath.

Who are these attackers, why are they here?! What causes all these enemies to align with Ilios? In time I learn the enemy Danaoi are not Danaan but men of Thrace, Thracian Greeks. But I never learn how Priam is able to call upon so many allies, and why they come. There seems no answer—other than greed . . . or fear of treachery.

*   *   *

The weekend after Hal's and my trip to east Vegas, as I sat at home drinking wake-up coffee I caught a glimmering of various elements in my life coalescing. An unseen pattern had likely been forming all along, and soon I might discern it!

Of course: this led me to think of money: the basis for everything besides sex and love and honor (and *they* entailed money). If I concentrated on raising funds, I thought maybe I'd be successful. Maya would provide useful lore. Yes, I was naïve about many things, but I knew that in affairs of the world money means everything—even more than disposition.

Money? —For what, the Party? Disposition? To do *what*? If I was serious about the Conservative-Reform Party making a beneficial impact on how we live, especially regarding that pesky matter of our planet heating up and drying up *and flooding* and dying, I might have to put myself out there and run for some high-profile political office to get the Party better noticed. Maybe this was axiomatic. I had to admit the notion thrilled me even as it gave my stomach a twist.

About mid-morning, on a whim I took a short drive instead of a walk. (My family *never* drove just to be driving.) I made sure to pass through a couple neighborhoods that gave me a sense of comfort before I drove to a nearby Regional Park called Rancho San Rafael. As I did, I found myself hoping that I would be wise; that I wouldn't screw up; that I would do meaningful things ahead. Ah, *hah*! That's when I realized I'd soon be making a weighty decision, never mind not knowing what I would decide *about*. Yet my decision would likely be affirmative.

Along the many ways I have sailed, beginning long before we reached this cursed place, I have come to value results of my actions rather than rewards (except for joy and pride). I can measure results by whether I achieve goals I desire. But first, I try to see if my actions will fit the design of my psyche and powers.

Thus I have come to believe all human plans, all tactics, all paths to objectives require graceful simplicity to win. Sometimes clarity must be imposed or a stratagem will come undone.

Thus too I have learned that actions by any man (unless he is a slave) should accord with the man's plan or vision—before demands made by gods or other men or the moment. A man acting solely because he must, in his desire to meet demands placed upon him, can often make good. But rarely is that sufficient. I know of better ways to live.

*   *   *

On the local TV news Julie and I heard an item about a professor Troy Culpepper from Oxford University in Britain arriving at our little university in Reno to give a short series of lectures about certain themes applicable to Bronze-Age Greece. I missed hearing what occasioned Dr. Culpepper's visit and started to disregard the fact until I heard Julie say, "It takes a real Brit to have a name like Troy Culpepper. I wonder what his middle name is."

"Did they say his specialty is Bronze-Age Greece?" I asked.

This Julie affirmed.

I uttered, "*Troy* Culpepper?" to which she nodded.

"Could be interesting," I said, "so long as it's not too esoteric."

Julie remarked, "Oh, maybe. It's not *classical* Greece— when they made all those quantum leaps in civilization we've learned about."

"Do you suppose the classical period just emerged from a vacuum?" I said.

Julie responded, "Yeah, I know context is important. But that Bronze Age, and the whole rest of the context, it's a secondary point of interest; you know?"

"Maybe to a lot of Greeks their Age of Heroes gave them a sense of clarity, a definition they could relate to."

"I'm sure that *Heroic Age* was pretty barbaric," Julie said. "Of course they all were . . . ."

"Well," I said, "those *were* heroic times. For some people."

We dropped the subject for matters more immediate, but it stayed with me because when I had woken up earlier that day, while Julie was getting ready to leave for work, just after I had pushed away phantasms of the darling daughter she and I had lost years before, a word flashed into my conscious—and when I said it aloud I thought it sounded like a name: *Iphigenia*.

Now, as fortune so often directs me, I knew of something I had to do.

HEROIC AGE

"Professor Culpepper, my name is Dan Hachek," I said and stuck out my hand.

A distinguished-looking fellow who looked like he should be named Alistair and hosting a Brit-lit-masterworks series on PBS, Culpepper took my hand with a genuine smile and a hearty greeting. The professor might have appeared tweedy in public, but now he looked dressed for a round of golf. We had met in the Liberal Arts faculty lounge.

"Do you know how your name translates?" he asked. —"From the Czech."

"I can't say that I do."

"Oh."

I saw no need to mention the Conservative-Reform Party, and the party name never arose between us.

Before this meeting I'd done enough background research on the 'Net and (some might say anomalously) at our central library to learn that Dr. Culpepper, a Yorkshire man, had spent substantial periods of time physically exploring Mycenae and Mycenaean sites. And once he'd even taken a sailboat trip to what had been Troy and trod upon ancient fortifications. I had a few questions to ask him and he was most amenable.

"Who was Iphigenia?" I said, and he told me she was a legendary figure: the youngest daughter of Agamemnon—perhaps also a legendary figure—who capitulated to his fellow kings and allowed her to be sacrificed by priests to assuage the gods and preclude sure defeat at Troy.

"Do you think a king would offer up his own daughter to be killed?" I asked.

"In context, I'm afraid that would have been a probability," the professor said. "After all, those were barbarous times. Precivilized, you might say. In those days, any group of people deploying rationality were like lamps in the night; they had a lot of darkness to overcome. Not just ignorance, but superstition and fears. We *still* have a lot to overcome. Obviously."

We let that subject evaporate. I was more concerned about other things and could only impose on this man for so long. Maybe that's why I didn't mention that I'd never physically been to Mycenae; I'd never been to Greece. But before I asked a couple key questions I mused aloud that the war against Troy held historical verity, as did the leadership of Agamemnon.

"Well," said the professor, "we do know that a mighty citadel existed near the Dardanelles and flourished during the Bronze Age. It was very small by our standards but virtually impregnable and well protected from outside the walls. The kings who ruled it—and the isolated tip of land there—seemed to carry incommensurate clout in that part of the world, mainly through piracy combined with, you know, strategic geography . . . ."

"They were rich?" I ventured.

"From what I could gather they were very wealthy."

Thus the professor continued: "In the late Bronze Age, despite protections they must have gotten from being part of Hatti—the Hittite empire—the Trojan fortress was evidently sacked by Danaan—that was a name the Greeks used to call themselves . . . ."

"I know who the Danaoi were. Also the Achaians."

"Right. Invaders probably from Mycenae, waging a trade war, say, around 1250 B.C. We don't know how the Greeks overcame the defenders. We have only the myths."

"Well, those *were* heroic times," I said.

Beat. The man glanced at me quizzically across the low table between us. I adjusted my posture.

Although I meant to ask questions, I heard myself say that victory by the Greeks might have been "elegantly simple." I explained: "That's earthquake country, right? The west-wall gate was relatively vulnerable. Didn't Pariamu have Thracian allies? They were *Greeks*. Maybe they weren't allies you could rely on during an earthquake, when the time might be ripe for joining the stronger side. Foremost, they loved gold and women."

Professor Culpepper regarded me oddly. At last I asked him my major question:

"What happened to a persona named Amphilochus?"

"Amphilochus?" He pronounced the name flatly, ignoring its musical quality. "A shadowy figure. Perhaps a commander fighting at Troy. We can't say that he really existed."

"He might be legendary as Agamemnon might be legendary," I said.

"All right. *Legend* has it . . . Amphilochus—and we have no documentation of this—legend says he emigrated to Cilicia in Asia Minor, what's now southern Turkey. Probably after returning to Mycenae after the war with Troy."

"Ah! But why would that be?"

"We don't know. We do know Mycenae was going through bad changes. You've heard what happened to Agamemnon upon his *nostos*."

"I know treachery haunted the land. The time of heroes had passed." I felt seized by sudden knowledge. "Even before Troy fell, maybe our man had learned of dishonor in the House of Pelops and could not abide it . . . . Maybe, over in—you say *Cilicia*—he had better access to raw materials for making bronze."

Again Culpepper regarded me oddly.

"Did Agamemnon really use a thousand ships?" I asked.

"Ultimately maybe half that number, in the aggregate. Depends on the length of the siege. In those days a war like that would have been a huge undertaking. Very profitable for ship builders, bronze makers, merchants, everyone. Getting from Argos to Troy, by the way, was usually a three-day sail unless the winds and weather were good, then two and a half days. It's hard to believe—Troy was such a miniscule state; the Hittite emperor probably tried to sustain it because of its location and wealth. It helped him maintain his realm, which was overly extensive."

"I wonder if this predates the 'divine-right-of-kings' notion," I said.

"For the most part . . . maybe. But look at Egypt. Under that concept they maintained a stable society for 2,500 years. Mycenae didn't last five hundred."

"Agamemnon's family relied mainly on their strong right arms," I asserted.

"That, and gold—all of it seized elsewhere. They were a very *spirited* lot."

"I thought the Mycenaeans were pretty down-to-earth," I said. "I hadn't learned they were known for being spiritual."

"I said *spirited,* which would be anything *but* 'spiritual,' although—who knows—some of that lot might have developed a spiritual basis for their wars and plundering."

Again I felt transported by sudden knowledge. "I think the Mycenaean strong suit was a capacity to *build on* whatever they had," I heard myself averring to the expert in such matters. Still I added: "Golden Mycenae might have really advanced civilization if it hadn't been subverted by maybe a change in climate or overpopulation, or maybe by mean humanity."

To my delight, I heard, "Yes! You have to immerse yourself—try to get *into*—their culture. You get a very real sense that for several generations, at least for a significant segment of time, something . . . let's say it was something *special*, something indefinable, came emanating from inside their Lions' Gate; that's the main entrance to Mycenae."

Culpepper paused, then concluded his thought: "We don't know what that indefinable quality was; I doubt that we *can* know. —I can't even be positive those animal forms carved on the gateway are lions."

"Those *were* heroic times," I said and considered rising to leave.

Beat. Beat. Now the professor leveled his hazel-green eyes upon my soul. He spoke deliberately, as though rendering dictation, actually for the delectation of us both. He said, "It seems Mycenae was the core of a kind of power, if you will, that I think we could define as . . . ."

He went silent again for a moment. I could almost hear his mind shoot out metaphysical tentacles through past millennia, and upward.

He spoke: "I think we might call it *transcendent*, for lack of a better term. There was a transcendent quality some Mycenaeans must have generated. As I say, you have to really get into the culture. Evidence shows they weren't all just pirates and freebooters, although they were that, too. They sacked so-called cities whenever they could."

"*Transcendent.* That's good," I said. By now I was feeling elated. At some moment I rose to leave

Dr. Culpepper had likewise risen. Together we strode the several feet to the open doorway and stopped to shake hands.

As I turned to leave I heard my own voice say quietly: "They are lions."

CHAPTER 16

POLITICAL?

When I left Professor Troy Culpepper I felt a strange new strength. It gave me the urge to buy and wolf down a large submarine sandwich before I went to my car. That afternoon I had learned something I had only intuited before: my very being—my existence—must hold more reality than I knew.

Before I drove home, a different concern that I'd submerged all day rose up to nettle me: I couldn't *not* tell Julie about my experience that afternoon. But she would want to know why I had undertaken it. What had *prompted* me to meet the professor? Good questions she wouldn't disdain asking.

At dinner that evening I introduced the subject of dreams versus memory. Then I simply told Julie what it was like to ride onto a wind-swept plain in a hostile land, trusting in my driver and the gods. I finished a brief description by saying,

"Sometimes the futility of this can be so overwhelming . . . you almost think it unreasonable to hope to survive."

"Tell me more," Julie said.

So I told her of many things. Those which are most important—facts in my story and truths I tell that are not facts—those things I have already told you here.

When I finished describing my Aegean experiences, Julie asked: "So how did you die? What took you out?"

"I have no recollection. Evidently . . . *legendarily* . . . it happened in exile."

"More than once I've heard you say that you feel like you're out of place somehow. It never occurred to me that you've been pushed out of a different time! To me, you seem so . . . *contemporary*. You know?" At this Julie smiled at me endearingly. She added: "Good thing you're adaptable. Over all those centuries!"

"Exile's not so bad," I said. "And sometimes you can't beat the company here."

From this desolate hilltop I watch as sunlight settles beneath the Bay of Baashik and Achaean sentries stir in their positions on other hills. We have dogs now; this gives me ease.

I can turn toward home or look to Ilios. First I savor mouthfuls of honey mead, then I try to see Golden Mycenae, three days sail from here. Drink helps me now, and I must wonder what Hittites—most from places far from here—are now drinking. We have planned no attack on the morrow because we have many labors to do instead. But if we are not assailed I will do a secret dance, for then I shall make bronze.

At last, I plan to start my true work. For this I need help from the gods to hold Hittites and Trojans and Thracians in their camps, and I feel that will come. I recall the many times Agamemnon told me we must do—no matter the difficulties—what the gods deign for us to do. For that we must exert our souls. I agreed, surely, for I serve the work taught me by my father, and his father, and fathers before. Yet I have wondered how we can know the will of any god. When I put this before my king he said, "I know to consult the priests."

To this I had no response and offered none. But long before we came to this Plain of Troia I was learning a different way to uncover knowledge a man needs. Our many struggles here—under burdens of danger and hardship and deprivation every day—cause my way of learning to become clear like morning air in the Argolid:

First I need look only within my Self, my whole self, for answers to questions a man must ask. Then—with my psyche laid open to every truth—I must look deeply at everything and everyone around me. If I demand no haste, answers come—and sometimes more questions. Priests are of little help. This much I have come to know.

*   *   *

"Running for any public office is a whole new way of living," Julie commented, her noncommittal tone masking dismay. Now I regretted having broached the subject.

"Do you have any idea what office to run for?" Julie asked.

"Nope. I don't even know for sure—*yet*—that I have to. We're speaking of an enterprise that's not exactly an integral component of my life, let alone my personality."

"But it does seem to be a result of maybe everything that's gone on with you," she offered. "It might be part of a pattern—say, an overall plan—that's not completely evident yet."

Now *that was* an interesting point.

"I don't know," I said. "Could be."

The thought occurred to me that I'd never really identified or defined my strengths. I just didn't care to know what they were. Simply testing myself over the decades built a good-enough inventory. (I fancied saying "My middle name is '*Guts.*'") Striving to act in ways that I was strong struck me as constraining, even oppressive. But I thought I'd be wise to pin down my strengths in case I'd need to use them down the road. Julie would know my capabilities, and she'd know where I'd be smart *not* to tread.

"I'm sure I've got to *earn* my alleged middle name," I said. "Absolutely, I've got to advance the Conservative-Reform cause. I mean, who else can we count on? I really don't have an option, so I think I'll be going public."

Julie fell silent, but I could tell what she was thinking-feeling: running for office to raise the Party profile shouldn't be up to me; I'd already done my part. Of course she was right, but maybe not entirely.

"How's it going with your personal-'transcendence' goal?" my son Doctor Jay asked me in response to Julie's or my mentioning that I might seek elective office. Jay was visiting our house at the time and conversation had naturally segued that way. A good-looking fellow (of course), I liked how his lean build never deterred him from hefting his motorcycle onto mountain trails. –My admiration for that recurred often.

"How do you know about my 'transcendence' goal? I don't recall ever mentioning it except to your mother."

"Uncle Harrison told me."

"Oh."

To answer his query I said, "Well, it might be implicit in what I've been trying to do. If not, I'll just have to worry about it later. My plate's really full; I don't need to keep trying to stretch myself."

Jay said, "Dad, you'd better do what you know you have to do. Your political work might be your share of the *dharma* talking."

He hardly ever called me "dad." Thus I gathered he implicitly emphasized his point. The kid might be smart.

I looked to Doc Julie; she nodded affirmatively, said nothing. Like when a car windshield wiper passes over wet glass in front of my face, the road looked clear. I thought, hey, that's it. As soon as I find a high-enough-profile elective office I could feasibly stand for, I *would* take a ride into The Big Tent going full bore. Of course I'd have to learn some basic realities, such as gaffes a smart man would avoid making—which I'd probably commit even if I ran for some public office unopposed.

CHAPTER 17

POLITICAL ANIMAL

The man spoke briefly to the clerk whom he evidently knew, and I didn't like what I heard. You might have taken the guy to be simply ignorant. I took him to be intentionally ignorant.

We stood almost shoulder to shoulder at the convenience-store counter where he had finished his transaction and I would pay for gas. I looked up at him and made firm eye contact.

"*Since when* can you say global warming—actually *global-climate change*—is a hoax?" I demanded. "Haven't you been outside lately?" (I was ready to bet that the work truck parked at the pumps out front was his.)

A still-youthful-middle-aged white man in work clothes. I thought him a little over six feet, maybe under 200 pounds. Well-formed, healthy-looking. He regarded me blankly.

Beat. "Well, it is. It's a damned fraud. Ask the U. S. Senators from Oklahoma or Texas or Nebraska! That's for instance. Don't you own a radio?"

"Look," I said, "anyone who thinks like that is a damn fool."

A dirty cloud scudded across the impassive face. The clerk behind the counter cautiously stepped away. Reflexively I turned my left side toward the man. (I was at least 30 before I'd learned not to face an attack fully-frontal.)

I almost wished he would have taken a poke at me. My intent was to block or slip it, then kick him or drill him with one or two (or three or four or five) good shots if I could get close enough. And if he landed one on me and I survived, his only consolation in the aftermath would be never needing to get a vasectomy.

But the fellow just gave me a disdainful look and walked away. If he had waited to confront me outside, I would have been ready. If he'd had some ignorant buddies in the truck to help him make sure I'd regret telling the truth too loud, well then, I thought, let's see what they can do.

This was the kind of mind-set I had been developing of late. I intended keeping it as long as I could.

I gaze at mountains of clouds sprayed by orange and red and turning purple in sea-blue sky over Ilios. Surely our sky over the Argolid is beautiful as this. And our hills—on one of which stands my home village—are many times more fair than anything we see here. We must bring victory to this expedition. This we know.

Only my desire for home, for things of life that are real, causes me to think we should not be here.

Under my orders we line ten chariots and horses—all at the ready—behind brush alongside one end of our trench. Near the other end we line ten more chariots, also hidden. Thus they will remain even after dark, for we stand warned of attack. Massed Hittite and Trojan infantry can yet overrun our position.

If they do that we will all die or be driven back to the sea (except for those of us who can be enslaved). Greek life will then wither by Troy's hand. This is sure. Yet my own needs—I yearn for my wife and son—and (again) our lack of sufficient food—make me wish to change our course while we can. I cannot say how. Only my desire is sure: I want us all to return home to Golden Mycenae. First we need to live and see more days.

I say to comrades, "Who cares about what we do here if we all die?"

Their answer I know before they speak, and I am right. Two comrades respond in words Achilles and Diomedes would declare: "Ages of men after us."

"And about them," I say, "why do we care?"

No answer comes to me. This I expected.

As we disband for our posts I hear a fellow captain declare my name. When I respond he says, "We must do all we can, sir."

At this I nod and lower my gaze to the walls of Troy itself.

*　　*　　*

CHAPTER 18

ACCEPTANCE

"**L**isten, Dan. If we're going to be *serious about* generating reform and reversing climate change—and that's gonna require a full-court press from everyone who claims to be rational—we need *you* to run for President. –Of the United States!"

Wilson Kocurek was saying this, and he appeared to be talking to me. I passed off the statement I thought I'd heard as facetious. But I saw earnest-looking faces turned my way. Heads nodding agreement.

Although I was hosting our meeting, I had let myself get bemused by a *trope*: Mr. So-Or-So has his "needle stuck on" a particular issue or point. This I dearly wanted to avoid being applied to me. *—Some jobs just have to be left to Al Gore!—* Right after I'd said this to myself I realized that I'd been absent from things happening immediately around me.

Wilson continued talking: "*Someone's* gotta do it. I'd say that's a sure way—maybe it's the only way—to capture public awareness of the real issues. Uh, what *we know to be* the real issues."

My attention devolved to the words "real issues." I believed I could state them definitively.

Then Mickey Caldwell was declaring: "Our reform movement needs a higher profile, Dan. You're best qualified to advance the Cause—put it up on center stage so everyone can see our banner. So wha'd'ya think?"

By god, he was actually talking to me; so was Wilson.

I said, "Yeah, yeah, yeah," and flipped a tiny wave of dismissal.

But I was hearing Kip Whitbread say, "We've got about two years to press our case, Dan. You're the one who got this started. You've probably got the strongest understanding of the *foundation* from which we can keep it viable. You implicitly know that any policy we'd propound is part of a comprehensive package."

I doubted his notion about "the strongest understanding" and said so. I still couldn't help regarding the proposition under discussion as a very lame joke.

With real conviction I said, "Hey, guys, let's get serious, shall we!"

(Reflexively I looked around for someone with good sense to dispel this travesty. Mitchell Freeman was not present. Hal was, but he sat regarding me expectantly.)

This was occurring just after we'd begun a meeting at my house, which had caused me to clear the place of clutter and provide various drinks and fattening cheeses and chips. I was willing to bet that had I put out donuts they would have disappeared quickly.

Jimmy Kestrel had not *suggested* we have this meeting when he'd broached the subject to me five days before. He had insisted on it, so I didn't consider declining. Subsequently I came unbalanced when Ira Blumenthal called me up and referred to Jimmy's request and asked if he could attend. Something was up. So I'd offered to host our "confidential get-together" even though Julie and I didn't relish having company over.

Ira was present. I had known for several days that Maya would be working for her primary clients, so she was elsewhere (probably at Tahoe). I learned that Mickey and Wilson had actually initiated our get-together after discussions with Kip and Jimmy. Alyssa was present in Mitch's place. Since I had told Harry about it, he showed up with Pancho to "offer technical assistance" as did—to my pleasant surprise—our party treasurer, a compactly built, masculine young fellow from Carson City named Daigan Kawakami. Until now I had not met Daigan; when he entered my house I'd had to infer who he was. As soon as we were introduced, though, I didn't have to infer his intelligence and good nature.

*   *   *

Of course after I'd heard Wilson and Mickey and Kip, I raised some demurs: I am *not a politician* despite my recent

forays into "political" activity. And why should we run somebody for *President*, for goodness' sake?

"Sometimes it's necessary to go over the top," someone
said, followed by manifold verbal concurrence. Plus I was
advised that my dissent lacked substance.

"Listen," I said. "Not only am I not a politician, I'm surely
not presidential material. Never mind that any one of us here
can do the job better than most of the yo-yos who want to
run for it."

"That's part of our point!" someone interpolated.

Jimmy said, "Wait a minute. Let's keep things real, now.
Dan's never been tested on the state level, even the county level.
So nationally, how are we going to . . . ."

Then I interjected: "Look at the shape this country's in;
look at the shape the *world* is in. Tell me anyone *in this room*
couldn't improve things. Ah, but that doesn't mean anyone here
should run for President! Me least of all."

Someone declared: "Well, the country needs Conservative
Reform. So we've got to broadcast it."

Someone else announced: "Dan is the Man!"

I could understand the apparent consensus. But the proposal at hand was flawed.

"I don't project a 'presidential' image," I said.

I was reminded of Harry Truman and Richard Nixon.

"I don't have the necessary height to be taken seriously,"
I offered.

"Wear cowboy boots."

"I *am* wearing cowboy boots!"

"You've got great hair."

That was a lie.

"Well, you've got good shoulders."

Curiously, nobody mentioned my good looks.

Eventually the point got driven home: Conservative Reform—the message, the platform, the party philosophy—*must* attract a great deal more attention. If it didn't, we'd be letting everyone down. (Guess who among us would feel the brunt of failure.) To gain high profile, someone from our party would have to stand for public office, the more public the office, the better. Our candidate would overtly shoot for the stars.

The next main point immediately followed: Would Dan Hachek declare himself our party's candidate for President of the United States? Again the consensus was that I should. (Again, "Dan is the Man!")

I really would not, and I said so. We were only the germ of a party; I disdained any exercise in futility.

But, I was twice reminded, upon capturing people's attention we'd grow. That's the path to gaining leverage to deliver our message. This surely seemed a worthy purpose. Therefore our job was to put forth an effective high-profile candidate. Surely, most surely, I was *IT*.

Sitting at my dining room table among close associates, I could see myself hustling to catch planes, or hunched over papers to get up to speed on all sorts of sticky, mundane matters so I could explain the Party's position on them. I'd have to buy and wear standard suits! My workout and nutrition programs would be left to wither. I let myself flash on a phantasm of me wearing a silver earring in my left ear lobe, an indulgence I'd been secretly intending and would have to postpone. But a real pang bore into me as I glimpsed a phantasm of Julie's delightful, smiling face . . . . *That* was a precious reality I didn't want to see any less frequently.

Again I balked: "We have to grant a couple things. Such as I don't have any of the standard credentials, as in national security or foreign policy. How am I supposed to represent myself as a plausible candidate for Chief Executive of *any* country?"

Wilson said, "Not much of a problem. When Maya Catchings puts you out there, you'll look like . . . El Cid. A modern King Arthur! With the right grooming, I mean this literally, you'll come across like—"

We all heard Ira exclaim, "*Maya Catchings*?!"

Hal nodded affirmation. I simply disregarded Ira's exclamation. We had weighty matters at hand. I rose from my chair and spoke:

"All right, everyone, now listen. As my brother would affirm, many is the time I've said that I really should be King of the World. If I were, well, of course we'd all be better off. The only reason I'm *not* king—of the world—is that I've never been told to be. Now *you are* telling me to be President of the United States. That's only a decent second place but, hey, I don't keep score. So provisionally I'll do what you say. 'Provisionally' means *if*—and this is a big *if*—my wife Julie goes along with the notion. I guarantee I can't do this otherwise. Is that understood, gentlemen and Alyssa?"

Yes, that was understood.

From Pancho: "*Si, se puede, jeffe. Ya arriba.*"

By this juncture I was already starting to regret the obvious time commitments and financial bleeding I'd incur by involving myself in a campaign to get attention. Maybe Julie would save me from all this.

My darling wife would arrive home later that evening, I announced. She and I would discuss the proposed stratagem and I would contact everyone within twenty-four hours. That was all I had to say about the matter.

My final words seemed to precipitate several minutes of people venting lofty ideas, even though our endeavor should be considered mandatory rather than high-minded. Finally we toasted the Party; then we toasted our country. This prompted me to think we'd have to work hard so the United States would *better warrant* such toasts.

As we disbanded Mickey and Kip each thanked me for hosting our meeting.

"Anything for my country," I replied both times.

Saying that felt right and I wished I could say it again.

CHAPTER 19

POST-ACCEPTANCE

I ra was the last to leave. He stopped and fixed his black-liquid eyes on me.

"What's your relationship with Maya Catchings?" he demanded.

I realized that Ira didn't know Maya was involved with the Party. First I simply declared that she'd been "at the very heart" of launching it. "Without her, we wouldn't have a campaign to speak of," I said. Then without preface I asked, "What's the nature of the bad blood between you two?"

Ira's luminous eyes searched mine for a long second. I found myself thinking I liked the fact that he was handsome and always elegantly turned out. Then I flashed on Julie's eyes looking similar to Ira's. I recalled my realizing that Maya's and my eyes were the same shade of blue.

Ira answered my question: "It's the universal story: the fight for love and glory." Then he virtually sang: "The fundamental things apply . . . ."

I chose to fill the gap: "As time goes by?"

"Actually," said Ira, "they're money and pussy. Maya supplied one. For a while, I took care of the other."

All I could say was "Really?" and cut a tiny laugh.

At that moment, seeing Maya in my mind's eye, I truly envied this man's experiences if what he said was true. But Maya wasn't Julie. The feeling evaporated.

Ira mused aloud: "At base, *all* issues come down to those two things. Of course they're intimately related."

I said, "Oh?"

With no preamble Ira told me that he and a former, long-time partner had developed a successful public-relations firm in Carson City. Concurrently they lobbied the legislature for select clients, with impressive results; eventually they also put their talents to work in Sacramento.

"We were stretched thin, but it was so lucrative we didn't care. Then we started making contacts in Washington that gave us even greater leverage back here. That's when we put on Maya—and the firm really took off. Before we knew it we were stretched thin again. She probably accomplished most of that; who can say."

Ira related that he had made Maya a partner despite push-back from his first partner, who eventually "just deserted us and hung us out to dry." Meanwhile, although Maya and Ira kept separate residences, they had become partners in another respect (telling me this caused Ira to smile unvolitionally).

Problems developed between them because for a couple months Ira had to spend frequent overnights in California.

"She *claims* I screwed around on her," said Ira. "She *claims* I hit on her cousin—who's way too young for me—which is ostensibly why I offered her a job one level below partner." Looking genuinely hurt, even vulnerable, Ira said, "She claims *all kinds* of things." The upshot: Ira and Maya dissolved everything between them except the firm (which declined considerably). Then Angela, the cousin, estranged herself from Maya. "She's my partner in the firm now," said Ira. "We get along pretty well." (This time a smile of satisfaction.)

Ira concluded: "Now Catchings and I are a lot more than *rivals*. Things between us ramified. Her family's involved in this, y' know, barely to mention a chunk of money. I had to make sure our assets—residual *and* potential—got prorated, uh, properly. It gets kind of . . . no, not *kind of* . . . it gets *really mean* sometimes. Even my son Brett, a good kid who's at Stanford now, gets caught in the crossfire sometimes. We'd had a few rocky years between us—Brett and me—but we were starting to, y' know, smooth things out. The trouble is, after I'd started working with Maya those two developed a rapport. So now I've got to be careful right *and* left."

He exhaled sharply and shook his head. For a moment he seemed to try staring through the top part of our living room wall. I had to empathize with him because of his dilemma. But the business between him and Maya wasn't supposed to be my business. I forbore expressing empathy. Maybe I got bemused by my vision that, together, Ira and Maya would have been an iridescent pair to behold if they hadn't let themselves go flying off separate rails.

"So what am *I* supposed to do?" I demanded. "I need you both."

"I don't know what else to tell you," Ira replied.

Paraphrasing a remark Mickey or somebody had made earlier this evening I declaimed: "You know, things might get really interesting—and messy!"

Ira shrugged and turned and walked off.

*   *   *

Right after that I set about clearing my mind, also the dining room and kitchen. Julie arrived about an hour later, not in the best of spirits after an intense (and tedious) meeting at her hospital. People who do real work *and* maintain other people's health—and save their lives—*also* worry a lot about regulations and budgets, barely to mention everyone else's ego. (For decades I'd predicated that medicos really have a higher calling.) When Julie asked me what had transpired at our Party get-together that evening, in one compound sentence of medium length I told her.

At first she appeared not to have heard what I said. As did Ira, she set her gaze upon an unadorned section of living room wall, expressionless. A couple moments passed. I said no more. She turned to me with an approving smile and remarked: "I've noticed you're crazy enough, so you might actually do it."

"Well, I need some advice and consent."

"Remember when you were getting your business off the ground; we didn't break even for a couple years. During all that time you still paid top wages—because the guys did good work and you were able to borrow the money. A lot of months the weather was bad, we went deeper and deeper in debt, but the guys got paid. Was that crazy, or what?"

I reflected on her words. I said, "Yea-uhh . . . ."

"Well, look where it finally got you. Now you have the luxury to get really pissed off, *and do something about it.* Maybe by doing what you think you have to do . . . you'll make a big difference in some people's lives, your own included." [That gave us pause for a moment.]

Julie continued: "Those terrible exertions you seem to remember from times past—fighting on the Troia Plain, as you call it, or else huddling there waiting to get attacked at night. The intensity of that—of everything happening back then—it *had to be* overwhelming if you can still recall it after your brain died. But you helped win the war and save your country.

"Now in this life, look at all those years you spent in school—and those decades operating a business. Utilize what you've got! *Put it to work* so it matters. No sense having all your background, all that development, and saying, aw, to hell with it. I'll just have a good ol' time from now on. —Of course I don't know about running for President of the United States! That might be a little extreme, but evidently that's what you've got to do."

At first I could only respond with "*Hmmph!*" Then I said, "I'll be damned. I'm shocked you even remotely approve."

"Well, I can't really say that I approve!" said Julie.

"Well, thanks, dear. We'd better sleep on it, so to speak."

I thought that capped the subject but Julie said: "Ah, sleep on it; now that's appropriate. [Beat.] You're a dreamer! Crazy people do what they dream about doing. You know?"

"Uh, to what 'dream' are we referring here?"

"How 'bout trying to set things right. Make life better for everyone. Maybe 'give back,' as people say. Probably you'd like to kick some butt, too."

I said, "Yeah. I want to do all that, even though it might not amount to much—I'm talking *ultimately*—you know, the Big Picture."

"Good. Spoken like a true dreamer. [Beat.] Who knows? What you dream of doing might not be so inconsequential after all—*if you make an impact*. You've heard of 'the ripple effect?' —Into eternity— It's why some teachers say they teach. Why some doctors try to be great doctors . . . . Not just for reputation, let alone money!"

For us both this was cognac time. Absolutely.

After an evening like this one I was too amped up to sleep well. When Julie went to bed I sauntered up the street to a spot from which I could gaze out at myriads of lights rained across a large section of Reno and the Truckee Meadows. I let myself dwell on lofty words I used back when I was enjoying the prospect of starting a political "movement." But now I was facing actuality: my comfortable vision had grown into bona-fide commitment. Could this be approaching my actual "destiny"?

Even now I see that might have been true. Embracing a really difficult commission calls for a capability that's more than just rational. It could be divine. But hugging a mad hope can also be the act of a naïf, and sometimes I have been known to be one. I have also been known to take myself seriously when reality has not borne me out.

CHAPTER 20

FRONTAL ASSAULT (PART C)

The morning after our meeting at my house I telephoned Harrison on some pretext to get his confidential take on Wilson's and Mickey's and Kip's Big Suggestion. Should I presume to raise our party's standard by announcing that I'm claiming to be a candidate for President—*of the United States*? Yes, maybe I should. But wouldn't that be an expensive exercise in futility?

Harry's response was purely positive. He said he knew that putting myself forward, stepping into the big arena, was something I'd secretly, deeply wanted to do for a long time. That *could not* have been true. I did mention that Julie gave me the green light.

"So you think I'm not just pissing in the wind?" I said.

"Even if you were it's for the better, all round. I'll tell Mom! Heeh-heeh-heeh-heeh . . . ."

According to Harry, if I ran a "hot campaign"—no matter *how* futile in terms of getting votes or political clout—it would have to "count for something. It won't mean *nada*."

"How is that?" I said.

"You should ask Julie about the 'ripple effect.' Ask her to explain it."

I told him I'd already done that, which wasn't quite accurate.

Harry exulted a little about the two of us reaching "*beyond* our little lives. Even if it's only for a little while. At least we'll have done it!" But my kid brother's agenda held an ulterior motive and he let it shine out:

"I betcha once we get your campaign rolling," he said, "it'll attract *all kinds* of chicks."

"I'd be surprised if it didn't," I replied, and why I said that I'll never know.

After talking with Harry, my first order of the morning was to indulge myself. So en route to Party headquarters (actually still my office), I stopped at the Safeway to buy bagels and a Starbucks mocha *venti* with a shot of hazelnut. (*All right!*) Almost all the adults in Julie's and Jay's and my life were chunky or chubby mainly from having ingested too many carbohydrates. Julie, Jay, and I were exceptions. Because I could, I took advantage of the fact. Heh-heh-heh.

Once I arrived at my office with my mocha *venti* (thanking the gods for Safeway installing a Starbucks) I got to work telephoning everyone who'd been at the meeting last evening to inform them (usually on their voice mail) that our stratagem was a "go-for-it." Julie approved; at least she didn't object. So I was open to be formally recognized as the Party's Presidential nominee.

In the process I got cagey by firmly requesting Mickey *and* Kip to phone the *Gazette,* our main newspaper, and two alternative newspapers to inform them about the formation (duly registered) of The Conservative-Reform Party, which, by the by, will nominate a candidate for President of the United States. *Personally* apprise the city editor and the features editor of each, please. And do the same for two newspapers in Carson City. I supplied the telephone numbers and backup Email addresses. And would you likewise apprise the newsrooms of the four television stations here in Reno and the stations in Carson. Harboring secret pleasure, it fell *to me* to inform Maya and Mitch of my new status.

Within about 30 hours all that was satisfactorily done. Then I had to be formally nominated as the Party candidate for president (by acclaim), after which I myself informed the local news organs of the *fait accompli* and my acceptance. Hal took up the job of informing news outlets in Las Vegas about our local political developments. Maya promptly connected with the University of Nevada to arrange for my formal announcement on campus there.

As soon as I could—partly to shore up my own commitment—I engaged a local craftsman to design and make two plain (but classy) metal signs declaring my office as Headquarters of The Conservative-Reform Party. Only two signs were required, one for the office door, the other for outside the building. I had to keep a close watch on expenses.

Achaean casualties were high for a day without true battle. Beside my chariot I gulp barley beer a soldier gave to me, and now the drink causes my mind to see our losses more clearly. Unseen weight presses my psyche.

Agamemnon gazes toward Ilios surrounded by fortifications and says we have come this far only to face a mighty acropolis. "But now we gain strength," he declares—"more men at arms, better supplies—and we are as clever as Trojans. Soon our Achaean ships will block all other ships from this Bay of Troia."

"Even Greek honor is not worth all the costs we bear," I say to my king.

"Perhaps not," he says, "but each man must decide that. Pariamu's subjects and allies strangle our trade to the north and northeast, also in other places. Every Achaean kingdom needs the trade we have lost."

"Wealth is hardly worth human death and suffering."

Agamemnon barely pauses to consider his next words: "I will tell you something you know but are not wholly mindful of, Amphilochus. As you and I grew to manhood together, and you taught me many things I value, you saw with your own eyes what I tell you now: Our Mycenaean power, all Achaean strength, does not shower down from the gods nor spring entirely from our character. We become mighty by using what we learn and receive and—yes—by what we seize from other peoples. What others have done we make our own and give it perfection. Thus we please the gods. Thus they reward us. I know this to be so."

My look of admiration for his words pushes him on:

"Ilios takes this power away from us when it blocks us from our sources of wealth. In time we will wither, perhaps die for lack of sustenance. We wage war to regain our trade routes. Only thus can we cultivate the gods' favor—we struggle to reclaim our way of living that makes us Greeks."

I never wonder why he is called King of Men.

*   *   *

Despite my intentions otherwise, about this time I found myself staying awake later and later night after night. Then I would sleep ill. Although I sometimes longed for Aegean experiences, I could not simply recall them. One afternoon, *sans* Julie's guidance, I actually went to a men's clothier and bought an expensive suit. I realized that I was coming undone.

One way I'd found to cope with anxiety was to refresh my perspective on what I was trying to do. Maybe I needed a reality check or attitude adjustment. Objectivity helps.

*

"All my years on Earth I've been exposed to your way of, uh, *thinking*," said Jay. "I can see how Uncle Harry has been afflicted as well. I meant *affected*!" [One has to admire the way he presents his thoughts.]

Jay paused to drain my growler of locally brewed porter into a tall lager glass, which only got two-thirds full. Julie lifted away the empty glass jug and swung it to the kitchen sink. Jay took a deep draught of the brew and noted it was beginning to go flat.

"It's still good, though," he said. "Got any Black Jack to go with this?"

"Not since last night. Or else early this morning."

"Well, D," said Jared, "you and Mom have inculcated in me the notion that there are some things each of us *must do* while we're on this planet. Some of those things are good in and of themselves, right? So we'd better *do* whatever it is we *have to* do, regardless of—"

Julie interposed, "We don't know if *anything* we do affects The Big Picture. [This from a nominal Methodist.] But, y' know, we *can posit* a 'ripple effect.'"

I said, "Unless, of course, you're a Mormon—or maybe a Methodist—you can't possibly know what The Big Picture *is*. All you can do, really . . . ."

"Is what you think is right, or *necessary*," Jay interjected.

That's my boy! I thought and nodded my concurrence at him.

While Jay and Julie cursorily discussed how the United States has been known to put ten billion dollars a month on the credit card for some foreign-policy fiat ("If we do that over several months, suddenly we're about 100 billion in the hole; after a couple years, we're talking real money!"), I caught myself mulling over Jay's use of the word "necessary"; it put hooks in me. The word *dharma* came into play.

Casually gazing into my face, Jay said: "Mom and you and Uncle Harry seem to have hinted that you're planning on doing something maybe wildly unusual, and you don't think it's very smart. If you don't mind my asking . . . ."

I let you—you to whom I address this narrative—complete the dialogue and extrapolate what follows.

CHAPTER 21

DEEP DIVE

Looking sharp in my dark-blue-pinstriped suit, expensive cowboy boots, and a white shirt open at the collar, I stood on grassy turf and gazed across the tops of perhaps two hundred curious souls. We had gathered this early-autumn afternoon on the quad at the University of Nevada.

Reno media had given me fair publicity that got my enterprise mostly right. Here at the university I could count on a friendly reception. Thank goodness I didn't have to cope with strong wind. I just had to quell my jitters.

Chimes rang the hour. Groundskeepers nodded to me. I nodded back: I was *born* ready. Before I took a step I tendered the audience a cursory—but real—*Namaste* and felt a sense of detachment, even liberation. *Here goes*, I thought, and strode the half-dozen steps to a microphone installed on a wooden podium that lent me a few inches of height. Then I took a moment—a long moment—to make eye contact en masse, an action that felt appropriate.

When everything looked right I spoke as levelly as I could into the single microphone: "Good afternoon. I'm Dan Hachek. I represent the Conservative-Reform Party, and I'm aiming to be your next President of the United States."

I expected polite applause and got a generous response. Scanning faces, I saw many looking back at me respectfully. The right venue for anything helps a lot. Some of the faces I'd seen at Party headquarters; a few (pretty ones) I recognized from local-TV news.

Three certainties descended on me: a small part of my audience was firmly *with* me because I'd already given them good reason; now I had to keep their support. Most people probably considered me a pretender, but the Conservative-Reform Party was a reality. At the moment I would have been lucky to garner two hundred votes for county hog inspector, but this was our beginning. Our mission was my message.

A short speech was in order so I gave one, trying to avoid banalities. It was not exactly a stem-winder but it was the best I could do. My objective was to broadcast the Party's stance on stemming catastrophic global-climate change and obscene national indebtedness. The main thing we had to do as a nation, I declared as crisply as I could, was transform our economy to a climate-safe one, and lead the world in *reversing* climate change. Avoiding dire asides, such as saying that dangerous effects of climate change have been permanently baked in, was difficult. The same held true for not citing too many examples of federal overspending and absurd priorities, barely to mention incoherent governmental (actually *national*) attitudes about countering transnational terrorism, which primarily requires that we deflate extremist narratives.

(I did manage to voice disdain for making America "the cop of the world" because, basically, "we simply can't afford to do that! It's also very stupid.")

Two days before this I'd resolved to state only a select list of the Party's other positions. So I homed in on relieving college-student debt and prioritizing rebuilding our nation's roads and bridges and airports and dams and water systems and, most important of all, the power grid—which must be set up *to preclude* digital hacking. "Everything my party and I stand for is elementary," I declared. And this really was God's truth.

Luckily for me the collegial setting lent me animus because I needed it. The Party's message *had to* get through; ideological crap was hardening the insides of our body politic.

Thankfully neither Julie nor Jay were in the audience because I stammered a couple times and had a little trouble shutting down. In a way, I contradicted myself: early in the speech I had declaimed, "We are *in* World War Three, and the world is losing!" Toward the end I declared, "We've got to *stop serving* our fears." Finally I exhorted everyone to register for the Party and what it stood for. Its presidential candidate (no great prize) merely waved the banner. A "Thank-you" and quick *Namaste* and I was out of there.

*　　*　　*

Right up to now, whenever I'd recall my announcement at the university that afternoon I'd feel an actual thrill—even though a rational person must wonder how I would have allowed myself to do that.

Only after the event did I learn that Hal hadn't been present, so he wasn't able to give me a *post-mortem*. Turned out that he'd sent me a text about a job he couldn't drop, but I never read texts. So Maya and I had to rely on media-news reports to learn how I had come across in my moment of fame. Evidently, not half badly.

Our mounted marauders confirmed my sightings. Agamemnon then granted my request. Thus we stayed low at the Xanthos until night fell, and we forded at my favored point.

Stealth in darkness could take us but a short way. Sentries with dogs listen on hills and watch from towers along our path to their city. Thus we pressed as far as we dared, then on cold ground we waited through night. Now as morning light rises above hills beyond Ilios we begin to move toward the city with care. For thin cover, our chariots carry boughs of parched brush placed here by my o-kas the day before.

We are nearly lined with the first tower of Ilios, along the edge of plain to the south. Already we have slipped undiscovered past hills with Trojan guards. I smell dying campfires on my left and my right sides—and I, and perhaps I alone among us, can smell something else. A faint acrid essence from the day before lingers in low spots of ground and brush bordering the Hittite encampments. For me that essence is familiar and reassuring.

Light has risen to reveal us. We can see ground on which we will drive. I wave my red cloak overhead and bound onto my chariot. Theron is ready at the reins to surge us forward while behind me a squadron of helpers mounts for action. I voice one word and we charge—and thrust—onto Hittite ground.

We have removed all chariot bells. Drums and banners we left behind. I hear only leather on wood, wheels grinding stones and sand, pounding hoofs. I hold my tower shield but no bow or spear. Both my swords are kept down. Theron knows the way to our goal, for we have planned this foray well. Just inside the Hittite encampment my o-ka converges on a roofed workshop that we surround, and we quickly dismount. My orders are sharp and clear.

Before enemy soldiers come to engage us we pull down the workshop and attach vats, a forge, and heavy wrapped bundles to our chariots. I direct us to place molds, hammers, calipers and other tools inside the chariots. Heavy pots we leave behind. Perhaps the camp has come alive while we complete this task. We cannot notice, as we work to depart as quickly as we came. I hear sounds of action, but we are the cause. A few of their soldiers approach us but hold back.

As I would rush a troop of workmen, I direct us to fly back over Hittite and Trojan ground to the river, then across to Achaean fortifications, dragging and carrying our gains. We have broken away unopposed. Greek horsemen—sleepy-eyed and scattered—come forward to aid our escape if we need them. As daylight falls fully upon us we complete our foray untouched.

We enter our encampment and I stop my chariot before the tent of my comrade-captain Lennaleus. Perhaps yet encoiled by a dream, he steps outside to meet my grin.

I announce to him, "We did what I said. Now we have means to forge and form new bronze."

My comrade stares at me amazed. He utters, "You have brought us a Hittite bronze works!"

I tap Theron's shoulder to move us on. "Heeh-heeh-heeh-heeh-heeh-heeh!" is all I respond.

*   *   *

POST-MORTEM

Doc Julie said she was proud of me after she saw me on TV news making my announcement and, notably, after she'd read about it in *The Gazette*. That was good enough for me. Maya declared that I'd done "real service" to my "Cause." And that was good. Hal said the predictable and asked if I'd "been taking politico lessons" [no response]. Jay's enthusiasm for my candidacy seemed muted but real. So I had to hope: I had to hope that from then on I wouldn't delude myself.

After I'd left the University of Nevada campus, I repaired to headquarters where I found dozens of well-wishers waiting to help me celebrate the event. They were there for good reason: rumor had it (somehow) that I had sprung for two kegs of microbrew and a load of catered chicken nachos and even a couple chocolate sheet cakes. The "rumor" was correct, and I would not have to see all that expense go to waste.

Media reporters were there and ate it up, so to speak. I was advised that there would be standard—but *objective!*—hype. Soon Doctors Jay and Julie managed to attend. Would Dr. Jay declare that he was proud of his dad? Yes, he would. In response to a reporter's question Dr. Julie was heard to shout that—*yes*—this development definitely "thrilled" her. ("I love my husband's message of 'conservative reform,' especially the *reform* part!") Here I should mention that good fortune has usually been my shadow.

Later, in the evening, I learned that Maya was happy about how my announcement went and the attendant publicity because now she and Jimmy Kestrel had impetus for aggressive fund-raising, primarily on the Web. (Their *mantra*: "Help save our country, help save our world—send five dollars, just five dollars!") I resolved to take advantage of every opportunity for publicity that came our way. If I could, I told Maya, I would speak to the NRA, the American Communist Party, the AIM, the LAPD, and any other bunch who wanted to hear our Party's message. I wasn't above addressing a convocation of the so-called Tea Party. An invitation to speak at Guantanamo Bay or Guam or Alaska would have set me to packing.

As it turned out, neither Maya nor Jimmy was working for free. Maya did most of the heavy lifting, so she paid herself modest fees for minimal hours charged—both of which she raised every couple months contingent on cash Daigan said was available. She also paid Jimmy a token consultation fee, which became less and less token, according to Daigan's reports. Thankfully, the three of them worked well together, with almost a private language among them. Daigan's reward was satisfaction in keeping scrupulous track of every dollar that came into the campaign. He was fabulous, so I dissociated myself from that aspect of the campaign although I was never shy about calling people to ask for contributions.

*   *   *

Less than a week after my candidacy announcement, I was up in Winnemucca, a fine, isolated town about a three-hour drive north of Reno, addressing a convocation of a few dozen local business people and their guests. They seemed friendly enough to me before I spoke, and when I introduced the Conservative-Reform agenda they appeared receptive. That is, at first.

But shortly after I'd begun speaking I felt connections between my audience and me simply fall away. And instead of recapturing them, ineluctably I lost more. I was mystified as to why. Could it be my manner? (I knew it wasn't my good looks.) Nothing in my delivery seemed amenable to adjustment. I quickly decided that it wasn't what I was saying that made folks disconnect me because my speech was basically the same one I had used in east Las Vegas. Regardless. When I finished (after cutting my talk a little short), audience response was tepid. My ego barely made it back to Reno, but at least I had learned that the same speech doesn't necessarily work twice.

By the time I returned home from Winnemucca the house looked dark inside, so I pulled off my boots and carried them in. I decided I needed a shot of cognac to smooth my frayed edges. A soft voice intoned my name with a greeting, so I looked into Julie's office to find her reading.

"How'd it go, sweetheart?" she said.

Whenever she asked me anything she really wanted answers, so I told her. She responded by stating obvious facts:

"You know, you've never been especially consistent . . . at anything. No matter how brilliant you might be in some areas, you're always a bit—how shall I say—*erratic*. I suppose it comes with the turf. —At least you don't screw up *big-time!*"

Julie was right about something else:

She said, "You probably think those folks out in the boondocks aren't much different from urbanites, like in Clark County or here in Washoe County. That's partly right. Let's say they're not *very much* different. You know what I mean?"

A person needs to grasp and internalize useful knowledge when it comes available. Usually I've done that, which is one reason I've survived, even thrived. So from that night onward I made a point of researching the recent political history of places where I'd be talking to people. Then I would try to frame my message accordingly.

Doing that was not easy because Maya was pretty successful finding speaking engagements for me here in the West and sometimes far afield (at events she called "absolute mandatories"). Beginning the next week I found myself addressing conferences and caucuses and "town-hall meetings" and rodeos and rallies and probably a fandango or two in Grass Valley (California), Las Vegas, Fallon (Nevada), Albany (New York),

Sacramento, Austin (Texas), Los Angeles, various San Francisco East-Bay cities, Phoenix, Boise, Boulder, and Santa Barbara. I went to Wisconsin twice (where I learned how to really put the "party" in politics).

Over the next few months I also spoke at several college and university events, mostly in Nevada and California. For me that was energizing even though participant turnouts were always small, sometimes outright disappointing.

Maya arranged for most of my speaking engagements with sporadic help from Jimmy Kestrel. To my surprise, some of them were the result of people or organizations soliciting *us*. After a while I grew used to the prospect that I might be in demand sometimes.

Consequently I grew compulsive about pursuing the first of our two immediate objectives: build Party membership in Nevada. (The second was eliciting donations so we could spread our message better.) Happily, Hal and Pancho made changing a person's political-party affiliation easy to do via links on our two Web sites. They also did a good job of coordinating their free times with mine to ensure a party officer being available to meet visitors at headquarters most days of the week.

By putting myself in their place I understood some of Hal's and Pancho's motivation for getting involved with the Party. To an extent I could also empathize with youthful volunteers who started coming by. Maya's and Jimmy's motivations, though, I couldn't really define.

One afternoon I arrived at party headquarters and found the door open; I heard some activity inside. Harry *y* Panchito, of course. When I stepped in, bright faces of two young men turned to regard me. I'd never seen either one before. They simply smiled my way and resumed their business. I presumed they knew who I was, if only from pictures of me on the wall.

"Hi, guys," I said. "Are you working here or what?"

They informed me that Harrison Hachek and Mr. Lopez were paying them to design and print out handbills explaining the Party and outlining the main points in two speeches I would be giving. Of course "Mr. Hachek" would sign off on the handbills.

"I'm Mr. Hachek," I said.

"Oh, we mean the *other* Mr. Hachek," I was told.

Al-l-l-l-*right*. Subsequently I met those same fellows and various young men and women (some actually still boys and girls) working unsupervised at headquarters. As I presumed, most of them were not paid anything. Later yet I learned that only "the supervisors" were getting paid. (I'd had no idea that "supervisors" existed.) By then, I rarely saw Harry or Pancho in the office.

Both Maya and Jimmy (and maybe Kip Whitbread) commented that eventually "the movement" would develop "*a life of its own*." During a late-afternoon conversation with me at headquarters, Wilson Kocourek asserted that we should cultivate an organization that would be "self-sustaining."

Just prior to Wilson stopping in, I had realized that I'd been spending too much time at headquarters—given that I planned my speeches, wrote letters, blogged, answered Emails, and did most of my reading at home. And I had plenty else to do at home, such as re-stain the back deck and replace some dead shrubs and (heaven soon willing) restock the refrigerator. My domestic dereliction was causing burdens on Julie.

"You know what I need that should be self-sustaining?" I said to Wilson.

"And what is that?" he said.

"My life."

*   *   *

"Listen," I said, "I'm no genius and I'm not informed enough to say much about this, but I know we need to use better sense. Do you know we can give the Mexican economy *a boost* by generating a whole new industry there: factories that manufacture 51-foot ladders with really strong rungs. We'd also give the pick-and-shovel factories down south all kinds of new business. You know how we can do that? By getting the U.S. government to build a fifty-foot-high wall the entire length of the Mexico border!"

That caused a gap in the conversation. My point was not lost on the locals I was drinking beer with after I'd addressed a Chamber of Commerce meeting in Roseville, a northern-California town near Sacramento. Probably some of the bunch had heard about Arizona's former governor (a fine lady) remarking similarly on the efficacy of walls to keep people out of a country. I thought that was all I had to say on the subject.

"Ronald Reagan said 'a country with no borders is no country,'" an old guy commented. I perceived tacit concurrence around me.

"Well, *that's* sharp thinking," I rejoined. "Add one plus Z and get three." I almost tried to make an analogy by saying "9/11" has meant fight terrorists, which meant invade Iraq, which meant defend "Iraqi freedom," which meant avert a "regional conflict" there . . . to protect freedom here. But was I fixing to muddle our discourse?

Fortunately for me someone stepped in: "We need to keep illegal immigrants out," a prosperous-looking fellow declared. "At the same time, we need 'em coming in."

A salt-of-the-Earth woman weighed in: "We sure haven't *stopped 'em* from coming across for a better life!" Nobody demurred; she continued: "If your family's in poverty and there's no way to pay for food and clothes—let alone medical care—you're gonna do something drastic. If it's *illegal* doesn't amount to a hill of beans."

I loved her for that.

No one said anything for a while until I broke the silence: "Look what they do in Europe, for goodness sake. The core E-U countries all have open borders. People can work or play, or whatever, anywhere they want. But they're still citizens of their own countries. That's where they go when they need to be where they belong. That's pretty much the case with us and Canada."

"It's a matter of documentation," someone offered. "But any document can be forged or faked. So here in California we have to pick up the costs."

I thought the connection between forged documents and "costs" might be tenuous, but people consider it real. Endemic bogus identification has been a fact of life across the U.S. at least since the second half of the twentieth century.

"I *said* I'm no expert, and I'm surely not a geek," I asserted, "but if we can't work out some kind of plan for electronic identification that doesn't involve paper and that's fake-proof, we're not trying. You take Charlie Smith's I-D code and fingerprints, for instance, and match it up with the same code in three connected databases, and it comes back Carlos Avila—born in Vera Cruz or Guatemala—maybe two of the three times; 'Charlie' is probably a citizen of Vera Cruz (or Guatemala City or someplace). And information like that we can already access, like, *instantly*. And there might be, say, a fourth database overseeing the other three, you know, just in case." I paused to let everyone consider what I'd just said.

I finished: "I'm willing to bet all this is possible. *Easily*. Maybe it's not a perfect solution, but documentation should be a *non*-issue. Trying to close borders just hurts people, on both sides. Hey, everybody knows it."

After a couple beats another well-kept fellow of about my age remarked: "I thought you were conservative. Isn't that in the name of your political party?"

I decided to respond with one of our Party lines: "We're trying to *conserve* and preserve things—like our national sanity. We aim to *solve* problems, not aggravate em." I also wanted to say that "we," the little bunch of actually non-political people I represented, were adamantly opposed to stupidity. But asserting that last point seemed a mite counterproductive. So I got smart: "That is all I have to say."

MANO-A-MANO

At about this same time I heard of a new buzz term: *blowback*. I registered it because I was sure it would soon be applicable to me.

Was I ever right. Somehow, a blog on my Web site had asserted that undocumented immigration to the United States from across our southern border was "understandable." Of course that is true, but I hadn't authorized saying it on my or the Party's behalf. Of course it became low-level news, like a sleazy rumor.

Blowback! Judging by my Emails and some letters sent to local newspaper editors by concerned folk, my attitude bit me in the glutes. I surmised that it cost the Party potential support from fence-walking GOP members and probably Nevada labor unions. I intended reproaching Maya for the "leak" but she herself was displeased by it. Hal could have done it but he denied it, as did Pancho although he said it "gratified" him.

In fact a couple days after the blog appeared, Pancho approached me to sign three affidavits asserting that his kin had been working for my old HVAC firm since a number of years back. His relatives needed this documentation to preclude trouble with the INS and to facilitate getting legal status here. Their need was acute. I said I'd be glad to help where I could, although these required notarization.

"Hey, no problemo," said my pal who, I then learned, was a public notary.

In fact my position on illegal immigration wasn't completely formed. And I knew that any stand I might take would cause more blowback.

Menelaos, brother to my king, has led charging infantry—flanked by my chariot squadrons—to strike at a narrow, hidden gate in their north wall—truly a bold move against massive defenses. We break through, an action surprising to us as much as the Trojans. But as we drive their infantry and archers back inside, the gate closes quickly and holds. Now we are stopped against their steep embankment and face sure attack on our flanks from forces outside the walls. We must turn and withdraw at once, and this we do. Still, we have tested their battle order and found weakness. At last our confidence rises.

Even while arrows still fly—some aimed my way—I steal admiring looks upon the workmanship spent on my swords, one inlaid with gold, the other with silver. I grip one and wave it toward Ilios so it can be seen. Agamemnon would say such weapons belong only at court; I say they belong with me, in action. Let Trojans envy my weaponry.

That is not all they must envy, for my shoulder armor and greaves are of finely wrought bronze showing (at very close range) artful etchings. Yes, I myself designed and fashioned the bronze, with help from my father, but left the etching to an artist of Mycenae. I take pride also in my boar-tusk helmet, a luxury reserved to captains. Yet for me such helmets lack sufficient grace. (This is badly true.)

Thus of late I have decided to change my form: someday I will don instead a bronze helmet of true grace fashioned from my own design. And it will be the product of my own craft since Hittite bronze workers one morning provided us the means for me to work. I stop and dismount my chariot to quickly gather up enemy arrows, for they show me what I must do.

*　　*　　*

Ah, if only we could battle stupidity on the open field with a fair chance to win, life would be so much better. And I'd have been so much happier.

Per my expectations I did receive mail—Email and the other kind—responding to my speeches and blogs and letters and "chats." I hadn't expected to get as much as I did, let alone from such unlikely places as Upstate New York or Great Britain or Israel. Most of it, though, was local—originating here in the West and Northwest (what I now liked to call "Ecotopia"). And not all of it was in my favor, and not all of it was reasoned—or even rational. You would be surprised by how vicious people can sound. A mean verbal jab at the Party or coarse remark about me seemed like only a whiff of stink compared to expressions of toxic spite and real malevolence that I saw or heard way too often.

After I developed thicker skin, so to speak, my besetting problem was how to ignore political attacks and personal affronts that simply begged to be skewered. But intentional stupidity—especially when it caused harm or would *support* causing harm—unnerved me. Every man has his limits. My getting lambasted for "subverting economic growth" on the basis of "some fallacious ecological theory" or for being "flagrantly unpatriotic," et cetera, et cetera, by "demanding we let the terrorists win" (presumably because of the Party's stand on capping defense spending) are examples of where my limits were breached. Even now, I'm not a bit sorry to confirm that the term "boobeoisie" may have escaped my lips and pen a few times too many.

"Y' know you might have screwed up a few times—a few times *too many*—with those rants about `intentional stupidity' and labeling maybe everybody in the country `the boobeoisie,' barely to mention `bunches of fundamentalist crackers.' [Beat.] Don't the words `intellectual treachery' sound a bit *shrill*? Who on Earth did you apply that to?"

Rebutting what Maya had just said would produce no good so I acknowledged it with a couple nods. She was entitled to her opinion; she was working for free. I said I'd buy her a latte and she accepted. We walked to a well-known Carson-City coffee house near her office and talked a little about recent blogs I'd loosened and letters I'd fired off to local editors.

Over coffee Maya informed me: "The donations we've gotten are pretty much spent. Publicity, y' know, costs plenty; even on our level."

I didn't press for details; we had established that I could always ask our party treasurer, Daigan, to disclose exactly how much money had been donated and spent. I knew I'd be mystified because I paid my own travel expenses and covered the lease on Party headquarters. Hal took care of Web-page costs. My priorities were getting out the Party message and defining *reasons* for the message.

Maya apprised me that she was planning a Party fund-raising campaign that would start with publicity generated by Hal and Pancho. That much would be cost-free. My role would be two-fold: help her do scud work setting up a pair of public events, one in Reno, one in Carson, and then appear at them as principal speaker and "host." I was busy, but I went along with it. When she mentioned that a major reason for mounting the events would be "to have fun," I heard echoes of her sister Alyssa lecturing her. I couldn't *not* concur.

Before I left Maya at her office I considered asking her what Ira Blumenthal would have done to generate Party money. Probably I was lucky I didn't. Abruptly Maya remarked that a "former partner" would have retained most of whatever we got. Maybe so, but Ira was savvy. I resolved to consult him (casually, perhaps covertly) although I couldn't afford the cost of his sagacity. There might be no expense because I intended seeking counsel more personal than political: Realistically, might I be wasting my time and life's gold by spreading the Conservative-Reform "message" the way I was doing it? (A smart man should step back and take a fresh look at his role in matters like this.) Ira would have to give me his insight, unvarnished, as a friend.

*   *   *

"Y' know it's possible you've been screwing up—*big-time*—with some of that stuff you've been trucking out like 'the *boobeoisie*'—okay, that's sort of good, but you sure apply it liberally. [Beat.] `*Intellectual treachery*'? What the hell is *that* all about?"

This was Jimmy Kestrel's turn to drub me. Still, he understood my contumely after I told him about the malevolence and intentional stupidity I'd been attracting of late.

"Put it all behind you," he said. "I know it's not easy. Even if you're like me, you never get used to it." This from a fellow human who truly understood malevolence.

I told him I'd work on it.

"Listen," he said, "how are the Party's finances?"

"Mostly out of my pocket."

He then apprised me that a comrade in the Gay-Rights movement, a deep-pockets businessman named Graham Reeves, had been induced (by Jimmy) to read two of my blogs and agree to meet me. The fellow might be relocating his manufacturing operation from Idaho to Reno and would be in town within a week. Of course headquarters rent was almost due; Maya had travel plans for me. I said I'd love to meet Mr. Reeves.

Per Maya's vision we mounted a pair of well-publicized fund-raising events, replete with local bands, beer, and speeches.

I gave the speeches, augmented by kind words from Mickey Caldwell and Wilson Kocourek. Maya even acted as co-host, which definitely enhanced our image in the media. True, we attracted some money, but our gains hardly seemed worth the efforts after we paid all the bills. Mainly we generated publicity for the Cause. And, yes, we enjoyed ourselves. Dr. Jay even accompanied me on stage during the Reno event, and he and I and Julie had a fine evening together. Happily for me Harry showed up at the Carson City affair, thanks to Maya's physique.

And, yes, per Jimmy's plan I did enjoy an expensive lunch at a casino restaurant with the well-heeled Graham Reeves. The only trouble was, our potential benefactor seemed to have never heard of the common-good concept.

"Where does your party stand on GLBTQ rights?" he asked me after too much talk about tertiary things. This occurred postprandially.

I said, "It's not *my* party. I'm sure the membership believes in equal rights for everyone. We don't make false distinctions."

Does the party have a gay-marriage plank, he wanted to know. Does the subject of GLBTQ rights appear in the party charter, was his next concern. I told him, no, our party doesn't have a gay-marriage plank, although it might in a few years; the subject of universal equal rights is not in the charter.

"However," I said, "that issue is implicit in our *raison d' etre*, in our philosophy."

"Can't you include it explicitly?"

I thought, great. His needle's stuck on one point.

"Our plate's too full; if we advance another issue we'll extenuate our impact."

"I'll be in touch," he said and stood to leave the table.

I'll bet you won't, I thought. I'll bet you won't even offer to cover my lunch.

Of course I was right on both counts. And rent for Party headquarters fell due the next day. Worse, I had no contact with Jimmy for the next two weeks. Even Maya couldn't say why.

CHAPTER 24

DEPTHS

The fellow had telephoned and Emailed me the day before, so I was there for him when he arrived at Party headquarters at precisely1:17, the time he had designated.

"You sure are prompt," I said, glancing at the wall clock.

"Part of my job; make a favorable first impression."

Jeremy Rakes and I shook hands and sat down on folding chairs against the wall near my desk, which I saw no reason to sit behind. We were the only people there. He had said our meeting was to be "exclusively private," and I aim to please when I can. The fact that young Mr. Rakes represented himself as Executive Director of Capacity Development for the public utility that services northern Nevada—and which I knew to be privately owned and very flush—might have guided my aim.

Just before sitting Rakes glanced up at the photo of Claude Williams on the wall.

"I heard him once in person," Rakes said with a head gesture toward the photo.

I was definitely impressed. I could tell he perceived that. He added that he'd been a fan of jazz fiddle "for decades," so in Kansas City several years back he'd seized a rare opportunity to attend a performance. "I'm older than you think," he said as a mordent. "I'll be pushing forty before long."

I whistled and looked heavenward in appreciation and spotted an unconscious flicker of smile. Then I asked him what brought him here.

"How much is your rent?" he asked, extracting a checkbook and pen from an inner breast pocket of his well-cut dark suit.

"About twelve hundred a month, give or take a few."

Rakes proceeded to write a check which he handed to me and promptly started writing another. I glanced at four nines, $9,999, on the paper. The second check was identical but postdated a month. "Here's a loan to cover it for a year," he said.

I said "Thanks" with a little nod and placed the checks on my desk, face down. (I can be *so* cool.)

"It's not just from me, of course. You might say we took up a collection."

"Who's it from?"

"Take a look."

So I had to pick up the checks for study. They were not personal drafts but bore the name Conservative-Reform Party and the words "Political Action Committee" in the top-left corner. The Party was also the designated payee. Rakes signed it with the appellation "Chairman."

When I replaced the checks atop my desk Rakes said, "Don't insult us by trying to pay it back."

"What's the quid pro quo?" I said.

"Funny you should ask! First you've got to promise that what I say here *stays* here."

I had no quarrel with that. Nor did I find fault with this young fellow's request not to publicize the existence of his PAC. Of course the fact of any PAC is a matter of public record; however (of course) no such fact has to be broadcast. His perspective: if people are to learn of it, let them find out about it.

"Let's say you have contact with, oh, let's say Wilson Kocourek," Rakes said.

(And of course he knew I did.)

"Well, you can just let Wilson learn about the PAC on his own; you needn't bring it to his attention."

I said I supposed I could do that. "So, what's the deal?" I asked.

Thus I was informed that our big power company would expand its capacity—quite robustly—if the county commissioners, who were usually such wussies, would go along with all the consequences. The main repercussion was that a much-expanded operation meant much-higher-water use. ("Which means someone's gonna get less, actually a lot of someones," Rakes said.) The county would fight this. Ultimately, if they didn't reject expansion, they would likely curtail the *scope* of it. Any curtailment would exponentially shrink the profitability quotient of the operation overall; it would also raise mountains in front of future company growth. An extensive public-relations campaign was therefore underway to achieve results deemed necessary.

"You see where I'm going with this?" Rakes asked.

"I'm not on the commissioners' board," I said. "I doubt I can even name half the members, truth be told."

Rakes' position: "We can't have you coming out against us while we're trying to build support. Later on, in the crunch, when it's up for a vote, we'll need your, uh, reticence. [Beat.] Notice—I'm not trying to buy your *support*."

"I appreciate that fact," I said.

"We *would* like you to help us promote our cause. You've probably got some well-placed contacts—in the community, City Hall . . . ."

"Now *that* I can't do."

"Fair enough. But you *could* change your mind. Here's how to contact me."

Rakes passed me his business card. Then he averred, "Not incidentally, some of us think you might be right when you preach 'conservative reform.' Look at our national debt! If you're serious about spreading your movement, I'm sure a number of my colleagues, myself included, are ready to back you financially—as much as appropriate."

At this point I decided to be prudent; I'm often a poor example of prudence, but I've learned the hard way to check surging impulses that are costly.

"I'll let you know if I *can be* reticent," I said. "No sense my cashing these checks unless everything's straight. How 'bout if I call you tomorrow afternoon, say . . . 1:16?"

"Use the cell-phone number. I might be in the fitness center working out. They expect us Directors to look like we're in shape. Part of our calling."

"What kind of working out do you do?"

Even under his expensive suit the man's physique looked whipcord. He told me he ran marathons and did yoga. I asserted that marathons put too much stress on the knees. They'll wear out sooner than later.

"Maybe then I'll take up salsa dancing," Rakes said. "Y' know there are *other* ways to stay in shape." A wink. "I'm overpaid, as you probably know. Here in Nevada you can get a lot of bang if you have big bucks . . . if you get my drift."

That very afternoon I contacted Ira and told him about the proposed PAC and what it entailed. He responded that what it *might* entail was of more concern.

"I can't tell you whether it's wise to accept their money or not," he said. "I *can* tell you there are always strings attached. This one doesn't quite pass the smell test."

Great. I didn't know what to do. I called Maya's number and left her a vague message about a political-action committee possibly materializing support for the Party. Later I received her voice-mail response saying that any PAC would be providential even if it stinks a little.

This would have been a good time to consult Wilson Kocourek but I was honor-bound not to, at least not yet. What *would* Wilson say? I projected that he'd concur with my take on the power-plant expansion plans: wussies or not, the county commissioners would have to reject the proposal no matter how well it is lobbied. Our water resources were already over-taxed. There was also the matter of where to put a larger plant. When someday we needed more power, we'd have to do what California does.

All right, I decided, I would go with my gut feeling and no harm would ensue. On the Party's behalf, then, I'd accept the PAC and, for my own sake, not feel stupid for having turned down money that otherwise would have come out of my—and Julie's—pocket. What's more I envisioned the committee being useful to our Cause further down the road. We'd do our best to keep it in a closet, though. And if there'd be blowback from our connection to Jeremy Rakes' bunch, I was betting we could fend it off. And if I was wrong, this was a fine time to live and learn.

DEEPER

About living and learning, in my conversations with Julie two words started recurring between us: "break," as in necessary vacation, and "Tuscany," as in Italy.

Julie definitely needed a break. I could see that long before she said so. We had never been to Tuscany because we couldn't see fit to go on tours when they were available. Now a good one had come to our attention, achingly available. And wouldn't you know, two of our friends would be taking it and wanted us to share in the pleasures.

"In good conscience, I can't go," I told Julie.

Hard enough that I was committed to attending affairs in Sacramento and Auburn and San Diego that conflicted squarely with the dates of our Tuscany tour; I couldn't pass up the *opportunity* those events afforded to get traction for the Party. Plus we were intending to make Internet videos.

Julie didn't try to persuade me otherwise. She realized as well as I that we—the United States, the world—had so much rectifying to do, with the odds rising against us and the stakes getting higher by the hour, that nobody rational could *afford to* just take "a break." For me this was also a matter of accommodating my share of the *dharma*, a fact that Julie understood.

Our Cause, embodied by the Conservative-Reform Party, might well have been a mad hope. Maybe in my case it was essentially an ego trip. Regardless. I had to uphold the agenda. That meant doing whatever it took to advance the Cause.

Thus resolved? I could only wish. For almost forty years I wanted whatever Julie desired; never could I abide otherwise. Now I knew, absolutely, that I wasn't coming through for her. The fact tore at my heart—and does still.

*   *   *

Barely had I wondered what would fly into my face next when I read Mitch Freeman's column concerning carbon-dioxide producers (facing caps and taxes and maybe no variances); his point was that effective control of emissions would require unheard-of simplicity, totally unlike, say, the U.S. tax code and more down the lines of Papal decrees. "Even conservatives such as those in the Conservative-Reform Party (Dan Hachek's fledgling political party) advocate a tax on CO_2 production based on a uniformly applied, simple formula," Mitch wrote. "And the costs cannot be legally passed on to consumers."

Well, I was unaware of the existence of a "simple formula," although I did maintain that CO_2 production should be penalized incrementally, without passing on the costs to consumers. But our position on that issue in the Conservative-Reform Party was still evolving. Mitch's column had let a genie out of the bottle, and I wondered where it would bite me, and I knew it would be in the usual place.

Almost everything I asserted in those days carried real conviction, but it was rarely profound. I might say that everything physical is finite; fresh air, fresh water, available money, available medical care, you name it. One would think this to be self-evident; the problem is, it's not. Another easy instance would be my saying the Earth can sustain only so much more population (*if* any more). Limits are inevitable. (They're finding that out, say, in Central America, but they're learning it slowly.) Thus the United States can absorb per annum only a certain number of permanent-new population (from all directions combined) because—words such as "physical," "finite," and "limits" *should* spring to mind here. Right? I say: *Right?*

Regardless. You can be sure that Jimmy, Ira, Maya, Wilson, Mickey and even Harry—and even Julie—often advised me to keep a public lid on some of my core beliefs. I used to habitually declare, "Nothing is *really* a big deal," and be confident that what I said applies to maybe all the struggles and striving we experience on this Earth.

But I changed my mind. Tacitly, implicitly, I wanted to help raise the quality of life for, really, everyone. And, yes, if we're spiritual beings—each of us with some kind of destiny—how we live *must be* important. So any success at helping improve people's lives *would be* "huge." I could say that without self-reservation.

*   *   *

Dozens of times over more than four decades I have discerned that every constituency, every interest group, can be animated by a mob mentality, which is basically mindless. Maybe losing oneself in a pack (or herd!) alleviates emptiness or offsets *Angst*. No matter. Whenever I'd see pictures of a unified mass of people, especially in live-news footage, I'd know—actually know—that every one of those turkeys in that mob needs a real life. (I bet most of them realize it, too.)

Probably *that's why* they'd become militant Shia or Jews or atheists or anti-U.S. homeboys—or whatever. How about all those rapturous Bible massagers? Or the rock-concert hordes? Or the NASCAR masses? (Julie refers to European soccer-match crowds, especially the Brits, as "rumbling hooligan gangs.") And, yes, I was strongly urged to *white out* this point of view once I'd entered The Big Tent.

Usually I managed to do that. All the while, though, (heh-heh-heh-heh) I searched out opportunities to declare that people should try to look at things from *Gaia's* point of view—as a matter of course. You would think this to be a pretty safe position, but I was staggered by the degree of blowback (some of it hostile, even venomous) I received or sensed. A claque of good souls, in the aggregate, must have thought I was plotting to subvert everything they held sacred (*Gaia's* sanctity of no relevance).

One afternoon, when Maya was in Sacramento, Ira Blumenthal stopped in at Party headquarters while I was there. For me, that was a treat. An expansive fellow, he offered me all manner of hard-earned advice—free of charge—his main theme being to narrow our focus in putting out the Party message.

"I know," he said, "that everything your Party stands for is derived from a philosophy—not just a political philosophy, either. Fine. That's great. Now, to attract people to the Party, especially when you put up political candidates, or a political *candidate*, to *attract voters*, you'll need a message that's clear and very simple. —Like something you'd see on a bumper sticker! For your actual platform, some of your philosophical tenets you'll just have to hold in abeyance because you can only put so many mandates out there. You don't want to be shot-gunning at the horizon, if you get my drift."

"I hear you," I replied. "I've been—*we've* been—trying to cull out planks that, you know, distract from our main thrusts."

"And what might those be, if you don't mind refreshing my memory."

So I inventoried the main points in the Conservative-Reform-Party platform, most primarily our advocating a full-court press—led by the feds—to eliminate carbon emissions. Since a lot of prerequisite technology and bureaucracy were already in place, the U.S. should implement a master plan to *use*—specifically—what's available, and then keep making advances. And we could *sell* our lore and technology, pretty much like we had claimed willingness to share how we'd make missile-defense shields.

As I went through the rest of my rundown I liked watching Ira lean back in the folding chair next to my desk and contemplate. A beefy, handsome man with thick black hair, always impeccably dressed (in expensive suits), he emanated substantiality and sagacity. Probably he voted Republican, I presumed, but with a liberal bias. After I'd finished we sat silently for a moment.

"How does expanding our national Job Corps fit into that agenda?" he said. "You're going to have to cull it."

I remonstrated. "It's an integral part of a coherent whole."

It's a distracter."

We sat silently for a couple moments.

"All right, it's a distracter."

"Are you going to cull it—with everything else that clutters the picture?"

"Yeah, I reckon so."

So expediency would rule, but not be for the better.

Before Ira left (rather abruptly) we touched on current hot-button topics, like who was going to be the next Assembly Speaker and where we would get our water given the reduced snow pack in the Sierras. I never got an opening to ask him whether he harbored enmity toward Maya, although I would have liked to.

WHAT IT TAKES

"Okay," Jimmy Kestrel said, talking to Maya and me through a telephone-conference hookup in Maya's office. "The Party's thrust is 'conservative,' right? Okay. So we can't even *think* about so-called 'open borders,' let alone maybe imply we'd advocate that."

This was my fault because publicly I'd mentioned, in passing, that the European Union had shown open borders to be feasible—analogous to our states here. I also said (in passing) that we could implement digital documents for foreign nationals coming over here (yes, even from Canada)—without being so onerous to everyone concerned. So, heaven screw me, I'd made a *faux pas*.

Jimmy continued: "Anyway, we have to streamline Dan's platform if we want to gain solid appeal that'll spread. That's a sense I've gathered here in Sacramento, before and after Dan's last appearance. I've picked up on that in other places, too."

Maya said she concurred. Truth be told, which I was not about to do, Ira had advised me likewise a day or two before this.

What I was doing in Carson City that morning defies logic because I could have induced Harry to sign paperwork for me at the Secretary Of State's office. I had no good reason to go to Maya's office, either, except as a courtesy. Maybe I'd begun feeling anxious because I had invested so many personal resources in our political party with no tangible return. The upshot was our telephone call to Jimmy in Sac that Maya initiated for my psychic benefit.

It didn't work, but it caused consequences. In this instance I wound up affirming that we *should* "streamline" our party's message. Unhappily, for me, another consequence was my assenting to never explicitly oppose (or even decry) the "war" on drugs, even though it's irrational and wasteful and working about as well as the Prohibition Act of the 1920's. On the subject of lapsed personal integrity, I could write a dissertation.

My pragmatism turned out to be helpful, though: Late the next morning at Party headquarters two well-dressed, vaguely menacing, authority-figure-kind-of guys came in to confront me about what they regarded as a libertine attitude toward federal anti-drug laws. Turned out that they were DEA agents, but not rank-and-file. These were Lead Agents who happened to be in town for a confab; by chance they'd heard of one of my early blogs that advocated legalization (and regulation) of the usual "drugs." A seditious political party, even a start-up one, that evidently attracted supporters on a university campus, mandated they take some kind of action, preferably before their lunch hour. So here they were, literally demanding that I spell out the Party's position on the issue.

I told them, hey, that was a blog I didn't actually write or even see. Or so I said. In fact right after we had launched the Party, Hal and Pancho put out stuff under my name in the blogosphere to fetch attention. It took me a few days to gain control of the situation. In all events, I said, I was on record supporting current anti-drug laws, which was a bald-faced lie I had no qualms about having told. The Party's position would never (repeat, *never*) propound otherwise, also a bald-faced lie.

"Well, we don't want to hear reports somewhere down the line that members of your organization might require surveillance," said one DEA heavy.

The other said, "Yeah."

I said, "Such a measure would be totally unnecessary— unless, of course, we have rogue members. If that happens, well, do what you must."

While they considered what to say next I thought, heck, my part of the *dharma* probably required me to compromise myself once in a while. But now I had *karma* to concern me.

Those musings evaporated when my visitors declared that generating a political party must require strong patriotism and *Chutzpah* on the part of everyone involved.

"I prefer the term 'guts,'" I responded.

It was time for them to find lunch. Otherwise, they said, they would have liked to learn more about the Conservative-Reform movement. I said that although our mission was to broadcast our message, the Party was registered only in Nevada. In no other state was membership yet an option.

"Maybe not for long," one of the fellows said. "*Somebody's* passing around petitions—I'm pretty sure with your party's name at the top—in Salt Lake City."

The other fellow nodded, then told me he'd heard (or read) references to the Party in Spokane, his home base.

At the moment and many times afterward I felt a frisson from thinking that possibly—*maybe*—people in faraway places, people unknown to me, were acknowledging and plugging into Conservative Reform that I (not incidentally) represented. In fact I'd given it birth. In different ways, can this be thrilling, or what? Words from unwelcome strangers that morning hinted I'd caused effects occurring in shadows, on the edges, beneath my vision.

Ostensibly I was on a quest, but with no concrete goal. For sure I was in the service of a "Cause," but one without parameters. Since I had torpedoed dearest Julie's and my vacation, I decided that my overriding concern should be making damned sure our movement wouldn't wither away on a dusty window sill.

In great fear my target, I think Arzawan, narrowly escapes my charge, for his mount starts at hearing chariot bells mingled with my shout. Then we swerve at a mounted young Trojan and I catch his left thigh with my spear. He falters sorely, and we pass by his other side and I slash him down with my gold-hafted sword.

We see a stream of enemy chariots making for the field to assemble a charge. I wave my banner to signal my o-kas to group for attack. This we do quickly, and we bear upon the Trojan column before they can find their order. They scatter like goats to escape our force, but we catch some. They can fight with spirit and try yet to escape, but their fate is short work for us.

I turn back to the low ground; my squadrons follow. Amidst our dust and shouts Hittite archers and infantry remaining on the field fall before us or run. My o-ka flank suddenly comes under mounted attack, but a squadron of Achaean horsemen, Agamemnon at the head, turns it away almost at once.

Without thought I raise my tower shield and fly at two Hittite horsemen. One turns to thrust at me and meets my shield and he is rammed from his mount. I slash at the other, miss, and we turn about in dust and ride over brush to charge him again. Now my shield is down, I grip my two swords. Skillfully my target turns his mount clear from me and picks his way past Greek fighters to make for city walls with his comrades.

At once, Agamemnon leads us in a mighty charge at the south gate; we know this to be a futile act. Thus we stop short and feint back as their archers line the wall tops. We pivot quickly to the east and our arrows find targets of Hittite spearmen we surprise at their barricade beside the great tower. Before our enemies amass their forces to strike us in the open, we depart the field in good order.

They think their wiles match their strength, but we can prove them wrong. Now they must be anxious, they must feel defensive. That is all we have intended for today—while our strength grows in other ways.

*   *   *

Thanks largely to Harry and Pancho from one direction and Maya (helped by Jimmy) from another, our quasi-political organization had actually become a viable entity with me as its figurehead. People were joining, many from the University; people were making efforts to induce other people to join; Maya was fund-raising and people were donating to a cause that some must have found compelling.

From what I perceived, everyday folk, especially youngsters not yet overburdened by living, want to do something "important" (a desire with which I empathized). At Party headquarters on some days, a growing number of acolytes would utilize a bank of five telephones; others might prepare mailings of my campaign literature that Kip and I had generated; usually someone would be sending Emails inviting persons to join us. The objective: disseminate our point of view. This *had to be* necessary work; thus it was "important."

When I did show up at headquarters I would always see someone I'd never met before. In time I learned names like Courtney and Brittany and Tiffany and Tyler and Reade and Slade. There was a suave young fellow named Blue. All in all, I met a wonderful bouquet of people. That alone kept me driving on track, which I tried to do passionately as well as plausibly because if there was anything I came to truly fear, it was letting them down.

The difficulty for me was having to focus my speeches and talks and letters and blogs on ecological matters, which might have been fine except that didn't leave room for much else. Yes, we have to save the planet from virtual death. Yes, we have to press a mandate: *implement* the national goal of

Zero Carbon. (I got to be facile in trucking out the steps by which to do this—starting with energy-efficient, new-building designs and with power plants installing advanced scrubbers in their smokestacks, et cetera, et cetera.) Since we *already had* the technology to get us rolling on Zero Carbon, my—the Party's—job was to insist on pulling it out of the closet.

Sometimes I'd point out that U.S. energy independence was a primary national *necessity*, which meant relying on so-called "alternate" energy sources—three of which happen to be abundant in Nevada. Sometimes chauvinism toward your home state can actually be a tool. It doesn't have to be just a pleasure.

Other major issues—such as Defense-Department spending caps and establishing an effective, multi-faceted *public-relations campaign* to counter extreme Islamic narratives—barely got vented. I had to tell myself that all the hassles I endured putting forth the Party's messages might not amount to a hill of beans within The Big Picture—but at least I took aim at objectives crucial to everyone right now. And they *are crucial* every minute of every day.

CHAPTER 27

ENTER A TROJAN

Unannounced, the well-dressed fellow walked into Party headquarters, introduced himself to me as Joe Crabtree, such-and-such assistant to our local U.S. Congressman, and took a seat next to my desk. He glanced at the back of a young man doing volunteer work at a desk halfway across the room and chose to ignore him.

"We really need to have this talk," Crabtree said. "It won't take but three minutes." A white man with reddish hair, early or mid-forties; apparently earnest.

I said, "Go ahead."

He said, "That total transition to a 'green economy' your bunch is advocating as being so urgent—it won't fly. It's full of holes."

"It's sort of like democracy," I said, "which is the second-worst system of government known to man." I didn't have to wait to see that he got my point. *His* point was that too many interest groups would oppose the Party's measures as harmful to their wallets.

"Look," I said, "some people don't have to get as rich as they think they do—even American doctors—and everybody needs, absolutely *needs*, a sustainable planet on which to live, unless we like seeing whole populations starve to death. The planet and people's lives shouldn't be so damned cheap."

This he conceded, and suddenly—catching me off guard—he insisted there were better solutions than universal Medicare, although he didn't offer one.

For a second I was on my back foot, but I took him up on his game and replied that our Medicare system—which is fairly analogous to a single-payer insurance system—seems to work very well, and that the government can guarantee caps on malpractice-insurance costs and malpractice lawsuit awards and offer providers all kinds of other benefits.

"Really," I lectured him, "some of the strongest opposition to a universal-health-care system comes from lawyers—who want to score big so they can move to the Caribbean and not have to practice law." I wanted to tell him to go away.

Finally I declared, "Look, we want healthy people. To keep that happening we need a health-care system that works. *Of course*, I think we should have that, as you should, but I've gotta tell you, Joe, my platform *does not include this* as a plank. The Conservative-Reform Party stands for other mandates."

"Now that you mention it," my visitor said, "now we're getting to why I'm here."

"Sir?"

"I'll cut to the chase: potentially, you're splitting the conservative constituency. Conservatives can't afford divisions in our ranks, especially since that GOP meltdown in 2020. We can't afford to be less than united. *Firmly* united."

For a moment I didn't know what to make of that. Finally I said, "Conservatives don't have to be in the Republican Party."

"Many people beg to differ," I was informed. "And the Republican Party can't allow itself to be weakened any further. We need to keep every voter we've got."

"So what can I do?" I said. "We're not going to dissolve our party here."

"You—your Conservative-Reform Party—can endorse local GOP candidates. Also GOP policies, which here in Nevada are conservative *per se*. You could do that as an allied entity."

"We *can*? [Beat.] I don't think so!"

"Sure, you can. Look. What is it you and your people want?"

This definitely threw me. After a pause during which I might have displayed some confusion I said cleverly: "What do we *want*?"

Yes, I was informed, "everybody wants something."

My brain finally kicked in. "I'm aiming to see the platform our party stands on gets implemented," I said. "It's not *my* party, by the way."

I waited through a few beats.

"That's all?" Crabtree said.

"That's all."

"Eh, bull shit. Look, your little splinter bunch is just screwing the pooch. The upshot of everything you might do is obvious, inevitable: you're gonna get nowhere. Nowhere at all. And you know it! While you're doing that, you give the damned liberals a better chance to win come the next election. Hey, now, is that good, or what?"

I regarded him impassively.

"You should know," Crabtree resumed, "we're bound to find *something* we can hang on you. While we're at it, we'll try to hang *you*, you know? What's gonna finally happen is that your little political movement, the Conservative-Reform *Party* [the last word almost spat at me] is going to just dry up and blow away. —Bye!"

Now I regarded him balefully while I groped for a rejoinder.

But he got the jump on me: "Just tell us what you want. You know, to, uh, help you quit."

"*Quit?*"

"Quit trying to fragment the conservative constituency."

"*Quit?*"

"*Quit.*"

Wow, I thought, this fellow has sure got some nerve. — Probably he associates with a swell bunch of retrogrades. I bet they all wear blinders.—

I arose from behind my desk and told him that I'd be in touch, but I didn't ask for his business card and he didn't offer one. Then I showed the gentleman out while doing my best to be amiable. Should I have been concerned about threats he said his boss's gang would deliver? Maybe. But threats to *what?* After the Congressman's "hammer" had left, I stopped at a desk near mine to make eye contact with the young man named Josh or Jeremiah doing volunteer scud work, sure that he'd overheard the preceding colloquy.

"Young man, you'd better find a cure for those aberrant tendencies you have for working outside the political mainstream," I declared and gave him barely a trace of smile.

The next day, late morning, I was in route to Party headquarters (actually now my campaign office), and again I decided to stop at the Safeway to buy a bagel and a Starbucks mocha *venti* with a shot of hazelnut, still exploiting the fact that lean Dan Hachek can do that *because I could*. Heh-heh-heh.

On my way to the checkout I braked at being addressed by a dapper fellow, maybe middle thirties, escorting a well-turned-out young woman carrying a bouquet of white tulips and office-snack supplies.

After we'd interfaced, the man informed me that I and my "political bunch" were mentioned in the business section of this morning's paper, which I intended to read at the office.

I thought, all right. Then I heard the fellow say, "Jeremy Rakes, the power-plant guy—who wants to befoul the air and suck up the water in the name of Progress—says your reform party, so-called, backs the plans he and his bunch have for building a new plant down river."

I needed to hear more; I graced him with my poker face.

"You can't be serious, man!" the guy resumed. "The complex they want to build would completely undermine the county's river-restoration project east of town. We know that project's underfunded, but it's worth *something*. They've barely got it off the drawing board; now you and that lot at the power company want to destroy it. Who *else* do you guys work for, by the way? Why do you call yourselves a 'reform party'?"

I tried not to miss a beat: "You should know I'm doing my best to help preserve our good life. As far as the expansion plans go, they're gonna get nixed. I'm not worried."

"Yeah, yeah. Thanks a bunch, man. You can't have it both ways." The stranger leveled a baleful look at me and turned to walk away, the young lady going along. After a stride he stopped and turned back to me. "Are you planning on buying a big house in Santa Cruz, or you gonna settle for a medium-size house on Maui?" he said.

I gave him my "hey-that's-*so*-low-rent-you're-annoying-me" look and they left me to fondle my mocha and wish I'd bought a fat donut.

"*Sheez!*" I said aloud maybe five times in route to headquarters less than a quarter-mile away. When I got there I dove into my bagel and mocha; in the process I checked my Email, which was mostly positive, supportive stuff. But one message called me a "tree-hugger" (basically true); another accused me of duplicity regarding something I couldn't define exactly.

My general optimism, I thought, maybe needed a reality check; perhaps I should call Mitch Freeman at the newspaper . . . . Ohk—too late! A creepy apprehension dropped over me: Might I be stepping into a big box with no exit? The Congressman's hammer who had visited me in this very office tried to make one thing clear: assuredly I was. Might I be doing something analogous to swimming in the Pacific Ocean and striking out for the horizon? Out came another audible "*Sheez!*"

All of a sudden two youthful volunteers were coming through the office door. My struggle to grasp reality had to be suspended.

The volunteers (Ryan and Amber) and I indulged in a brief discussion of Party philosophy in conjunction with recent U.S. energy policies (mostly nonexistent in fact). Again I had to face it: kids are much more sophisticated than my generation when I was young. That's barely to mention how clever they are.

I showed them the work volunteers were doing. They were willing and able; they asked a few astute questions. Sweetness and light prevailed for me again. I excused myself and simply left the office and headed for my Honda.

CHAPTER 28

MANIC HOPE

Now we know of Thracian Danaoi allied with Troy—among those many groups of Hittite warriors arrayed against us. Even men of Phrygia and Lydia fight for Troy. No reasoning can tell us why. Our surprise by this adds only bleakness to our prospect.

"We dared coming to this wretched shore in numbers never before seen in Greek lands," I remark to my king, "but Ilios is more powerful than we knew."

Agamemnon nods and gazes toward darkening sea, toward home. Our Mycenae lies farther away than ever, for we cannot return without victory.

"I knew," says Agamemnon. "But my knowledge meant little, aside from more work, also more daring as you call it." A thin smile. "We must do what we must do."

I rarely disbelieve Agamemnon, but now I question that he knew of Troy's might, its many allies.

"I knew," he says simply.

"You knew of Thracian soldiers riding against us?"

"I was told they might be allied, yes. Still their presence surprises me, I grant this. But I am prepared for surprises."

"Yet we are here," I say. "This is not daring. This is something different."

"Oh, this is different," says Agamemnon. "Our expedition, our struggle, our many, many sacrifices—we, I think all of us, see the truth, and I will state it."

Arms at my side, I wait for his utterance. I think to gaze homeward as I hear carefully chosen words:

"We know this to be a mad hope."

*   *   *

As once before, I needed a solitary drive. This time I did a double loop taking me through maybe four neighborhoods where I could count on knowing at least a few people living in each. My junket turned more extensive than I'd intended although it lasted barely thirty minutes. The areas I traversed probably covered the middle-class spectrum, including some beautiful houses beyond Julie's and my financial reach.

I wanted to make palpable why I was doing what I'd been doing. This turned out right. After a few minutes I realized that now I'd begun trying to apprehend—grasp with clarity—the actuality that underlies and pervades the *human reality* spread before me. Perhaps then I would appreciate our lives better. If this required using some imagination, I was game.

Basically I saw all around me family life with countless ramifications:

People pursuing careers and practicing professions and, I hope, doing real work at a wide array of jobs. Probably many of those souls worshipping a higher power from within the folds of some faith. Undoubtedly everyone intent on attaining a variety of pleasures, most of them wholesome. Love and courage and industry and creativity and (I expect) good humor implicit in the fabric of all that living.

And everything is worked out, albeit imperfectly:

Here in the U. S. we've got the Constitution, the courts, the hospitals, the schools and colleges and universities, the levels of government, the political parties and election machinery, the media. We've got venues for the arts and we've got trade unions and trade-regulatory boards. Most of the food we eat is good. So is our water. We have technology that's everywhere, including controlling traffic-signal lights and inside every moving vehicle. As the majority of us *schlep* along, we depend on scientific breakthroughs—that really are breakthroughs—to save and enhance our little lives.

Yes. I saw all this as intrinsically good. But is it *important*? That's a question I always ask. I had to conclude: Yes. If an aspect of reality is good, it must be important. *Good* in the universe does not just happen at random, much as art would not occur without context.

And if my conclusion is not true? It's true.

Driving back to the office this late morning, I thought, oh, yes, I'd better embrace the work I had accepted. A spasmodic little tremor bumped my right hand up from the steering wheel. It wasn't caused by palsy from old age.

CHAPTER 29

LAYING SIEGE

y "vanity announcement" (so called by the main San Francisco newspaper and some on-line pundit) that I was running for U.S. President under the aegis of a "fledgling political party" in backwater Reno (which is all of 450 miles from Las Vegas, which is not exactly a model of civilization) generated mild effects in Nevada. But it caused noticeable ripples in "Ecotopia" (northern California on up to Canada) and down in the Southwest. The main reason for that, evidently, stemmed from what people thought the Conservative-Reform Party represented. I gathered this mostly from the Web.

Someone in Tempe, Arizona, sent me an Email attachment (which I almost didn't open) showing a newspaper report titled "Start Small, Grow Big" and implying simpatico with Conservative-Reform-Party themes. Some media reports alluded to David (of Goliath-killing fame) or a mouse ("that roared") or, of course, Don Quixote. I decided to accept what I could get. At Party headquarters the day after I got the Email attachment, I declared "Start Small, Grow Big" to be our party mantra. We'd post those words all over town—and beyond, I said.

*

Out of the blue, two days after I'd shown Joe Crabtree the door, a pair of FBI agents stationed locally, a youngish man named Trent Wheeler and a young woman named Crystal McGee, presented themselves at Party headquarters. They happened to be in the vicinity, they said, and felt a duty to stop in and learn something directly: did this new political party advocate *no restrictions* on the kinds of guns people could own?

I responded that the Party supported current federal (and state) laws regulating sale of firearms. We weren't Libertarians.

"That's good," said Trent, "because we don't want people looking for a public excuse to buy machine guns! [Beat.] Really. If people think they've got an excuse, they'll break the law. Sooner or later guess whom that helps—the bad guys."

Trent and Crystal looked so earnest and attractive I gazed at them dead-on for a moment, then I said, "Do you mean to tell me that people *don't need* to own pistol silencers and machine guns?"

I beheld a lot of teeth in two bright faces. Crystal deferred to Trent who offered some ironic response. Then Crystal asked me what kind of firearms I owned.

"I don't own any," I said. "If people want to own guns, they've got the right. —Who am I to say nay?— But I don't keep any around."

"Why is that?" said Crystal.

"Having guns around is just asking for it," I said. "If you got 'em, there's always the chance you—or *somebody*—is gonna use 'em. That's when benign, totally delightful things happen— which might explain why so many people get shot and killed every year. In the U.S., I've heard over 10,000 a year. —God knows how many get wounded. *I've seen* how a bullet can tear through a once-intact body . . . ."

A little pause. Crystal said, "I think the figure is 12,000 a year. Firearm deaths in the United States. I've seen no figure for woundeds, although I'm sure it's out there."

Trent said, "Yup—12,000 a year, most years. Guess where that ranks us compared to other First-World countries. And guess which country has a populace that owns enough guns that we could invade Western Europe . . . without even using the military! Might there be a correlation, one could ask."

"Well, it's heartening to be way *over* the top of the heap in something," I said.

Our conversation shifted from gun-slinging to the aims of Conservative-Reform, a subject more suitably discussed over glasses of cognac or pinot noir, which, not surprisingly, also became subjects of discussion. The talk among us would have been more free-ranging, presumably because of different individuals' brains operating primarily on the same electrical waves. But my guests were on the clock.

To cap the proceedings, Trent and Crystal said almost in unison: "Why are you standing for such a high office, Dan?"

I lied outright by replying that I just liked the attention it got me. They knew that wasn't true but they understood it facilitated our concluding. Crystal and Trent arose; we shook hands and they left. I found their visit so pleasant (and ultimately ironic) that I have reprised it here.

*   *   *

Lest we forget (I sometimes reminded myself) the reason I was alleging to run for the highest office in the land was to call attention to the Party. Before I could get on the ballot in Nevada—and do justice to my mission—I had to collect certifiable signatures from two thousand registered voters. My take on the requirement was that a person or party could collect twenty signatures petitioning for something cool; but then try to get two hundred . . . . Because the potential voter pool for a minor party was marginal, inducing *two thousand* souls to commit to us seemed probably futile.

When I telephoned people to ask them to sign the petition, the aggregate of answers I got almost caused me to rethink what I was doing. Most citizens probably thought I'd entered politics for my own aggrandizement. I would have liked to announce across the state that, hey, to me, running for political office was almost as pleasurable as learning street dentistry or running a garbage-recycling plant. Local people didn't seem to realize that Conservative-Reform stood for actions and beliefs they really valued for good reason.

So we counted on a cadre of maybe three dozen vital young people eager to "make a difference in the world" and ready to circulate petitions and canvass potential voters. Fortuitously, somebody paid for pallets of pizzas and truckloads of soda to be consumed at Party headquarters. Oft times that was I, but not all the times. At "the shop" I did my best to maintain a festive atmosphere. We always kept a C-D player going. When office space came available across the hall, I leased it so we'd have room to specialize our functions, like working the Web or phones.

Meanwhile I had to congratulate Maya and Kestrel and Hal and Pancho for putting out the word: the USA *needs* "conservative reform" immediately. So everyone needs Dan Hachek. I thought I'd be sanguine to envision our "movement" developing a life of its own, but eventually that seemed to happen.

Campaign contributions came in, although I didn't know how modest or copious was the inflow. One day Ira telephoned me—quite unexpectedly—and addressed that subject to advise me about something I kind of knew: if I could show myself to be a big money-raiser, I'd be regarded as a legitimate candidate. (A potential winner attracts money; and people *look to* a potential winner; so if I wanted to be taken seriously I'd better focus on attracting large donations.) Ira said he felt impelled to convey these truisms to me because they might be useful. Then he asked me a few questions about our fund-raising and what I was doing. I gave him specific answers, and he commented "Good" or "Good for you" a few times before we casually rang off. I felt a bit flattered by Ira's attention, especially since it was gratis. Only days later, after my intuitions had delved into this occurrence, did I see that Ira's telephone call might have been aimed at gleaning information about Maya's activities.

Still, Ira's words struck me as correct. Raising more money could mean raising our number of supporters. Unless we got a lot of supporters we wouldn't be getting out the message. (According to the Secretary of State we were playing in the "minor-party" league, which means preaching to our own choir.) But we had to be effective, and I didn't want to generate just sound and fury even though it signified plenty.

CHAPTER 30

WORK!

"My point is, after the Web we need to be using *media* to get out your party's message—mainly to induce people to support it with cash," Maya declared from across her stacked-up desk.

I had claimed to be merely stopping by her office on a mind-clearing drive to Virginia City, where I used to do occasional business. This was not true. Mainly I was there to ask Maya, on a personal (*vis-à-vis*) level, how we could attract more campaign money, which I did. Thus came her point.

"What do you mean by 'using media'?" I asked.

"You know, advertise—on TV," she replied.

"Oh. On TV? Nah, I don't think so," I said.

When she asked why not I said that I didn't think we could raise the money that would cost. We left the issue there, although Maya said she could readily get numbers, like the cost of making political ads and buying air time on local television stations. She said she thought Daigan had remarked that we had a few thousand dollars in our war chest.

One thing I didn't mention to Maya was that I simply would not abide cultivating a public persona, an identifiable *image* designed to meet mass expectations. That would be stupid. Besides, I had my limits.

But personal limits can be vague; my bully pulpit bled away plenty of my dollars and time. Besides traveling to profess the Party's position whenever I had to, I did plenty of blogging and sent countless Emails and—eventually—"*tweets.*" I hoped doing this was enhancing our Party's platform effect. And I had a bedrock hope: that I wasn't deluding myself.

While I soldiered on, I usually received moral support in various forms. But during the span of one month at least a few dozen people took my announcement that I was running for president, sometimes using the content of my blogs and letters to editors, as their license to wax irrational or hateful or mean. About half of those messages were stunningly incoherent. Some were outright disgusting.

Two of them were alarming, one via Email (sent from a public library in Las Vegas), the other by posted mail. The lesser alarming note called me unprintable names and advised me to always check behind me on the street and to buy a pair of Rottweilers for my home because I "*would be* getting visitors" who planned to do the public a service by getting rid of me. (Why? I wasn't told.) The other tersely informed me that even if I would always wear a bulletproof vest and helmet, "no way" would I live to see the day of the next general election. (Why? Because I had it coming.) I thought, *great*; I wouldn't even know where to find a bulletproof vest let alone such a helmet. One cannot totally ignore such threats, and I had to tell Julie about them because she needed to be alerted. Eventually I told Jay also.

Maya and Mickey and I resolved to get endorsements of the Conservative-Reform Party from about ten prominent Nevadans, plus ten who were less well known. Despite kind words from a few of them, whose names I wasn't given permission to divulge, we came up empty-handed. Even now this disheartens me. Having to face eternity with recollections of futility might cause anyone to feel a bit, shall I say, deflated.

But I did get *morale* support—which gave me definite reason to go on. Often it substantiated our party's positions on key matters (sometimes with astute advice, like what steps to propound toward best implementing a general conversion from petrol to biofuels) or it came in the form of good wishes (with occasional cash donations) for my presidential bid.

Contacts came from points as scattered as New England and Kansas. Two souls, one from Georgetown, Texas, the other from upstate New York, dubbed my crusade a "boutique campaign." Pretty often I couldn't help being charmed by the warmth emanating from messages I got; sometimes they even included digital photos of a sender's family, home and pets.

After about a month into my boutique campaign, I concluded that many people found reason to be optimistic about the Conservative-Reform "movement." I was not sure why they were optimistic, but I hoped they were right and understood things that I didn't.

Work! Now perhaps I can work. The challenge—truly a test— lies in doing my best. No allies can help me except in small ways. Gods can grant me help only by allowing me unburdened time.

And thus they are doing, for a thigh wound makes me take rest. Bad food and dirty water have distressed my innards (as are most Danaoi afflicted here). I am now spared from combat, and spies tell us of no planned attack against us. (Instead we see stronger Trojan and Hittite bulwarks rising outside Ilios walls.) Beyond the bay, Troy's banished vessels and those of Troy's allies might attack Achaean supply boats and war ships, but we can learn of that only later. A kind of peace hovers atop conflict and tumult. For me the time is right.

I look into a vessel of a kind I know well: my Hittite cauldron for casting bronze (with a silvery metal yet unnamed). I have just now uncovered it from a smoldering hearth. For days I have tended my forge and at last the metals are melding properly. Ah, hah-hah! Even such lowly work is central to my craft as well as necessary.

Agamemnon is right: because of this war the house of my father—built on bronze-making, as was the house of his father and fathers before—prospers, as do many who make things we need for living and war. (At times I wish my family built boats and ships, but I am happy to craft bronze when I do it well.) Indeed my king's "fate," as he deems it, causes my house to prosper because of the great need for foundered metal. Yes, our Achaean bronze comes to us from Hellas—but for now, not all of it.

*   *   *

"That internalist conference in San Diego in two weeks: I told you about it a few times, you might remember. I'm going to attend, as I've mentioned. Here's the good news: looks like I'm actually going to present that paper I've sweat blood over. Finally!" Julie said this to me as we were preparing for bed midweek. Feeling unpleasantly worn out, I was focused on business of the moment and could barely process what she was saying.

I felt blind-sided when I heard Julie's main thrust: Would I attend the conference with her? If we took a red-eye to San Diego, she said, we would break off only two days of normal living. I tried to give the matter some thought even though I couldn't feature myself going.

"I'd really like you to come with me," Julie said. "I'll need your help, and we'll have a good two nights in San Diego. I'll rent us a car so we can get around after hours!"

"How would you need my help?"

"Oh, you know. Carry my computer and projector. Carry the bags. Be the 'trophy husband' and look like you're having a great time." Pause. She turned her delightful, darling smile on me and added, "I want your company."

Could I reasonably presume to tell her "no"? I could *never* voluntarily tell her I wouldn't do exactly as she desired, nor—as long as I kept my faculties—would I ever. But that is just what I did. I had three commitments pending for the week in question. Of course I was busy in other ways, too; some of them sticky, time-consuming. And there was so much at stake! This was not a time to welch. So I roundly disappointed Julie—and my soul got cleaved.

Sometimes I've been known to be a funny guy, rightly so, but in no way could I make light of this disaster.

CHAPTER 31

ANOTHER TROJAN

Maybe I was amenable to reopened discussion of whether to put out a TV ad touting Conservative Reform—and therefore my presidential candidacy—because I was worn down from being too conscientious. (Really.) After barely a couple months of campaigning (on top of my partial life), I might have been afflicted by adrenalin depletion.

"Priority number one is to make sure we can get enough signatures to put Dan's name on the ballot." This was Wilson's point. Probably I concurred.

"I bet we can do that readily if we just concentrate our resources on increasing party membership." This was Kip's point, and I probably agreed.

Jimmy was there (we were at Party headquarters). He said, "Publicity's the key. Believe me; I know." This made good sense to me.

Maya weighed in: "That's what gets contributions. But Web publicity only gets you so far. [Beat.] Janet and Johnny Q Public need to see *a face* in their living room! Immediacy makes them feel connected."

I could see where this was going. "What kind of publicity are we talkin'?" I asked.

Consensus: We needed at least one good TV ad if we were serious about recruiting membership in the Conservative-Reform Party. Putting our candidate for President on the screen for people to see in their homes would surely generate interest. People would wonder: Why on Earth is that man claiming to run for President? What's his point; what's the point of his party? What does he—and the bunch he represents—stand for? We might stimulate debate.

But could we afford such a tactic? I posed this question and was informed that Daigan said we could.

Sort of a Devil's-Advocate kind of question I felt impelled to ask: "Couldn't I just continue to put out our message the way I've been doing it? I'm pretty sure it's been effective."

The consensus: Yes, of course. So far, good job. Now we have to get more serious. ("The damned *U.S. Congress* won't do the work that needs gettin' done," someone muttered, "so we've gotta enlist people power.") With this I had to concur, although later I wondered if I'd been prompted by a hidden desire for ego massage. After a few predictable confirmations we wrapped up with Maya and Mickey arrogating responsibility for setting our new maneuver in motion.

*　　*　　*

Exactly two months after I'd announced I was standing for President on the Conservative-Reform ticket, I got summoned by a local staffer of our junior U.S. Senator—whom I considered a good guy even though several years earlier I'd seen him on TV applauding happily when his GOP President had come to Reno to deliver all manner of inanities. On my voice mail I heard Karla Rucker tell me her telephone number for my response.

Normally I returned telephone messages, but this one I saw fit to ignore. (Anyway I was busy.) Darned if the next day I didn't get the same message, this time with a vocal hint of irritation. (But I was still busy.) A day later the lady reached me directly and virtually demanded we meet soon, which struck me as . . . well, a bit queenly. I thought it wouldn't hurt to comply, though.

"Your place or mine?" I said.

We settled on the following day, late a.m., at Party headquarters (mine). I'd forgotten I had an appointment elsewhere during that time. If it hadn't been cancelled I could have missed meeting the darling Ms. Rucker.

I was glad we did meet because she was good-looking in a stereotypical WASPish-GOP way, and she brought an interesting message.

"In the first place," she informed me, "the senator's chagrinned and perplexed by what you're doing."

"How is that?" I thought I knew the answer but I wanted her to vent the issue so I could apprehend it better and respond with my typical wit.

"You're *possibly* eroding the base of conservative voters in the state. It's possible that you—and your minor party—can cause a rift, or little rifts, in the state Republican Party. This at a time when we need unity the most."

I sat trying to look profound in one of the folding chairs beside my desk. She and I sat shoulder to shoulder. "I reckon the GOP needs every vote it can get," I said.

She replied, "Absolutely. Especially in national races. In all events, the *Party* needs to be unified. [Beat.] Ever hear of Ralph Nader?"

"Oh, you mean 'the Spoiler.' Y' know it's possible—I think likely—he and his lot contributed directly to utter catastrophe —on a world scale!"

"Uh, ye-uh. Of course that depends on what you mean by `catastrophe.'"

"I think you know what I mean," I said. "I'll bet deep down you agree."

For the moment Ms. Rucker was stymied. I proceeded to inform her that I had no sympathy for the national Republican Party. None. Still I added: "I know it's got some good people, at least here in this state, in this county. I'm just totally disgusted by what the Party has done, and lately what it stands for. I don't care what happens to it."

"You just opened the door to another issue," Karla Rucker said. "Now the senator feels he might have to divert some of his precious resources—mainly that means some of his time—to repairing damage *you're* trying to cause."

I asserted that my disgust ran deep. But being a "spoiler" was not my designated role. My job went "way beyond chicken-shit politics."

"Then what is your job?"

"Advance the cause of our Conservative-Reform Party. The name says it all."

Now Karla was the one to sit looking profound. (Which she did a good job of.) Then she went to the meat of her message:

"Look, we can play ball with you and your party, *and* we can offer you a really attractive deal. We can do that *if you play ball* with us."

I might have been mildly interested, out of sheer curiosity, in what she meant by "a really attractive deal." All I said was, "How are *we* supposed to play ball?"

"Simple. In about two weeks, when the senator is back in town, after he announces for re-election and who he's gonna support in other races, you and your cadre come out for him."

"And how do we do that?"

I was told "Simple again": the senator's office would arrange for certain people—myself included, ostensibly—to be present at a press conference; this would give the party I represent a perfect opportunity to declare our senator the state's premier-conservative standard bearer. I might be asked something about the national context. Likely there would be some follow-up publicity ops. That, too, would give the party exposure.

I said, "Oh."

"It'll all be rather pleasant," Rucker said. "And quite rewarding . . . uh, for everyone concerned."

She graced me with a smile that I barely noticed. I had heard enough; my disgust threshold was low. One small point did pique my curiosity: "Does the senator know you're, uh, consulting with me?"

"No. But I'll tell him when he gets back in town. I'm sure he expects me to do something like this. But I consider it part of my job to spare him details until the time is right."

Again I said, "Oh." Without appearing unfriendly I simply stood up and proceeded to show the lady out. I had nothing more to say to her.

Rucker, though, had a few more words to say before walking away, and without animus she used them to convey two elements of interest: our senator was on the IRS oversight committee and chaired one of the IRS-related subcommittees; thus he often consulted with IRS *officials* responsible for specific districts. He had a first-name relationship with the Director for Northern Nevada and California. Element Number two might hold more immediacy: the state and county Republican leadership would surely make strenuous efforts, *possibly* under the covers, to reverse any adverse effects wrought by a "spoiler." I now stood advised.

Ms. Rucker handed me a business card so I'd know how to contact her when my thinking gained more clarity.

"By the way," said the lady, "your wife's a medical doctor, isn't she?" Before I could answer she named Julie's hospital, mentioned two federal grants, nodded slightly portentously, turned and walked off.

Afterwards I wasted several minutes sitting behind my desk, then pacing outside the office. I thought I could discern a threat as well as the next man, but I couldn't tell my wife about it as readily. So I debated whether to tell Julie that this development had occurred; it was so rankling and petty. Eventually I lost the debate and had to tell her.

CHAPTER 32

WHAT IT TAKES II

It's easy to understand that after I'd acceded to the mandate to put on a suit and present myself at a makeshift studio at appointed times to shoot campaign ads (on the cheap), I hated the project. The hassle was bad enough, but a thirty-second promo required me to water down the Party's message, which caused me acute pain, so I came to hate the process even more. On top of that, for me to earnestly deliver sound bites made me sound fatuous. Surprisingly, Jimmy showed up to watch three of the four sessions (all of which were a grind), and he said he was pleased with how my parts turned out.

We finished with two products for our trouble. In one I address the camera with background footage of northern Nevada and northern California and all sorts of ecotopic images going on. My job: deliver inanities urging support of the Party while appearing statesman-like. The best part is the end, when I wish everyone well.

The second one barely showed me: We see pictures of smokestacks and cars and trucks and jet engines belching out crap for us to breathe while we enjoy the benefits of trapped heat. We see vibrant young families in a park and a pristine wooded setting—about to have their lives undone. We see dirty sky, incredible wild fires and raging hurricanes. This is all stock footage edited to fit the platitudes in the script. An attractive blonde woman with a lean, finely lined face does the voiceover before she appears up front for the final ten seconds to urge people who care about the Earth to join (and donate to) the Conservative-Reform Party. We see only two candid images of me, each from a different side, talking to an assembled crowd (digitally entered), with my name emblazoned beneath my feet and "Candidate for U.S. President" in a large subtitle.

Before and after we made these "shoots" I explained to Julie and Jay and Harry (and probably others) that I got involved in this enterprise for the sake of my party and ultimately our country, although my pride was at stake, too, because I feared underperforming. For me, "performing" mainly entailed writing and approving the scripts (with a lot of input from various people). This was not easy because everything in the process turned out to be sticky or tricky.

For some reason, my writing seemed more emphatic, punchy, in the second product, particularly when the thin, blonde lady (whose full-time job was in a bank across the street from our so-called studio) declares: "We *can* save the planet. We *can* regain the financial strength and core values our country has lost. Together, *we* can do it!" Of course I wondered whether she believed any part of it.

To my delight, Julie eventually saw the ads and said she liked, really liked, seeing me on TV. So this disagreeable project carried an upside, which I had anticipated because Maya saw the ads before they were aired and she acted quite pleased. When I asked her whether she thought people would consider me an "attractive candidate," she responded, *"Of course!"* Coming from Maya that caused me a psychic boost.

Truth be told, an experience I had after our first promo shoot caused me guilty pleasure in private moments. The production crew and I had repaired to a brew pub on the south side of town to unwind and find some food. Maybe it was the beer inside me that set me talking. After we'd been at our table for a while I found myself descanting to crew members and interested wait staff about issues salient to my "boutique campaign" (such as how to avoid sounding superficial). For a coda I let myself go and declaimed: "I think I'm gonna grab onto this little star that's come my way and hold onto it as tight as I can—and just keep *holdin' on*—'til people hear me and listen!"

I saw nods, traces of smiles. Someone immediately averred that corn is simply not the best source of ethanol. Plenty of concurrence there. Ah, but sugar-cane ethanol might be used in fuel cells—a subject *worth* pursuing. My hearty declarations of a few moments earlier had gone the way of a belch.

Later I thought, well, how much of our human experience is *not* superficial? If we defined the things that are *actually* important, we might count them on one hand. Still, whenever

I mentally replayed my words to those virtual strangers over good brews that afternoon I felt a surge of pleasant warmth. Until now. *Even* now.

*   *   *

Before I say or blog another word, Kip advised me, I must get my ducks in a row.

"Um, which ducks are those?" I asked.

Dead space for a moment. In my mind I saw him rubbing his forehead in the funny manner he had. (We were talking on the telephone.) "All right," he said, "let's put it this way: you still have to set your house in clear order."

My turn for dead space. After I asked him to explain, he told me that I needed to stand on my own platform; I should propound my own agenda, beyond (and subsuming) our party's program.

"You've got to come forward and say exactly what you would do *if you were* President," Kip asserted. "Tell us your plans for when you are elected."

That sounded good except for one sticking point:

"What are the odds of that?" I said.

"You never know. Right? Regardless; you must act as though you were a serious contender. Get straight your *primary* talking points, the main things you want people to hear. Then you refer to the Party because the ones you've hooked will want to know more."

Kip's drift: we'd been propounding our message effectively; now we should aim for optimally. Or so I thought I understood.

I said I would take his advice, which he expanded by saying we would Podcast my proposals—all the more reason they had to be precise and specific and demonstrably interconnected.

And so I went to work crafting (as some people say) the message I would have liked to hear from all U.S. Presidential candidates. With broad strokes it covered three steps by which I thought the U.S. should *take the initiative* in arresting global warming (thus rendering obsolete any treaties designed for that end because they were actually half-assed).

My message proposed specific caps on U.S.-government spending and so-called "entitlements," while calling for more effective support for things that really matter like making sure we cultivate teachers and train technicians in all the trades. It advocated creation of two "banks": one for investing in rebuilding the country's infrastructure, the other for funds to help retire college-student debt.

This was brain-numbing work because I couldn't bear to realize down the road that I'd put out less than my best. I sequestered myself at home to hammer it out. Other than calls from Julie, I answered the phone only once because I knew the caller was Harry. And *of course* it threw me off stride.

"You'll never guess what happened," he said excitedly. "So I'll get right to it: we've scored a large—totally *unexpected*—uh, donation . . . kind of a loan."

When I asked for specifics I sat in astonishment as Harry related his being approached at Party headquarters by a representative of the greatest, most hated robber baron in Nevada history—let us call him Pantera, Cassius Pantera, who was only beginning to appear in history books because he was still very active.

It happened that Mr. Pantera was keen to meet the Party's presidential candidate (and our Party's chairman) to bestow both a donation and a "loan" upon our campaign, the latter with less-than-minimal-repayment terms, no strings attached. Add: use of a company helicopter and pilot, 24-7. Was this a fantasy? Was it too good to be true?

CHAPTER 33

ENTER TROJAN GENERAL

Of course I wondered aloud whether Cassius Pantera's donation and "loan" to my campaign (barely to mention use of his helicopter) were real.

Said Harry: "Oh, they're real. But you'll be able to confirm that yourself."

Conviction in his voice made me chary. "How's *that*?" I said.

Harry explained that Pantera's lieutenant, named Graham, decided to expedite his boss's offer by allowing Harry, as a Party officer with the same surname as mine, *to accept* part of the offer on my behalf. "It's a done deal," Harry said.

"What part of the offer, if I may use the term, is *done*?" I asked.

"Call it lunch—with The Man. Probably he's paying. I said you'd be glad to treat him to lunch but there's no chance he'd let you."

From me a couple mindless vocables.

"There's more," said Hal. "Graham and I set it up for the day after tomorrow—instead of tomorrow—in case you've got to cancel something to keep the appointment. It'll be downtown, so that's cool and I'd say considerate.

"Then right after Graham left, before I could call you up, who drops in but—wooh-wooh!—the beautiful Amazon—your mentor, Maya Catchings. She said she happened to be in town and was on her way back to Carson. I was amped up about what just transpired so I told her about it although I spared her some details."

"And what did she say?"

"She said don't do it. Not yet. It's probably not worth the benefits, given The Man's reputation et cetera. She seems to be down on people doing things to make money."

"Did you tell her about your accepting *my* lunch date?"

"That was a detail I spared her. Incidentally she said you should not even meet the Big Guy. She said he's very persuasive. The point is, if he causes us any publicity and we're linked to him, she thinks it would be highly detrimental to the Party."

I didn't know what to say other than our campaign had bills to pay and I could use a big lunch for a change (usually my lunches were Spartan). As a fillip I mentioned that I would take along my credit card and hope not to use it.

My brother, the man of action, said, "Don't tell Maya what you're doing until after the fact. That chick can be overbearing, let me tell you."

Damned if I could rejoin Harry's remarks.

*   *   *

Some things about Mr. Pantera were well known, some were suspected. I knew he owned a mega-ranch in pristine high country south of the Black Rock. I presumed that he exploited thousands of mountainous acres mainly to capture millions of feet of water per year. I'd heard that he was in the process of selling water to a power company building a coal-fired plant in the desert . . . on land he leased to the company for undisclosed (maybe bottomless) returns. He was an avowed right-winger suspected of co-founding and funding a militia of notable strength. Everyone knew he took advantage of untold dozens of "immigrants" who sought refuge on his contiguous ranches, although (aside from second-hand verbal reports) that was never proven.

While we talked of many things over escargot (before a fine lunch of braised steak, pilaf and vegetables, which we both ordered) I learned that "Cassius" was quiet-spoken, had a good appetite, a decent sense of humor, and would have been insulted to have not paid for lunch. These were points I appreciated. I estimated his age at late-mid-sixties, until he mentioned that he'd recently turned seventy-five. His hair still held some black although his small trimmed beard was all white. He certainly appeared hale and energetic.

What I had to appreciate about Cassius, though, were some opinions he alleged holding: The U.S. government must become proactive in stopping carbon (and other) emissions. Since part of the government's job is to *actuate* national-energy independence, it necessarily has to implement nation-wide 100% reliance on alternative forms of energy. (I thought, *Right on!* The man sees the real picture.) Open borders are inevitable, north *and* south, so we need to use digitalized identity checks. When he said he espoused this, I told him that I'd been persuaded to streamline the Conservative-Reform-Party platform, so we probably would not advocate that for maybe two years.

At that Pantera nodded affirmatively and finished off the escargot. Then he ordered pinot noir.

Did I like California wines, he asked me. Of course I did. "Well, we grow some good grapes right here in Nevada," he said, and he'd been doing that as a sideline recently and selling batches of varietals to established vintners to bottle. I thought, *cool* and told him so. Presently he asked me about the Party's campaigns: Were we gaining membership and raising funds to support my candidacy? I told him that frankly I didn't know the numbers, although I'd heard that we were almost out of money. Well, he said, he could help us a little.

I listened with interest as Mr. Pantera offered me a loan of $50,000 with obscure "repayment" terms—to come due in forty-four years. Since his business integrated some limited partnerships, he was sure two of them could make Party donations of $10,000, the legally allowable limit, and he was empowered to do that. Would I be amenable to those amounts? Even before he said this he had fetched out three checkbooks and a pen. My response was a display of stalwart prudence. ("But of course!") And would I perchance have occasion to use one of his company's helicopters along with a pilot? I had only to allow about eight hours lead time when requesting such use. Again, my answer showed firm prudence.

Cassius Pantera never said or implied that he wanted me to do anything for him. (I had my antennae out expecting he would.) So I felt at sea: I didn't know exactly *what* special interest I was making myself beholden to. I simply presumed there would be bills I'd have to pay. Long after we'd parted it dawned on me that I should have asked him *up front* what he wanted from me and the Party. Only a naïf would have neglected doing that.

My work calls for inspiration as well as skill. During this conflict my hard-won skills have lain fallow and grown flabby. Practice should restore them. But inspiration I now take from enemy arrows. I simply must choose the best one.

So I do: Trojan and Hittite arrowheads lack a cutting edge seen on our Achaean missiles. But two kinds of their arrowheads hold a grace we see in art. One—made of obsidian perhaps from nearby hills—I cannot resist, and I fashion my mold—already carefully measured—to accord with the grace of the object resting in my palm.

Will this effort bear fruit? Only by completing the product will I know. My tension almost overwhelms me as I dip into my forge . . . .

Pouring, working, then shaping this bronze almost completes my labor. What I see, what will be my finished product, lends me joy beyond language. I have only to trim edges of eye slits I placed straight up and down on both sides of the face. Back of the crown I shape a small eye for hooking a crest.

Now I behold the most beautiful helmet known to man. It is proportioned, I think, perfectly. The lines and curve and roundness of it (to fit closely upon the head) are pure grace, I think. It will protect the head and face, although I hope it will not block vision much. Until it cools it lacks only the felt lining and leather chin strap (for which I have made a bronze plate I will inscribe with the logo of the House of Pelops). The crest? That will be made of Trojan-horse hair.

A number of my comrades come to view my work. Most utter hearty admiration. Workmanship such as mine we know uplifts our lives. We, all people, need it for living well. Beyond that we know something else: products of art and craft—such as this—prove the glory (and goodness) of our civilization. This is what we can do!

Again Agamemnon is right. Love of homeland and family and self we make true, for we produce beauty. All the gods must be pleased.

*   *   *

CHAPTER 34

STARTS TO THICKEN

Since Julie's work schedule had turned hectic, I didn't get a chance to tell her right away about my having met "Cassius Pantera." But the next morning (beautifully cold and crisp and clear), when I told Maya about the event over cappuccino in Carson City, I was skittish about how she would react.

She took the news evenly, saying that we needed every penny we could get to keep the campaign public; moreover our range of exposure shouldn't be just Nevada and the West. Soon I realized Maya considered herself in no position to remonstrate with me because of something she herself had done the day before.

When she divulged what that was *I* didn't know how to react. (For one thing, I was distracted by her twitching smile as she started relating details.) Somehow this dear and voluptuous associate of mine had made contact with—and arranged to physically meet—a Las Vegas character, whose name, not to be mentioned here, would be synonymous with promoting first-rate sleaze. (I had to grant, though, his public persona struck me as engaging because he always seemed so happy.) A good question would have been *why* she had met with him, but I didn't get a chance to ask.

"He said it's true that he's got more money than God," Maya explained, "so he says some of it could go into one of his partnerships that will comprise a PAC, you know, a political-action committee. It, in turn, will make a loan to the Conservative-Reform Party—with an understood proviso about how the money will be spent."

I managed to ask what that applied to.

"Well, the Party has to spend it on our—on your—campaign."

"Specifically for President?"

"Correct. It's to be used entirely for getting publicity. That's the only string attached, although I'm sure he'll find some way to capitalize on his PAC's loan, sooner or later."

When I asked the Big Question, I was surprised more by the actuality than the amount: a mere $110,000.

"For him, that's chump change," I said, "but I've gotta wonder what motivates him to do this. Did he say why?"

"No, he didn't. We can only conjecture. Why does anybody do *anything*?"

"Usually for money or sex," I said, a phantasm of Ira behind my eyes.

Maya apprised me that Mr. Las Vegas had been an occasional client of her current and previous PR firms. (Indeed, Ira had initiated that.) And it was possible, she offered, that the man had made personal overtures to her in the past. (She did not say they'd been rebuffed.) Connecting with him for a meeting had been easy, and apparently pleasant.

"Did he write a check or anything?"

"Actually not. But he got on the phone to one of his attorneys, then one of his accountants. He told them exactly what he wanted and gave them instructions. The check should be in the mail. —It'll be a cashier's check to the party's account.— Hope that's okay!" As she said this her explicit satisfaction touched me.

"Well, let's hope we can keep this whole thing under everyone's radar," I said.

"Of course. We don't need word of this to get out. But it *is* public information."

Then the plot got even more interesting as Maya rolled out additional facts:

According to Daigan, our party treasurer, people were donating to the Conservative-Reform Party in small amounts (average \$22.51) but in substantial numbers. Evidently "the movement" was catching on. We were developing a war chest that could enable us to make an actual impact on the public conscious.

I might also be tickled to learn that Maya's big client in Vegas told her that he not only knew "Cassius Pantera" very well, he knew that Pantera was intending a donation to the Party. And Mr. Vegas would not be outdone by a hick rancher. That hick rancher, Maya learned, was expected to hire a high-profile PR firm to grease palms in the state legislature to facilitate resolving certain issues per his satisfaction. This wasn't public knowledge yet. In Washoe County, though, the newspaper had reported that Pantera was pressuring county agencies for all manner of environmental variances.

Maya's final assessment: Her sometime client in Las Vegas dealt sleaze; that was unsavory enough. To some degree we could obscure our connection with him; people would mostly excuse it anyway. But consorting with that robber baron so close to my home would be scandalous if that fact were to become public knowledge. And bad press for the Party would *surely be noted* throughout Nevada and probably in northern California. In short, our party's impact could simply evaporate.

I said, "It's possible I screwed up."

Said Maya, "We'll see soon enough."

My take on all this, as I explained to Julie in the evening, was if we declined big donations, we might fail to reform any-thing. Publicity was the key; publicity costs money. So I would accept money from almost *every*one on behalf of the Party and let the chips fly. Sure, public knowledge of my getting into bed with certain unsavory characters could tarnish the Party name and impugn my integrity (except among far-right wingers); I simply would risk that happening. I stood on safe ground, I thought, because I had not agreed to be anyone's lackey. But I knew I might be naïve about this. (I perceived Julie felt likewise.)

As for whether I had actually caused a hole in my integrity by accepting Cassius Pantera's beneficence, that I could rationalize: for the Party, anything goes. The Party was working for the world. After I'd told Julie this, I heard her dear voice assure me of support in whatever I had to do, but with this proviso—"so long as it's not demonstrably wrong." At that instant I profoundly hoped I wouldn't have to *prove* that what I'd done was not wrong.

*   *   *

Holidays always caused me joy even though I don't believe in most of them. Luckily for me, holidays (especially Christmas and New Year) always provided an opportunity to take a deep breath, loosen the inner cords, and enjoy my wife's and son's presence, and maybe reconnect with old friends. (My friends were few but the best. After I'd embarked on my unlikely political odyssey they seemed to regard me with a special kind of respect mingled with a tincture of amusement.) Two days after New Year's, I eased back into trying to change the world by meeting Maya for lunch in Reno at a laid-back fish-taco establishment downtown.

Maya had marching orders for me and counsel regarding how to cope with blowback from my accepting donations and "loans" from disreputable donors. I should simply ignore any criticism but never lie about what I'd done. My mandate: get back to work and be cool. I would soon be going to Phoenix and Fort Worth, by the way.

Before we broke off I felt expansive (good salsa and beer do that to me), so I remarked that I was surprised by the degree to which Cassius Pantera and I shared points of view. We seemed to have no disagreements, politically.

"Maybe that's how it appears," Maya responded, "but his priorities are all self-serving. I guarantee that. He's especially afflicted by a bad case of greed. I can *definitely* guarantee that."

Within that moment I determined she was right.

After a pause Maya continued: "Greed fills up a life; it affects how a person eats and drinks and screws. I should know; you could say I've been there. My ex-partner taught me all about it, big-time."

When I asked her how, she related that when she and Ira Blumenthal were partners "in every respect" (a phrase I let pass), he would nick her for money in various ways. (After a while, she told me, she started gouging him in return, as a sort of challenge.) When their partnership and firm dissolved, Maya said, she took some real economic hits in terms of client relationships, assets, referrals, reputation, even paying overdue office-utility bills. She felt she'd been attacked, and still felt that way.

"Wow," I said. "That's a lot of sound and fury . . . for next to nothing."

"What d' you mean 'next to nothing'? We're talking my livelihood. I've got a daughter, you know; she's ten now. —I like to be accessorized!"

"Yeah, I know." (Actually I hadn't known about her daughter before this.) Pause. "Listen," I said. "We've got this incredible cosmos around us. And beyond it there's *more* cosmos;

all of it beautifully organized. It's imbued with non-material force—look at human spirituality: it's not caused by any *thing* or *things*. So we *are part of* the cosmos; it's necessarily got laws built into it. So we have to do what humans are supposed to do—*given* how we're designed—or we might as well be turnips or goldfish."

"Oh. [Beat.] So?"

"Somehow I don't think slashing at each other for money is part of the scheme. It's bound to be counterproductive. When you get enough bread and beans and beer—and, of course, accessories—it's time to figure out how to live. And do it."

I thought, well, it's happened again: Danny Hachek explains it all for you. A still moment passed between us. Maya shot a straitened look at me that I wasn't meant to see. I could tell she comprehended everything I'd said but would be damned if she gave it much weight.

She remarked, "You're a spiritual man."

"No more than you."

CHAPTER 35

HEROES

Maya and I walked to her car in the parking garage across the street from the fish-taco restaurant and finalized logistics for my immediate future. The wind was bitter. I wanted to be home.

As we approached her car she said, "You know my gynecologist has a Yiddish name, and he and his folks came from a hellish situation in Europe."

"Yeah?"

She resumed, "If Mr. Ira Big-Bucks were one-tenth the man my doctor is, I might still like him despite everything. You know?" [Beat.] "Do you know, Bloomen-bucks and I were actually *full-time* partners—outside the firm—for four years. You might say he screwed me every way he could."

As we stopped by her car inside the cold garage I almost wanted to say "I gotta envy him." I always tried to be honest with people close to me, but saying that to Maya might have skewed our relationship.

I did say: "The thing is, your doc is doing real and necessary work. That removes him from all kinds of struggles and mean situations. He's *exempt from* a lot of crap most people have to deal with; he doesn't have to sell himself."

Maya said, "Look, I sell services that are basically nonessential to life and human aspirations." She paused to reconsider. "Although *sometimes* what I do makes a real difference for some folks." [Beat.] "I'm no doctor or mechanic or farmer or scientist; I'm always aware of that. So I do the best I can with what I've got. I work real hard at doing a good job, and my clients, also my associates, are glad for it. Where would *you* be without me?"

"That's true."

For an instant she looked into my eyes earnestly; I didn't know why. So I gazed back at her. I hoped she would never have imagined my next thought: Could I get *this woman* off? Yes, I could. Screaming, crying and laughing. Ah, but she wasn't Julie.

"Well," Maya said, "I'll do my part in keeping our message alive and thriving." She opened her car door and prepared to step in. "Answer your damn Emails!"

After she'd settled into her car and closed the door, I gave a little wave and smile from outside her car window and got bemused: she had used the word *"our."* In fact, I didn't know whether Maya was a Party member. I thought to find out, but I cannot say I ever did.

A swift force of Trojan chariots struck a daring blow at two of our largest ships on the beach. The crafts lay mostly unprotected, guarded this day only by a thin company of soldiers laboring at building a breastworks. Attack from the direction it came—from beyond us to the south, then driving at our outpost overseeing our west flank, then to ride away onto the plain—was truly unexpected. Their speed and order appeared natural, well-practiced.

Yet they were unprepared for the outcome, for the men of Iolkos—with hurried aid from men of Attica working aboard the ships—held their own. Our crafts took little damage from fire as my o-kas sped to repel and almost enclose enemy chariots at their work. A phalanx of Hittite archers came forward to hold us back—at great peril to themselves—and the raiding dogs made good their retreat, but only narrowly. Bodies left in the dust this day are sure to be of Ilios.

I see Agamemnon's teeth in a grin as he rides toward me. We pull our chariots side by side, wood still creaking, bells falling silent, foreign dust settling about us.

"Hah-hah! We taught them some things," says my king. "Now they know—to attack us, even by surprise, invites them into danger. If they cannot drive us back, one day they surely face doom. Only the gods can change this, unless we lose our will."

I ponder this briefly and choose to hope he is right. But can we sustain a long campaign? Meanwhile his mind leaps beyond the mountains of dangers yet standing before us.

"Mark what I say, Amphilochus. A thousand years from now in cities far grander than Mycenae or Troy men will celebrate what we do here, and yet will do."

Perhaps that is true. Already, no doubt, we have done famous things; the costs alone will be long remembered. So I smile and nod. My right thigh burns from my spear wound.

"Very good," I respond. "Good, good."

Always do I yearn for my lovely village on the nearest hill beyond the west wall of Mycenae. I yearn for my father's and my workshops, for the houses and gardens. I need to see my wife Shadia. I am sure she awaits our return anxiously, and this aggrieves me. My wound is slight but she would be horrified by it. Barely can I picture my son's face for my long absence. Agamemnon understands this, I know.

I say to him, "We, all of us, our dead especially, desire to protect the life we know in our Hellas. But I am mystified. What good lies beyond that?"

"Our glory!" answers my king. "Our fame."

He turns and drives away, escaping my response.

*　　*　　*

Julie tried to cap our conversation about the unnecessary travail that lately had been dominating her practice of medicine. She said, "Given that—however rare this is—we got the wrong results after we did everything absolutely right, and now we're gonna get hammered for it in court, which is *not* a rarity, can you envision something—*anything*—that might offer us a ray of hope?"

For a moment I pondered before I said, "Well, life's a bitch and then you die, but *right now* we can have a good day. — Uh, let's see— I'm sure that after we've passed from this Earth, you will still be remembered as a doctor who *did a good job.* Uhm . . . how much more *hope* do you need?"

After reviewing my profundities Julie remarked that my "obsession with elegant simplicity" was both "perverse and un-American, barely to mention passé." Then to my surprise she asked: "So how do *you* wish to be remembered? To put it differently, what kind of tributes would you like to hear about yourself, even if you believe they're of no real value? Have you ever thought about this?"

I told her that I hadn't because "all the noise and sweat we spew while we're trodding on Mother Earth won't amount to the proverbial hill of beans when our days are over—so why bother?"

"Well," said my wife the *uber*-doctor who had deep reasons for everything, "I'd like to know what you'd want people to think about you. So give it some thought."

*　　*　　*

The rancor that I'd perceived between Maya and Ira was so damnably counterproductive; reflecting upon it actually hurt me. Plus they were violating the *dharma*, as Buddhists would say, while they caused adverse consequences to themselves. Sound and fury signifying meanness *has to be* disturbing.

That might have been an underlying reason I ran my yammer—and really enjoyed doing it—just before we wrapped for the night at Party headquarters a couple evenings after my last meeting with Maya. Usually I tried not to waste words, but I couldn't help myself when I overheard the uncle of one of our volunteers (who was there to modify some office desks) loudly denigrate jihadists, which he flippantly equated with all of Islam.

"Actually, I'm *awed* by Islam," I declared. "Big deal; I'm awed by Judaism as well. Come to think of it, I'm awed by Mormons. [Beat.] I'm sure some religions make certain groups of people stronger; like in Japan when everyone got together under their sun-god emperor and almost conquered half the world. You can bet the Aztecs and Mayans and the kings in West Africa (maybe Central Africa) back a long time ago did all kinds of wondrous things . . . largely *because of* their grand religions. Look at the ancient Egyptians and Nubians . . . ."

Someone demurred with a reasoned statement connecting religions and illusions. I corrected her by saying that, at least to a Buddhist like me, "*delusions*" is the better-applicable word. At the moment I had just sat down amid a knot of six or eight hardy souls who'd have to brave frigid winds to get back home. Most of them were probably university kids doing scud work for my campaign. (One could tell this from the empty pizza boxes and energy-drink cans.)

A lot of college students are religious, so in the spirit of conciliation, I declared that anything in the realm of spirituality—*including* the major premise of every religion on Earth—*is* possible. ("Look at the cosmos; it's way beyond impossible. Check it out!") But people shouldn't get carried away as they did in the Crusades and the Spanish Inquisition (which, strictly speaking, was still in effect until about the time of our Civil War). Jihadists are great at getting carried away. While I was at it I graced the room with a gemstone of wit concerning

Catholics, killing, and Ireland. I tried to cap the last point by noting that even Sunni and Shiite militants make no distinctions among themselves when they're on *hadj.*

Maybe for a third time I was sure that I heard a sweet little plastic *click* on some electronic gadget. I thought nothing of it and didn't look for the source. Only much later did I learn that someone had been recording all this.

My logorrhea persisted a while longer because I was sick of reflecting on "simple-minded retrogrades" (who, of course, don't have lives) murdering people for reasons not self-defensive but usually delusory, like Basques killing Spaniards and Kurds killing Turks and Israelis killing Palestinians—and Palestinians killing Israelis—and Chechnyans killing Russians and Micks (I managed to use the term with impunity) still hoping to kill Brits, and a bunch of *jihadis* wanting to kill Americans (*any* Americans).

I declared that if humankind has been "redeemed," we had scant evidence of that. Likely proof of *the opposite*: a valid case could be made for "renditioning" a former President and former Vice-President of the United States to stand trial for crimes against humanity and the use of good sense. ("Remember hearing about 'Shock and Awe'?") To me, much worse, though, was corporate profits having become *so sacred*—let's say to Exxon-Mobile or British-Petroleum execs and shareholders—that "somehow they're worth killing Mother Earth!"

I thought I'd heard the little *click* again. A few of the kids offered something to say along the same lines as mine, and it was time to go home. I had no idea that one of the workers in the office this evening was a staffer on the new alternative weekly newspaper that Alyssa Bender (whom I hadn't seen lately) and some other young people had engendered. I'll call it *The Reno Chronicle* (a fictional name).

A week later I learned that *The Reno Chronicle* was heartily endorsing my ("not-so-Quixotic") candidacy for President; moreover, their editorial stance was firmly aligned with positions taken by their political party of choice—Conservative-Reform. And, *voila*, the *piece de resistance*: a charming story about Dan Hachek that could have been construed as a public-relations coup.

In the feature story about me (highlighted by a mobile-phone photo of me speechifying), *Chronicle* writers allegedly drew upon various sources—one of whom reported verbatim "unguarded" utterances I'd made after hours at Party headquarters ("while relaxing among staff and Party members"). They used my words to depict me as "deeply spiritual," "edgy," and "passionate" about critical issues and affairs. The writing was not bad, although the word "caustic" was used twice and I had a quarrel with that.

Fine. I decided to let the story stand. Of course I didn't know that we had a trio of fugitive-Basque ETA members, a Chechnyan jihadi (also a fugitive), a militant Irish Unionist (deeply Catholic), and a sharp-shooting Serbian nationalist—all living in northern Nevada and without sufficient occupation. I didn't learn of this until the coming spring. Nor did I suspect the degree to which "big oil" was sensitive (and *alert*) to criticism, and that they secretly employed their own versions of jihadis to remedy such adversity wherever it appeared.

And who would have dreamt these people even perused, let alone read, *The Reno Chronicle?* Certainly not I.

THRACIAN PREMIER

Maya's short-term strategy of using the Internet to publicize the Party and attract speaking engagements for me buttressed a vision she shared with Jimmy Kestrel: generate Party *cells*, initially by forming alliances with politically active environmental groups and *proactive* conservative groups wherever we could find them (as we did in Boston, St. Louis, Atlanta, Seattle, Chicago; Burlington, Vermont; Portland, Oregon; Tempe, Arizona; Madison, Wisconsin; and Austin, Texas). If they offered to pay my way to be their guest speaker, so much the better.

Some organizations with which we had contact were transregional, like Earthworks or The League of Conservation Voters, barely to mention the Environmental Defense Fund and chapters of the Sierra Club. I would have been glad to speak before meetings of the Audubon Society, but I was lucky to distinguish a buzzard from a meadow lark.

Our primary objective was to expand Party membership in Nevada, but we wanted to plant seeds in other states, too. In the process we solicited donations from specific individuals and groups, most of whom we uncovered gradually. ("They're out there!" Maya emphasized. "So *get* 'em.") Of course I continued to Podcast and blog and put content in links that Hal sent to Reddit (called *subreddits*). When I wasn't speaking in places I didn't care to see, I wrote letters.

One day, as a member of a four-person panel, I addressed a journalists'-awards dinner in Tampa, Florida; two days later I talked to a high-school-teachers' convocation in Lubbock, Texas. ("Oh, joy!" I told Julie, "I've always wanted to visit the Texas Panhandle in winter.") An attitude I forced myself to internalize was that I was bound to find surprises almost everywhere; some of them will be good. —It turned out valid enough to be useful.

This adventure took a strange twist after Maya told me about a meeting of the United Synagogues Alliance in (interestingly enough) Las Vegas. My attending that function was absolutely mandatory, said Maya, because "they're a serious-minded bunch of fellows, and some gals, who need to hear what you have to say." The mayor himself would be there, I was told, and he's a virtual media star.

Before she consulted me, Maya had finalized a bid for me to be one of the featured speakers. My topic: potential macro-economic gains from implementing large-scale measures to arrest and reverse global warming. (At first I thought she was joking.)

So I went to speak at the meeting, superficially prepared and a little anxious because I was barely conversant in my subject. But I only had to hold forth for ten minutes, which I could have cut short—and which I didn't because I'd become a "politician" and always had cogent points to make. It went well enough, and they gave me good food.

Two days later, though, I learned that I'd gotten the *last* available speaker slot at the meeting because, perhaps through some chicanery, Ira Blumenthal's invitation to address the same group reached him too late to accept before all the slots were filled. So they listened to me instead of Ira's "crucial message" about bills that would be pending in the legislature, which his clients had great interest in advancing (because, of course, those bills were important to Nevada). I learned all this because Ira told me.

"What it comes down to," Ira declared loudly across my desk at Party headquarters, "is I didn't come through for people who *pay me* to make their case. The Alliance meeting gives me an ideal forum; it's tailor-made for me. I've been attending it every year, for years!"

A fool couldn't miss that he was irate and that to his mind I bore some responsibility for his reason to be irate. So I declared my innocence, but Ira wouldn't be mollified, which caused me distress. I was glad a volunteer named Omar came to my desk with a question to interrupt us briefly.

"Y' know, I bet Catchings had something to do with that miscarriage," Ira asserted. "She'll do anything to stick it to me. *Anything*."

I asked him why that would be so, even though I had resolved to stay absolutely clear of their conflict. Good thing he didn't answer me.

"Be careful whom you associate with," Ira declared. "And don't take advice from a tyro, although it was a neat trick she pulled off; I'll grant her that much."

Shit! I subvocalized. I didn't want him feeling that I was siding with Maya—against him—or that I didn't need his friendship and counsel.

Standing erect, Ira muttered something to the effect that some people are thoroughly devious and grasping. Then he gave me a little wave, turned about, and departed the office, leaving behind an acrid smell of anger comingled with frustration and other undesirable feelings.

*   *   *

"So," my wife the physician casually asked me, "have you been able to recall how you died back in the pleasant Bronze Age? Any idea what took you out?"

"Nope. Sometimes I've tried to recall that, but nope.— Nothing. Maybe I pitched off my chariot and broke my neck, but not at Troy. I've been led to think I finished up in some land to the east, in what's now western Turkey. Professor Culpepper—the Brit—helped me get that."

Julie said "Oh" or "Ah." We were relaxing in the living room before going to bed. Her bemused expression told me she wanted to learn more. Probably she refrained from further questions because the premise of our discussion was so implausible. In her shoes, I would have dispelled it. Finally I decided to volunteer information she might find interesting:

"I don't specifically recall our leveling the citadel at Troy. It seems like the job was partly done for us, say by an earthquake. Of course we had to finish the job. I don't recall returning home to Mycenae, either. And I don't have a clue as to how long we were gone, although it probably wasn't more than a year or two. We probably came back as heroes."

Now Julie looked captivated as she peered into infinity before she spoke.

"However evanescently, I know we're all connected to the past," she commented. "In different ways, to various degrees, et cetera, et cetera. Okay; that's axiomatic. For you, though, connections aren't so evanescent! Can you remember anything specific that might be relevant to *now*, today? —For instance what happened after the heroes returned?"

"I don't remember going into exile after Mycenae got subverted."

"Subverted?"

"Yeah. From within. Agamemnon was right: At Troy he told me time and again there was much to fear at home, from without and within. Barbarians might land on our shores out of the blue sea, in masses maybe too large to cope with. Still, I thought he felt confident he could deal with that. But when jealousy and covetousness and greed emerge as primary motives

246

among the very people you depend on—well, sooner or later they're gonna put you down. Agamemnon didn't last long after we returned from Troy. The myths say he was murdered by his own wife and kin. Probably they would have come after me, too. Maybe that's what drove me to exile."

"Do you think you went volitionally—or purely by necessity?"

"Beats *me*. [A deep breath.] I think I can say this much: The king, my comrades, I—we were *all* acquisitive. But not obsessive about it, you know? We weren't necessarily greedy—like the Trojans. First we wanted to advance a good way of life, and not just for ourselves and our families. Agamemnon's concern encompassed all of Hellas. But he had a lot to worry about right there in his own house. This much I know: our friends—even our families, at least Agamemnon's family—provided no comfort, let alone sanctuary."

"You know this?"

"Yes."

Julie whistled softly. Telling her all this was causing me wholesome pleasure.

And for a long moment I felt—tactilely—my sword haft in one hand, arm sinews to my elbow taut and exercised, muscles up my arms into my shoulders well used and pleasingly tired, my beautifully crafted leather torso protector (preferred to bronze armor) lending me a sense of strength—much enhanced by the mantle I wore of lion fur (*a gift from my king*). Inside me I felt a surge of some kind of power rise from below my belly into my chest, stretching out the encasing leather. With no more thought I spoke quietly:

"I know also there was heroism for a cause not to be lost."

*　　*　　*

You might say that what follows is a case of hubris, which is true but too kind:

My heart has usually been in the right place. Usually I have operated on principle, or so I thought. But until the following began to unfold, I didn't really know how low I could grope.

First Daigan Kawakami in Carson City Emailed me then telephoned to say that he'd heard from an employee at the local airport that in three days Ira Blumenthal was going to be flown—in "Mr. Pantera's" plane—to Pantera's ranch (his headquarters and home) northeast of Reno. Of course I wondered what on Earth would *that* be for.

Recently Maya had mentioned that Ira's firm was soliciting the rancher for a contract to lobby state legislators to get specific bills passed. (Measures Maya said she would never touch.) Still, something bigger than that must have been brewing if Ira was going to be flown to the ranch.

"Pantera doesn't care if he drains the state dry and contaminates the air *and soil* while he does it," Mickey said with bitter inflections after someone had alluded to Pantera as an exemplar of "A Local Problem Gone Global." This happened during an *ad hoc* brainstorming at Party headquarters involving me, Mickey, Wilson and, to my gratification, Jimmy Kestrel (who'd been diverted here on his way to Sacramento from Las Vegas).

"That fella's not a scum bag; he's pure poison," Wilson declared.

"I've heard he's pretty toxic, all right," Jimmy said.

That's when I had to muster real courage to say: "This might sound strange to you all, but he's a big donor to my campaign."

As I expected, the room went devoid of oxygen. I proceeded to confess the full nature of my (therefore *our*) association with Mr. Pantera. It was tough, but at least I could say I had promised Pantera nothing. I might have overlooked mentioning the perk of using his helicopter (pilot included); probably I forgot to describe my good lunch experience. Harry and Panchito entered the office during my exposition, which I concluded by asking: "Does anybody know *why* Ira might be going to see Pantera?"

"I think I can guess," said Jimmy, "but first I'd better use your telephone."

CHAPTER 37

TURNED COATS

We had to wait while Jimmy phoned Maya and had a brief conversation with her about Ira's vagary. Looking dismayed, he returned and confirmed his "guess."

"The long and the short of it," said Jimmy, "is that he wants to discredit us—the Conservative-Reform Party—to get at Maya. Or maybe he's gonna do it the other way around. In all events, he wants to get at Maya. Dan's candidacy—the entire thrust of your Party—would probably wind up as mere collateral damage."

His explanation got a bit complicated but made sense: By taking on Mr. Pantera as a client in Pantera's highly visible push to get measures through the state legislature, Ira was attracting commercial attention and more business; some of that business probably would have gone to Maya. (She said she expected to get "cut off" from at least one lucrative mining contract because of this.)

The real rub would be Maya losing ecology-conscious clients because of her connection with . . . the *Conservative-Reform Party* because Ira would ensure that our association with Pantera would get exposed, even publicized, every way he could. Tarring the Party by doing this would be unreasonable, of course, because I'd accepted no *quid pro quo* and Maya had twice in recent years declined to lobby for Mr. P., but that wouldn't cut soft butter in the public arena.

Something else surfaced: In barely two weeks I was supposed to address a coalition of "green" advocates gathering in, yes, Las Vegas. Publicity from my doing that, according to Maya and Jimmy, would be a rich lode. Probably the Party—and I—would become more newsworthy nationally. But by then our Cause would be damaged goods if the Party's connection with Pantera were widely known. A clear-cut case of guilt necessitated by association.

In short, our credibility—the future of our movement—was likely in jeopardy. And for what? To get at Maya, to whom I owed so much, and to "knock down big bucks by shilling for an enterprise that's utterly unwholesome—and probably outright evil," to use Mickey's words regarding Pantera's push for environmental variances and other incentives that would induce investors to build the coal-burning power plant he wanted built.

Someone raised an additional rub to which we had to accede: Pantera might *get* what he sought from the Legislature because he always pulled out all the stops. He'd won improbable concessions in years past.

"Boy, this whole thing stinks," said Wilson.

"It's certainly intolerable," Mickey added.

"We shouldn't have let ourselves get into this fix," Jimmy said, "but here we are. Isn't there some way out of this?"

Nobody said anything for a while. I tried to find words to cap this situation when Mickey rose from his folding chair next to a desk saying, "Well, I'd best get going. No sense wasting time until we see what's gonna happen, see where we stand."

Wilson said, "Let's just see what we're up against." He stood up also.

Apparently both men had more consequential business elsewhere. They bid the rest of us a "great afternoon," wished us good luck in seeing our way through this, and left the meeting.

"Well," I said to Jimmy and Harry and Pancho, "looks like your local grass-roots political party has a bit of a *situation.* [Beat.] Does anybody know what to do about it?"

Jimmy said, "Well first we've got to dissociate ourselves from Mr. Blumenthal, very publicly, very loudly. Then . . . I'm not sure . . . ."

"You'd better whack him before he whacks us," Harry said, and Pancho nodded.

At the moment I was thinking about Maya, who had a stake in all this. Taking her side in her conflict with Ira was now a given.

"We really need to squelch him, right away," I said. "Once he meets my number two benefactor, he's *bound to* go public. And he might sing about our other connection."

Harry and Pancho regarded me inquisitively but I said no more. I was thinking that if Ira really wanted to smear the Party to bludgeon Maya, he wouldn't stop at revealing Pantera's support for me and the Party; he would also drop public references to my campaign's big donor in Las Vegas, the high-profile character Maya had enlisted to start a PAC we hoped to keep obscure. *Look at who Ms Catchings gets dollars from—to support her political client . . . .*

Not rhetorically I added, "How do you squelch *anyone*, short of strangling 'im?"

Pancho spoke: "I think I know a way."

Silence. (Beat, beat, beat.)

"What's that?" I asked him.

First he mentioned needing "three documentation letters," and I thought he was referring to letters I'd been induced to write on behalf of his aunt and two cousins, attesting that over a decade ago they'd had part-time, long-term employment (as "associates") with my late firm. (Some of this was fiction.) Now they wanted to substantiate their claim of continuous residence in Nevada, USA.

I said, "I wrote 'em. I thought I'd given them to you."

"I need three more."

"Oh. Write out the particulars; send me an Email. Uh, what is it you say we can maybe do? You know, to whack him."

"I know a guy—"

Hal cut him off. "Oh, not *that*, man! Get real, Frankie."

"This *is* bein' real," said Pancho. I know a guy who knows a guy who can definitely help us. You just have to pay him enough. He can make *the Pope* look bad!"

"This is getting too sordid for me," Harry said and turned his chair away from us.

Jimmy said, "If he's got a way to handle this, *go* for it. I know Ira. I know what he's capable of."

"Tell us more," I said.

"Have you ever heard of Avi Rubin?" Pancho asked.

"I'm out of this, brother!" said Harry.

This time we have caught two columns of motherless dogs bearing supplies toward their north gate. In early-morning light they move quickly but are far short of first defenses beside the walls.

My o-kas spring on them and cut down mounted soldiers at their lead. Quickly we turn on the infantry guarding their rear, work that is savage. Soon only their supply porters are left to us, mostly boys, preparing to die for nothing.

I give no order to hold back our arms. We simply stop killing. I look about for Agamemnon or Achilles who would disapprove; both are back in our camp. Finally I say it: "Cease!" The wretched supply bearers and a few remaining soldiers, all of them Trojans, we allow to move on without their cargo. We need no more slaves. One day, I think, we will starve Ilios to submission. Perhaps that will stop the need for savagery and slaughter beyond our Achaean limits. I take some pride in hopefulness.

As I finish my thoughts, exactly as our story-tellers would sing—a wide cloud of dust rises over the curve of hill before us. We hear pounding hoofbeats and know mounted enemy are coming to rescue or defend.

I tear a glance to our flank and see two well-armored horsemen descending a rise, intent on attacking our lead chariot. For the moment this chariot is separated from my o-kas *by the escaping Trojans, and it is mine. I mark the horsemen about to press me as Helladic: men of Thrace.*

Before I can meet their attack with attack of my own they pull up short, their attention on my doings. A full company of horsemen arrayed before us stops to watch. We allow Trojans to scuttle away from us.

Enemy numbers here are perhaps not superior enough to soundly attack chariot squadrons. And Achaean horsemen are already approaching to help us. Two Thracian horsemen can yet attack me, for my position alone is exposed, but their horses stand quivering. One such warrior holds his sword loosely, pointing it downward.

In a loud voice I declare: "I am called Amphilochus of Mycenae."

I hear no response, but the man holding reins in both hands nods to me. The other quickly raises his sword to shoulder level then lowers it in salute. They turn their mounts and return up the rise and are gone.

The enemy horsemen spread before us gaze toward the sound of our Danaan drum roll. These are Hittite and Arzawan tribesmen mixed with Thracians. All have come from far away and might die here for no cause but greed. We hear an order given, then another. With little haste they all turn about and leave us the field.

Thus I sense need of a word we have yet to know: defection.

CHAPTER 38

TROJANS ALL

The man walking toward me struck me as intense and what we called "bookish." He looked to be medium-sized, middle-aged. Aside from his appearing intelligent, I saw nothing distinctive about him. He was neither well nor shabbily dressed.

When he stopped before me and sought eye contact I thought, *this must be the guy*. We stood outside the Safeway I often patronized, next to a newspaper dispenser. Only occasional patrons bustled by since it was dinner time. Cold wind had subsided.

"I bet you're Dan Hachek," he said. A meager smile.

I affirmed that and he said, "I hear you've got a job you might want done."

"Did Pancho give you any particulars?"

"Pancho? Who is Pancho?"

"Frankie. Frankie Lopez. Did he tell you what I want done—uh, what we *need to* have done?"

"He did. It'll be no problem. I just need to confirm a few details and collect some cash. —Don't worry: I'm not wired or anything. I guarantee we're not being recorded."

Aside from Ira's exact name and address and my needing the "job" done within thirty-six hours—before Ira would be flown to Pantera's ranch—details were necessarily vague. Avi Rubin's task would be to make Ira look bad, very bad. If Ira were to be suddenly regarded by his community as worse than an unreliable fool, he would be too preoccupied to concern himself with anything else. That's what I wanted.

Did I have anything specific in mind? No. I still felt wary of being recorded. "Just *do not hurt him physically*," I declared loudly enough to be heard by a kid passing near us. "Don't do anything illegal," I added and gave a bald-faced wink.

The cost came up: twelve thousand dollars, cash.

"I'm good for six," I said. "That's hundreds of dollars per hours worked."

We settled on $10,000—half up front, half when the job was done. I pointed the way and we walked to an ATM in the same shopping strip as the Safeway. I had already put together about four thousand dollars from other personal accounts, so I needed the balance.

Before I handed Avi his money I asked how I was to know the job had been done, and done right. And how was I to make the second payment.

"You'll know. Just get a newspaper for a couple days. Watch any news out of Carson City." I proffered the flat clutch of bills which he took and slid into the breast pocket of his gray suit coat. Then he said as a post script, "Make notes of anything specific you want done." He peered at his wristwatch. "You'll be filling in my associates in one hour and twenty minutes, right here, at this very spot. They'll be doing the actual work. You'll pay them when it's done."

"Your *associates*?" I said, taken aback.

The meager smile. "I don't *do* the jobs."

"Oh. Of course."

And his "associates" were . . . Logan Hunnicutt and his lady, Wren Topley. I would know them when I would see them. (A clue: Ms. Topley was Nordic.) Avi Rubin tendered me a curt nod, stepped past my shoulder, and walked away.

He was right. One hour and nineteen minutes later I approached two youngish people at the designated spot, a well-dressed, Ivy-League-looking man and an anorectic-blonde woman in faux fur and high red-leather boots, and I knew they were Logan and Wren. Logan graced me with an eye-tightening smile; Wren simply looked at me. After we finished our brief transaction I could not recall Wren having said a word.

Did I have anything special in mind for "Mr. B"? No, so long as he wasn't hurt physically. Then it hit me that I really wanted Ira thoroughly discredited so he could do no harm— at least for a while—to the Party, to my campaign, to Maya. He had put me in this incredibly distasteful, maybe pathetic situation. Okay, I wanted him smeared all over the place and looking like a pedophile-meth dealer with BO and fudge in his pants—whatever that might involve—and with some dismay

I said as much. Logan listened and nodded empathically as Wren looked on.

"I'll handle it with alacrity," Logan said.

"I'd be grateful," I said.

All right, I was told, we should be able to meet again at this very ATM in . . . . Would forty-six hours be convenient? I looked at the clock mounted inside the credit-union window where we stood and nodded affirmative. Some kind of inspiration took hold of me.

"I think I can spare an extra thousand when it's done right," I said to Logan.

"See you in 46, right here."

That evening and early the following day, at the office and on the street, in ways as subtle as I could muster, I mentioned Ira's name in tandem with declaring that the Party (and my "boutique campaign") could never afford the services of high-dollar consultants and lobbyists such as he. This was actuality.

And it so happened on the day after that, probably every politically connected person in the state was shocked—disgusted—by Ira's arrest on charges of controlled-substance possession (crack cocaine), unlicensed concealed handgun possession (under his car seat), illegal handgun-device possession (a used silencer), and heavy-duty child-pornography possession (a lot of it in his car, evidently for distribution, and some of it stored on one of his hard drives), barely to mention the traffic stop for driving with a broken headlight and broken taillight that triggered all this.

I had to wonder where Ira's massive possession of child porn actually came from, but I didn't see fit to ask when I paid Logan $6,000 drawn from my straitened accounts. The only expense he asked me to cover was sixty dollars he'd paid for a "Saturday-night special" and "a few shells," items he called "props" for his and Wren's "latest prank." The used silencer, Logan said, was "thrown in" so he could be rid of it.

*   *   *

From then on, nobody would mention Ira's troubles in my presence. Harry, Pancho, Jimmy, Maya: all had nothing to say about that. I simply joined into the sense of ignoring the whole affair. It hovered outside our orbits, a totally detached entity. Anyway, we were busy.

On a few private occasions I considered telling Julie that I felt bad about Ira's travail (she knew I looked up to him), but that maybe I was glad about it, too, because I suspected he would have willfully discredited our Conservative-Reform Party to undermine Maya (probably) and to help him attract high-roller clients—and now he couldn't. But I chose not to burden her with unsavory details and never raised the subject before her.

Simply put, I had to protect our Cause. "All the good" our party was trying to do (and might be doing) was not the issue. *Necessity* was the issue, and it was at hand. We in the Party were obliged, mandated, to press our Cause. Debasing it could not be allowed.

From my viewpoint, Ira's propensities could have laid waste to our efforts and expense in launching our fledging party. But what stabbed at my root was realizing that *Julie* actually had borne some of those costs by having been denied things she wanted and needed because she was married to a "political animal." I would have preferred dying than to abide her incurring that for nothing.

Of course I knew that Ira now faced disgrace and lost reputation and maybe lost livelihood, so I thought the old query about whether any means justifies a desired end could be answered affirmatively in this case. Maintaining the Party's well-being *by quashing* Ira's likely plans were definite goods in and of themselves. As to my *method* for squelching those plans, I used what I had available. Period.

I tried to take solace in thinking Ira probably would not do prison time if he got convicted on those charges against him. But that dog wouldn't hunt. Ira had been mauled badly even if he regained his shadowy trade. Worse, I'd caused his soul to be lacerated. Was that acceptable anywhere in the *dharma*? Of course it wasn't.

Coincidentally, a few days after Ira's arrest Mitch Freeman put out a column lambasting Mr. Pantera's designs and implacable greed, and calling "shameful" anyone who helped him. Ira at least escaped that association.

I had to wonder whether Mitch had somehow gotten wind of a connection between Pantera and myself. That kind of concern causes dread, so I simply dispelled it. Still, I tried calling Mitch to invite him to a policy meeting we had planned for the coming weekend; he didn't answer the phone so I left a message and he didn't return my call. This was a hard fact for me to atomize. Thrice I tried to contact his protégé Alyssa to invite her as well, but she was out of pocket.

Lo and behold, in my voice mail I heard a message from—a chill wind blowing—Cassius Pantera voicing relief at having heard that I (and the Party) had disclaimed association with "that scum-ball political shyster, Ira Blumenthal." Since he was on the phone Pantera wished me good luck in my campaign, he wished the Party well, and he said he wished that Ira had never contacted him (and vice-versa) because he had a reputation to maintain.

CHAPTER 39

ARTFUL PRACTICE

The klieg light of my life, Julie my wife, pounded two pillows and slid her flannelled body under our bed covers on a cold, blustery night while she tried to speak matter-of-factly.

"I know," she said to me, "you're just trying to be a proverbial shot across the bow of the major political parties—and for that matter the whole ship of state, so to speak. I know you have no intention of being a `spoiler,' presuming that's even a possibility. Obviously you don't have the so-called `credentials' in national security and foreign policy. Okay, granted all that. But y' know, you might be the best man for the job, really."

As I loosened my side of covers I said, "We are talking about what, may I ask."

"Aren't you running for President of the United States?"

In fact barely two hours earlier I'd returned from a speaking engagement Maya had set up for me in Salt Lake City, and (this seemed anomalous to me) Daigan our party treasurer had paid for my flight tickets. I couldn't very well demur.

After I lay myself alongside her, I remarked to Julie, "I'm more of a political outrage. The Party is the 'shot across the bow,' not me. What differentiates me from the real candidates are a few signature issues, provided I don't *lose* 'em."

That last clause I tried not to utter ruefully because I didn't want to be asked to explain it. Often I felt beset by challenges to the Party's platform; I had to keep it intact. And I had to make sure the Party would not lose its soul, which was a real danger given how I had recently allowed my own soul to diminish—a truth I planned never to heap on Julie.

Said Julie, "You're not just advocating U.S. 'energy transformation,' and financial . . . what's the word—*solvency*. It's the way you're trying to shift the paradigm of political conversation. The name of your Party kind of says what I mean. It's not just your 'signature issues' that make you different."

Probably I would have corrected her linking *"your"* to *Party*, but she immediately asserted, "You don't *need* a lot of experience in what they call foreign policy. It's already been totally screwed up by experts. A cool Buddhist can take the long view of all the crap that's going on in the world, and empathize with everybody the world over, and leave 'em all alone. You don't need experience in security matters; there's manuals and books about that. There's a whole Pentagon full of advisers champing at the bit to earn their pensions. [Beat.]

"Your heart's in the right place, that's fairly obvious. I can say you're probably honest. Nobody need know about your visions. [I chose not to ask her the meaning of that.] I happen to know," Julie aimed to conclude, "that you're good at making people think it's worth their while to do what you want them to do. It's a *gift* mostly unknown in American statecraft. I think it stems from rectitude, being *right on*. For that alone, you should be a contender."

In the dark I uttered to the ceiling, "Gee, I should da been a *contendah!*"

Then I thanked unfathomable powers beyond me for helping me refrain from commenting about Ira's recent disgrace down in Carson City.

King Agamemnon whistles with admiration when he beholds my work of hand and art. I must share in his admiration, for the beauty of the shape we see and mastery of skill needed to make art such as this cannot be overlooked. Now it is complete, and I show my king the felt lining and attach the leather strap. A slave hands me the black horsehair crest fashioned to fit on top, a little below center. When I attach this to the helmet we—king, slave, and craftsman—fix upon the whole of my work to seek out flaws. Instead we see perfection.

"Sometimes," says Agamemnon, "I feel we turn blood drunk. Now I must truly fear the same of our foes when they see your helmet! They will kill to get it. They will die . . . just to hold it."

"I will not wear it, sir, until I have made another exactly the same."

We have a history together, Agamemnon and I, reaching back to before we became men. I see his eyes widen, teeth flash through his beard. He understands what I said. I reach both hands forward, palms turned up. He raises off his boars-tusk helmet and I take it and scowl, for it looks graceless, lumpy, now unfit for the King of Mycenae. But it will serve to shape a mold to the size of his head.

We step inside my workshop (a sorry, hastily built affair) where I show him how I work the lump of clay that I will bake when the size is right. I take different measurements, then we confirm them. While we do this Agamemnon tells me he always envies my bronze-making skill, but now he envies more my art.

"I have no such skill as yours, Amphilochus. Nor your art, as plain I see!"

"My father once commanded chariot o-kas, but he values more his mastery of molding bronze," I respond unnecessarily, for Agamemnon surely knows all this. Still I add, "Of men's affairs, my family most honors hard-won skill, but mingled with art."

"My family most honors skills not necessary for life but for living grandly," responds my king. "Behold, Golden Mycenae. We are royal—I speak for my family—but we earn our royalty with deeds. Not all our deeds are force of arms."

We know he must repair to his tent for a council—from which I am today excused. (Heh-heh-heh-heh.) But thoughts hold him. He stays to speak:

"You must know, my mother's father's mother was of the Perseid family that ruled long before we Pelopids took command. Knowledge and lore come to me down long chains. Thus I never say my voice is that of the Lord and Father of the cosmos, or of any gods. All who hear me know this. My voice is that of my family, and no more."

This is true. I never heard our king declare he spoke for the gods. He simply does. We all know that. In our own ways, then,

I and my comrades do as well. This is sure knowledge, worth knowing, and I think to say so as I work.

*　　*　　*

Daigan down in Carson outdid his usual pranks by Emailing then telephoning me to announce that he had a piece of *extremely* unexpected information.

"You'll never guess or believe how much we've got in your war chest," he said.

I almost considered making a guess. Instead I said, "Right you are." In my mind's eye the figure fifty thousand appeared. Then it morphed to my fantasy figure: one hundred and fifty thousand. So I asked him how much money we had.

Instead of his saying what I would have said ("Come on, take a guess!") he blurted, "One-point-three *million!*"

I said nothing. Daigan added, "Would you believe?"

I stayed silent a couple beats until I uttered (with a noticeable scratchy thinness), "That should buy a lot of beer and pizza."

Probably after nodding affirmatively, Daigan replied: "That'll help us get you on the ballot in other states. {Breath] I can't wait to tell Maya about this; it'll blow her skirt up over her face! [Beat.] Heh-heh-heh-heh! Maybe she'll want to go out to dinner and talk about it."

"Hey, good luck on that, and let me know what she says." And that was all the wit I could summon.

*　　*　　*

"Of course with the right publicity you can be on the ballot all over the West, unless we concentrate on California and Nevada." —Maya speaking to the Party cadre assembled in Julie's and my dining room. This I could have predicted she would say.

Kip speaking: "Putting out our message in California might be like telling kids of Asian descent to work hard in school. Even at that, we probably still wouldn't get you on the ballot over there; it's too big a state. But if you could be an actual *candidate* for President in a couple-few states, *so what* if they're not California—that'll get us real traction. People are gonna have to take notice. That could affect the next congressional elections, maybe the next Presidential election. We can possibly start shaping elections!"

Time for some leavening. I retorted: "Then we can all go to heaven."

"That might be the ultimate point," Wilson rejoined.

Hal was there, this time without Pancho. He said, "I'm all *for* a barrage of 'Net publicity. That's what's been getting us results."

Maya declared to everyone and specifically to Hal that a bona-fide campaign would be different from "a lot of 'Net pronouncements."

Hal said, "What d'ya mean, 'just a lot of 'Net pronouncements'?!"

Maya said, "I didn't say '*just* a lot of 'Net you-know-what.'"

Maya and Hal then enjoyed a brief interchange. To me they were both right. But between them emerged a large burden: I thought, who's going *to do* all this work? Maya had an answer ready:

"We should hire Paragon," she said. "They'll make *sure* you get maximum exposure for every buck spent. And that'll help us get more bucks."

We summarily learned that the Paragon Agency in Las Vegas specialized in generating political publicity. They would make ads for television, they would direct Podcasts and put me on pages in *facebook* and *MySpace* and whatever, they would even text-message selected potential voters, and they would coordinate these activities to cause optimal impact.

"My brother and his pal do a lot of that, and they do it very well," I asserted. "How else do you suppose we attracted all the donations we've gotten?"

"Your brother's work has limitations," Maya replied. She turned to Hal. "Harry, you keep doing what you've been doing. We'll launch a real campaign alongside you."

I didn't catch Harrison's reaction to that. But I did hear expressions of concurrence from Wilson and Mickey and Alyssa (whom I was delighted to see this evening). A few prominent volunteers I'd invited to our meeting murmured vocables of approbation.

"Oh, man!" I said. "We can't really afford a 'real campaign.' A million, even a million-point-three, can only get us so far. —Even if we get the biggest bang for the buck."

Maya's point (with which some attendees concurred): we would attract a lot more bucks by investing in extensive publicity, say in Salt Lake City and Phoenix. The West is a fertile garden for a good cause. (To this Mickey appended, his eyes putting a grip on mine: "So long as Dan won't be too public about his Buddhism!")

At the moment I tried to feature myself campaigning full bore; *not* a desirable picture. For me to get in the thick of politicking, which would happen if we were successful enough—which was certainly our objective—I would impair my health and risk undermining my marriage. At the least, both would be impacted adversely. Who could want that? Not being shy, I voiced these concerns with a tincture of disdain.

Pushback: the notion of "shape the debate" rose to the fore.

Pushover: another apt term. It imbued our discourse and applied solely to one person.

Daigan offered some financial insights as our party treasurer. Proposals were advanced (Maya told us what we should do). Consensus was reached (we promptly agreed with Maya's plan). Basically our strategy would entail hiring Paragon while we maintained our modus operandi.

"Harrison, the handsome brother to our equally handsome presidential candidate, has been doing a stellar job," Maya declared. She didn't have a hat to tip at this moment, she said, so she was giving him a little bow. (Token accomplished.) "It's time he got some assistance, maybe some relief. Paragon's got a roster of real pros; they'll show us what to do."

I glanced at Harry and thought he looked impassive as Maya brightly advised those of us who wanted to be on TV in the near future to get our hair done and lose weight; *now* was the time to start. One thing Paragon always did exceptionally well, she told us, was telecast movie-quality commercials. "Looks like Dan Hachek is going to be a media event," she announced, "and we can *all* get in the act!" Smiling Jimmy Kestrel nodded total approval.

Before we adjourned, though, while we stood around talking and drinking my imported beer and noshing, Jimmy looked anything but serene as he listened to Hal's and Maya's discussion about some apparently arcane subject. Harry's back was toward me but I looked past him to see Maya speaking intently with her brow furrowed. I feared I would learn the upshot of this soon enough.

CHAPTER 40

COSTS

As a man formerly of leisure, I faced doing hard jobs and making tough calls. Maya (presumably assisted by Jimmy) usually had some kind of marching order for me. Does going to Minneapolis in mid-winter sound like a desirable enterprise? How about Chicago and Des Moines? Usually I drove to events in California so I could detach and refresh.

At home, when I cleared the blogs to be released over my name (often written by Hal, with some help from his friends), I had to elide any hint of my opposition to the death so-called penalty and my support of laws banning use of assault-style weapons by our puissant citizenry. Of course I dared not advocate the only realistic way to deal with illegal immigration to the United States.

At the same time I was acutely aware of neglecting a person who needed vigorous exercise and stringently proper nutrition, barely to mention fiddle lessons. (I could not allow myself to even think the word "Tuscany.") My saving graces were a penchant for doing pushups when an opportunity arose and my relentless hatred for saturated fat. Usually I avoided excessive carbohydrates. That bagel or scone in the morning, though, often got the best of me. And some types of locally brewed beer taste so damned good.

These were blithesome matters compared to my realizing that I wasn't doing justice to Julie. When she wanted to spend a special night (or pair of nights) at a casino-hotel in town, guess who was too busy to take her up on it. Ditto, of course, when she had to attend a function out of town and dared to want her able-bodied husband to accompany her. Almost as bad, I was depriving myself of the pleasure of her company. These realizations I had to swallow.

Honoring Julie and causing her to smile every way I could: *that* was actually my primary "mission" on Earth. Probably that's why I was alive. (I'd confirmed this countless times over the years, so it looked valid.) Often I have marveled at the degree of outrageously good luck a person needs to consummate his or her role in the *dharma*. I had to accept that my good luck had gotten thin.

My destiny, my lot in Life (and definitely my *bad* luck), also entailed making open-throttle efforts to fulfill my political "mission." Had I known the cost of that beforehand, I would have thrown in my jockstrap and opted for watching NASCAR on TV.

*   *   *

Conversation between us—about our strategy and how it was playing out—had been brief and business-like. So I faced Maya across her desk (black-and-chrome-Nordic design), told her that I was about to return to Reno this blustery mid-afternoon, "but first," I said, "I think it's coffee time." She would understand I was referring to a *barista* shop three blocks away.

Maya arched in her chair for two seconds to stretch her back and neck, giving me a breathtaking view of her breast capaciousness and shape. I feared she was debating whether to accept my invitation and was losing. When she leaned her blonde head and broad shoulders toward me to stretch the other way I glimpsed weariness and age lines (unless they were an effect of snow skiing in sunlight) etched on her face. Not surprisingly she declined.

"I've got some coffee in a pot in the room behind me," she said. "Help yourself."

This fairly alarmed me. Something made me suspect that I'd been taking Maya's assistance and, yes, friendship for granted. But if that were so, it wasn't totally true.

"You doin' all right?" I said.

I knew that she knew my query was genuine. She told that she hadn't been getting the business she'd been expecting lately and she was a little too involved in my (she used the word "your") campaign. Explaining the latter, she let slip that she was put off by how she perceived my brother regarded her.

Was something going on outside my ken? Maya strove to drop the matter but I pointed out Harry's tender age (although he was a few years older than she) and begged forbearance toward "a benighted upbringing down south." His genetic makeup might have been deficient, too.

"I don't mind so much the way he looks at me," Maya said, "but since our meeting last week I don't like the way he talks to me. I'm trying to do the right thing, the best thing. —So far I've been kind of successful.— I haven't remotely considered superseding him or depreciating the work he's done."

So something *was* up. "I'll certainly talk to him about this," I said. And I meant it.

"You'd better tell him not to take Jimmy too seriously—except to show him respect." No elucidation; just silence. Unsaid by her: something else was afoot, too, bearing large warts.

Maya rose from her chair and said she would get us "something warm to drink" and stepped into the tiny utility room along the wall behind her desk. As she did I resolved to refrain from even glancing at her backside, with scant success. For a long second I fantasized what I would find if I could check out, thoroughly, what she packed in her black slacks.

"I stay in shape pretty well," she said glancing at me over her shoulder. Then she asked, "Do you mind tea for a change? It's pretty good."

We sipped hot brownish liquid the color of branch and talked about money. Nothing profound. Maya regarded money as symbolic of success in her line of work, and I couldn't quarrel with that. It also bought shoes; she liked to be accessorized, as we'd discussed previously. And she had a ten-year-old daughter who was "very demanding."

"Like her mother?" I said.

"Like her mother."

I said, "Fine!"

My tone must have surprised her. She couldn't know that for two years I'd had a daughter.

She disconcerted me by saying, "I used to be married—before I met Ira B. Never again!"

Any further mention of Ira I wanted to sidestep.

She helped me out: "You're married, aren't you?"

"Of course! I thought you knew."

As if she were asking me the time of day she said, "Happily?"

Beat. "I can't honestly imagine being with anyone else. Even for an hour."

We allowed a little space for me to further my response. So I added: "I can't imagine actually *living* unless Julie's right there with me, or nearby."

"Really?"

"Really."

"Interesting!" She arched her back in another stretch, this one too brief. Then she regarded me evenly (the tea having relaxed us) and said, "I'll 'fess up to being several years older than my sister Alyssa. But I haven't gone through 'the change' yet. It's still more than a few years away."

Beat. I could only surmise she told me that so I would know her better since I'd just revealed part of myself to her. If this were true, I now esteemed her more.

"Well, I'm a *lot* older than you," I said. "That's all I'm gonna 'fess up to."

Before I left Maya's office, I knew that for me our connection now was basic.

*   *   *

Driving within Reno on the south part of the loop, I felt guilty satisfaction in noting a billboard that asked in black on white, "TIRED OF GOVERNMENTAL INACTION AND WASTE WHILE MOTHER EARTH HEATS UP? HELP THE CONSERVATIVE-REFORM MOVEMENT! VOTE . . . AS YOUR CONSCIENCE TELLS YOU." Both words in the Party name were boldly underlined with a broad band of red, white and blue stripes. A part of the sign I would *claim* to deny loving was the medium-tight, flattering photo of me in the upper-right corner, as though I beheld the hordes of motorists passing by there daily. Next day I spotted an identical billboard on the north part of the loop. The Paragon Agency had been hard at work.

During a morning telephone conversation, Harry acceded that publicity for the Party—and my campaign—was intensifying. Whether that would pay for itself we both considered problematic. I tried to address the issues between Harry and Maya, but Harry abruptly declared how our mother, who lived in suburban Phoenix, Arizona, would delight in seeing our publicity if she were properly exposed to it. We could only try to describe it for her during telephone visits since she had difficulty traveling and lacked interest in Web matters.

"Maybe it's worth getting yourself pushed around," Harry said.

"Would y' mind clarifying that for me," I said.

He did so adamantly. His point of view was that for some ungrounded reason Maya had taken hold of the reins of our Party and gotten too big relative to the rest of us. We always did whatever she declared we do.

"I'm sure that's only half true if it's true at all," I responded. Unpremeditatedly I added, "She gets a lot done because she's not alone: she draws on help from Jimmy—"

I planned an encomium about Jimmy's contributions but got pulled short:

"Hey, listen, I don't want to see or smell that faggot anywhere near me, man."

Beat. "How's *that*? Hey, what in the world's goin' on?!"

Hal's vehemence threw me. I hadn't heard him call someone a fag in probably over twenty years.

Very emphatically he explained that he never could "abide queers, even though some of them are all right." But Jimmy's personality grated on him, he said, and when Jimmy "tried to put the moves on [him]" all the wrong buttons got pushed. "Maybe it's the *way* he tried to do it that really got to me," said Harry. With that, I knew not to press for details.

"Listen," I said after taking a second to frame my response, "be good to Maya. She's great, and we need her. She's crucial to putting out The Word. [Beat.] You know she relies on Jimmy! I'll talk to him, so keep cool."

From my brother—"Ukh! First we get that pushy bitch, who needs to have her panties chewed off, now we've got us a snotty fag whose face I'm gonna *tear right off* next time he gives me half a chance."

Summarily we rang off. I knew I had a problem, but I presumed all parties involved were civilized adults.

Since our objective was to promulgate the Party's position on crucial issues, we replayed locally and in Las Vegas and Sacramento the two TV ads we had made. Ultimately we hoped to get national exposure that would help reshape the narratives in next year's elections. Our ads looked professional but they were not really compelling. Maya informed me that producing and broadcasting a "major message" for television was going to be the top priority of our hired publicity agency "when we have funding in place." And that would be fairly soon.

Our penultimate objective kept me preoccupied: getting my name on the ballot in Nevada—and we intended other states—for the presidential election. Too often, though, people imputed my campaign to personal vanity ("Dan Hachek's ego trip"). So often I resorted to righteous indignation and got on my bully pulpit, and that was good. But sometimes I felt my spirit for this exercise start to wane—if only because *"vanity"* can mean more than just being vain, as a distressed fellow named Ecclesiastes once famously averred.

*   *   *

Slovenia: a small alpine nation adjacent to Austria; home to about one and one-half million hardy Slovenes—a very estimable people. When that country was part of the former Yugoslavia it accounted for about 26% of that federation's GNP.

Slovenia was the first component of Yugoslavia to break off for autonomy, and when it did the central government in Belgrade basically let it go (unlike what happened when other Yugoslav components broke away). This speaks for the Slovenes' formidability, as do their Olympic skiers' prowess and the beauty of their women (especially, one notices, those who ski).

One day, let us say, a cohesive but diverse group of about ten thousand Slovenes chose to form a separate community, a hidden settlement, on part of the Alps where no civilization had existed before—for reasons unrecorded in surviving histories. They were enabled to do that, we do know, by global warming that made the enterprise feasible. So they did it, with great success. Basically they detached themselves from their own country, evidently were pleased with the results, and at some point cut themselves off from the rest of Europe. And there they flourished in splendid isolation for maybe three hundred years. Whether members of the community had commerce with their home country—and whether outsiders could gain ingress to the settlement—is unknown. In all events, this aggregation of Slovenes appeared to be totally self-sufficient.

They actually had everything: access to the Internet, satellite TV, apparently their own technological inventions; somehow they had sufficient food and adequate medical care; they lived in a pristine environment (which may account for their having removed themselves from the rest of civilization); they must have had romance—there were schools for youngsters, and they had churches (each one different); they patronized concert and beer halls (utilizing a couple breweries and a distillery and somehow getting Austrian grapes for vintning); they even made movies and produced plays and took time to read books (for this size community theirs was a fine library). Evidently the atmospheric climate in this part of the Alps allowed for very viable living.

Until it changed again: erratic weather patterns triggered a series of snowfalls of historic proportions—with the attendant series of avalanches. The "settlers" must have known this was coming and evacuated just in time, for they left no corpses (even of animals). Their Shangri-La not only got buried, and reburied (and reburied), it stayed buried—until 200,000 years later when Earth warmed enough (presuming she still lived) for post-human explorers to detect and eventually investigate the well-preserved remains of that alpine community.

Of course the explorers' discovery astounded them, but especially after they dated when the settlement was last inhabited.

"Would you look at all the cool stuff those people had!" one of the finders gushed. [Somehow English had survived those many millennia.] "And that was so incredibly *long ago!*"

Said another explorer: "We *can* call 'em 'people,' can't we?"

His partner commented, "Yeah, I suppose they were 'people.'"

Another explorer on the team couldn't help bubble: "Look at all they were able to do, given their subhuman development. If you ask me it's positively freakin' amazing!"

Ripe with wonder, a silent moment passed. Then all three finders declared simultaneously: "So *big* [bleepin'] *deal!*"

This is a perspective I have tried to keep on just about everything.

CHAPTER 41

ARTFUL

No matter how blasé I tried to be about this, I always succumbed to gratification when I saw young people circulating a petition to validate the Conservative-Reform Party's candidate for U.S. President. No doubt, when Bernie Sanders stood for U. S. President in 2014-2016, he must have felt this exponentially in double digits. That was good.

One day I learned that in Reno, Vegas, Carson and Elko, cells of volunteers had formed to hand out publicity urging people to sign my candidacy petition; other cells presented the petitions for people to sign. Once again, I had to congratulate Maya (with her hired guns) and Hal and Pancho for putting out The Word about "Conservative Reform" and thus my campaign. Julie explicitly touted our progress. Just as important to me, Dr. Jay said he took pride in seeing my candidacy going forward so well. Hearing this would have been worth killing for.

Agamemnon's helmet is smaller than mine but the difference cannot be seen without measuring inside. This surprises him, and I ask how a head less large than my own is able to command this army against an alliance of foes as strong as ours . . . also the fleet that protects the many ships that bring supplies to us.

Somehow he chooses to think on this long. Finally he answers: "Amphilochus, I do not know. Ask the gods."

"If I ask the gods," I say, "how can I know their explanation?"

"You can ask them to become men. Thus they will speak or write. Perhaps you can go to Delphi and the priestess will divine what they say and tell you, if you have means. Or you can pretend you hear their words as they speak only to you. But then you must go about and tell everyone to believe what you hear so you will believe it also."

We smile at this as my king raises up his new helmet and fits it over his head. Together we bend to see his reflection in my tub of tempering water. The image is startling, for it is handsome and graceful and fearsome. Mere sight of a man such as this can frighten even me, and I know him well. Very simply he thanks me for my work and art and generosity.

"Now you truly look like the King of Men," I respond.

"Now I believe that. Can you make such a helmet for Achilles? I would pay you grandly."

"Achilles needs a better helmet, I have no doubt. But first I must founder more bronze, for his head is large! I have seen his helmet size; it exceeds belief!"

At this we both smile. I raise up my helmet and don it to match my king. Then Agamemnon speaks on a thought.

"*Trojans—and all their many allies—will want to kill us only to claim our helmets,*" he says. "*This is certain.*"

Now we grin through our beards beneath bronze nose plates and neither of us speaks, for each knows the other's thought on this.

We think, So let them come forward!

*   *   *

According to Maya, who almost succeeded in keeping a poker face while she related this, Ira's life had gone into free-fall since his arrest. The details were dismaying. I tried to push away what I'd heard about the charges against him and the likely consequences to his business (which he used to refer to as "a hustle") and his relationship with his son, who had recently telephoned Maya, she said, to inquire whether she thought his father would actually do those things charged against him.

As I recall, the young fellow goes to Stanford," I said. "What did you tell him, may I ask."

"I told him no, but I also said nothing Ira might do would surprise me. Brett seemed to accept that."

Maya and I had met in a small parking area outside Party headquarters and talked as we walked inside. I went silent as I reaffirmed, maybe for the twentieth time, my conviction that my role in torpedoing Ira's fortunes did not stem from one of my better decisions; it was simply necessary. *Somebody* had to preclude that man from—we were pretty sure—discrediting the Party, rendering it collateral damage. Predicating this, I profoundly hoped everyone I cared about would never, ever get an inkling of what I had done. Plus I had a bona-fide fear: the

Party would implode if my machination ever came to light. In short, my own greatness astounded me.

Inside the Party office Maya capped all this by saying, "Ira has very few enemies, believe it or not. He sort of specializes in me; and he knows his enemy. Now it's possible that someone, someone I don't know about, *planted* crap on him so he'd get sucked down a sewer. I'm sure he wouldn't seriously suspect me of pulling that because he knows I'd never play *that* dirty."

I nodded while I secretly wished I could claim likewise.

*   *   *

In Winnemucca, in Elko, in Sparks, in Las Vegas, in Henderson, and (especially) on the UNR campus, people in our party's "cells" wanted to know: Who would be the Conservative-Reform Party's *Vice*-Presidential candidate? All kinds of unlikely rumors about that swirled like dust devils. I made a tentative attempt at blaming Harry, but he denied starting any. When he asked me whom I had in mind for a running mate, his query came at me from around a corner.

"Who do you think?" I said.

"Nobody. Nobody I know of," said Harry.

"That's whom *I'm* thinking of."

Until Hal's query, I had casually considered the subject maybe twice; it was outside my realm of reality. When I asked Hal if *he* had anyone in mind he said he didn't. Soon after this I asked Julie, then Maya; neither could (or else would) suggest a name. Ditto result when I broached the subject to Kip, to Mickey, to Wilson. Jimmy said he thought he could suggest someone, but not at the moment. I almost considered placing an ad in local alternative newspapers: *U. S. V-P candidate wanted, any color, either sex.*

By happenstance I mentioned this problem to Dr. Jay, who earnestly paused to think about it. When he said he knew just the person, I thought he might be using irony.

"Look," he said, "you've got a basically *guy*-centric campaign going, even though maybe half the volunteers are women. You want to diversify, appeal to a wide demographic. So make the Party look, y' know, 'demographic.'"

Jay continued: "I know an attractive woman—nice-looking and lively, but not drop-dead gorgeous—she's part Asian, by descent, and part black and can speak Spanish; I guess sometimes she uses Korean. She used to be married to a guy of Arabic descent and she keeps her married name. The beauty part is she belongs to our Party, or so I've heard."

"Cool. —Who is she? I can look her up on the Party roster."

"Kim. Kim Something or Other."

"Don't you know her last name?"

"That *is* her last name. It's hyphenated; I don't remember the second part. Her first name is Savannah. She's from the South."

I got right on it, did a search, and found Savannah Kim-Sheikaday, who lived in Sparks and denoted her occupation only as "service industry." After difficulty contacting her I finally reached her by phone. She was lively, all right, and Southern. I found our phone visit very pleasurable.

After I identified myself and determined she was receptive to my contacting her, I explained that to vent our Party's position on issues and capture broad appeal we needed someone—like her—to be named as our Vice-Presidential candidate. Would she consider becoming "a very public person for a while?" The aim would be public service.

After my overture we went silent for a few beats. Then she said, "You're asking me to run for Vice-President of the United States?"

"Yes, ma'am. Actually I'm asking you to seriously consider it. We need to name someone as my running mate. I'm thinking you could fill that slot nicely."

"Well, thanks," Savannah replied, "but I don't know . . . I don't normally get involved in political things."

I quickly explained that my campaign was not really a "political" undertaking. Nor was the nature of the Party actually "political," regardless of its name and *modus operandi*. She seemed to understand my position.

Abruptly, Savannah reeled off her qualifications for representing herself as a candidate for public office: a double-major degree in communications and international relations. She then informed me that she could speak two languages besides English (with smatterings of two more); that she had "extensive" business experience; that she was a single mom of two grade-school kids. I thought if she was half as attractive as Jay had averred, I desperately wanted to meet her.

Savannah added that, "absolutely," she would like to do public service, but as a breadwinning mother—she had to work. She couldn't allow "politicking" to interfere with her job. And I acceded that I should have anticipated as much.

Then I asked, mostly pro forma, "What `service industry' do you work in?"

"I help run, I'm co-manager of, The Wild Bunch Brothel. You know, I make sure we turn a profit and the girls stay healthy and pay for their board. Put me down as a `hospitality-industry manager.' What I do might not accord with our Party's aims, but I've got *all kinds* of expertise."

"Ah," I said and did some quick thinking: All right, she wasn't a seamless prospect; so be it. Then I told Savannah that she would enjoy meeting Maya and key members of the Party, and that *I* would like to meet her, and doing that would get her a good lunch. I wasn't surprised when she accepted. The hard part was arranging a time to fit our schedules, for we found the next two weeks impossible. We agreed to make contact after the next week.

"Now don't be a stranger at The Wild Bunch," she said in ringing off, and I honestly didn't know how to reply.

I never learned what connection lay between my son Jay and the lady with *all kinds* of expertise. Presumably it was professional, from one standpoint or the other.

*　　*　　*

Shortly after I'd gotten naive enough to think a particular matter that had been vexing me might have died by default, Jimmy Kestrel surfaced like a Super Bowl umpire throwing a flag.

We spotted each other at the lunch buffet in the Silver Legacy Casino. Business had brought Jimmy to Reno; he was amid a company of suits and haircuts. We touched on the subject of our being unable to contact Mitch Freeman, and I invited Jimmy to stop by Party headquarters before he went back to Sacramento. He did just that, and we spent most of an hour discussing Party matters (mainly the vagaries of my campaign) and he told me about weird clients he had in Sacramento. Party volunteers were working across the hall from us, so we had some privacy.

"On the subject of weird personalities," I said, "what on Earth could have touched off *my brother* after our meeting a few weeks ago? He seems, uh, bent out of shape by something you said or, I don't know, something . . . ."

Jimmy cut a token laugh and smile. "Your brother Harrison always strikes me as someone who's feeling incomplete. Don't you get that sense about him? I would think you must."

"He strikes me as a lot of things. I don't know if 'feeling incomplete' is one of them." Beat. Beat. Both my hands fluttered up emphasizing perplexity. "What happened?"

"Well, if he hasn't told you by now, you might say I violated one of my principle rules: mingling pleasure with business matters. —Not that I consider your political enterprise 'business,' strictly speaking.— Well, when our little get-together at your house was just about finished, I couldn't help feeling that Harrison needed pleasant company *après*. If you get my drift."

"You put your moves on a hetero man?!"

"How can anyone tell whether *any* man is hetero? I certainly can't. Let me say that I was thoroughly unprepared for the violent response I got! [Beat.] Well, it was *almost* violent. It could have been violent. I still recall feeling a little rattled, you know what I mean?"

"Well, Harry's got some issues, no doubt."

"'Y' know some of them involve Maya, who by the way was also astonished—shocked—by Harrison's reaction to what I'd call my kindly suggestion."

I simply sat nodding. It would be nice to end this now, I thought.

"Make no mistake about it," said Jimmy. "If Maya is going to be put upon, as she was by your brother—this was before he reacted to me—I simply won't stand for it. She won't either; I guarantee that. If she's out of here, *I'm* outta here." A shrug of finality.

Maybe a vulgar expletive escaped me. Was I in a box? I regarded Jimmy levelly. I said, "Let's keep everything cool. It's for the common good."

From Jimmy a token shrug; "Okay," he said. We paused as his mind arced to a distant subject: "I've been meaning to mention," he said, "Maya's got plans, I think, to hire a high-powered so-called political consultant. We don't have Ira B. to lean on anymore, and I can recommend this guy Maya wants. He's based in San Francisco."

To my mind we could afford no such consultant. Nor did we need one. I didn't even want to know his name. It was Trevor Butts.

CHAPTER 42

TREMBLOR

"Hey, look," said Harry, "we're probably making too many enemies; more than we can afford. Even before Dan gets on the ballot we ought to consider that."

Hal was addressing the strategy meeting we needed before we planned our next big move (using Maya's parlance). This time we had gathered at her office in downtown Carson, late afternoon, which turned out to be an imposition on most of us. Our logistics were not quite rational. That's why Wilson, my sage-most colleague, could not attend.

Jimmy suggested that we "suspend" Harry's point about alienating certain groups of people and declared that the Party "must not lose its soul"; our publicity has been accomplishing exactly what we wanted. Maya concurred with Jimmy. I didn't know what to think.

An unfamiliar voice sounded among us: "The first fellow's right. You've got to figure out ways to *disarm* your critics. At the same time you'll be covering up vulnerable spots from potential opponents. In retrospect, you'll always be glad you did that."

This was Trevor Butts, Maya's newest "investment." A likeable-enough man, plainly astute, otherwise difficult to describe beyond "white, maybe early-middle-aged, a bit overweight."

He seemed to make a point of not thrusting himself at us while he spoke in neutral tones: "Regardless of the large numbers of people you intend to benefit down the road, right now you're alienating everyone who might be connected with the defense establishment. [Beat.] You know, the ol' `Military-Industrial Complex'! —And that's barely to mention doctors, corporate hospitals, federal and state bureaucracies, entitlement beneficiaries, *anyone* who milks the system; and that's barely to mention everyone who absolutely, necessarily, needs a big RV. There must be a lot of not-so-hardcore Republicans—and, yeah, a lot of Democrats—who've heard of you and prefer to see you dry up and blow away. Then there's always the bunch that doesn't have a life except for getting real excited over what they hear on talk radio—they're gonna fantasize *actually doing* the blowing away, so to speak. My point is you should try never to offer critics an attractive target. They'll find plenty of targets without you helping 'em."

The man could make a point. For a while we discussed how many mountains we had to climb to accommodate it. Finally the Sage of the American West spoke up in my usual tympanic tones: "We've got to stay true to principles our Party is founded on. Otherwise why bother? I suggest that, once again, we *put out there,* for *everyone to see,* exactly where we stand. We do this as clearly, as cleverly, as we can. If whirlwinds do arise, *eckh*! I'll reap 'em later. —That is all I have to say."

I felt sort of good about what I'd just said.

Our business of the moment then became how to best state that the U.S. government must take proactive steps ("*this week*") toward arresting global-climate change and getting us out of debt (which happens to be a national security threat that's real). Thus we pressed the necessity that the federal government develop a plan for cultivating small businesses and another for fostering scientific and technological research for specific national objectives. Tangentially we deemed the U. S. badly in need of a foreign policy that steers clear of nation-building and giving away dollars, regardless of who expects to get them. (This is where Harry or Pancho said if the U. S. did that, we'd have to start up "a new earplug-manufacturing industry" to cope with "the massive waves of squealing" we'd hear from our client countries and, their champions).

When I got the chance I suggested that we insert a one-sentence preamble to our platform stating that our Party's overriding objective was to foster the common good. Shockingly, I got pushback from, of all people, Harry, seconded by Pancho, both of whom claimed not to know what "commonweal" means. Darned if I didn't have to define it. Making a top priority of rebuilding our highway system and bridges would be a fine example of aiming to benefit everybody. So would an energy policy that enables the whole country to rely exclusively on renewable energy sources. Kip or Trevor (or someone with *wonk* credentials) hooked up the common-good notion with regulating financial dealings such as "derivatives" while *help-ing* investment banks loosen their tight money but precluding them from going belly-up.

Meanwhile someone said that U. S. military power was essential in quashing the potential ISIS (or ISIL) "caliphate," but someone else (seconded by me) said that simply wasn't "our job." Hal spoke up: "Hey, *nota bene.* That kind of enterprise *is not our job*! If it were, we could just send over the Chicago or maybe the Los Angeles Police Department and get it done. They might not even need air support!" Without actual discussion we reached the consensus that the U. S. role *vis*-à-vis Islamic extremism is to take out terrorists. Wherever they are.

Implicitly a question rose before us like a wall of wet steam: Were we presumptuous in professing that we knew what the hell we were talking about?

Once I realized the question, I took up our banner. "Look," I said. "We're here to tip off America: America needs to be smarter; we've gotta *stop doing stupid stuff*!" Of course I knew that a lot of people would take serious issue with me when they'd get the opportunity.

After a few hours of brain-numbing work, we needed a break—say for a week—so we adjourned until eight days later at my house when we'd resume inscribing granite. Those of us who would have time and psychic space to dwell on our proposals during the interim might then suggest points we hadn't adequately discussed or hadn't raised, such as how to propose feeding and rebooting people displaced from obsolete energy-extraction industries. We should "try to show that [we're] not a claque of worthless do-gooders—callus to human aspirations like paying the mortgage and buying bread and beer." (Trevor's words.)

When we agreed to adjourn I felt deflated because we had not even touched on what I considered a centerpiece proposal: building a job-corps-peace-corps-hybrid organization that would eventually operate *sans* borders to teach people how to fish, figuratively speaking. (Ex-President Jimmy Carter liked to use the trope that contrasts giving a man something *vs.* teaching him how to get it. So he talked a little funny, but he was one of my heroes.) To do constructive work a person must learn how. People all over the planet gainfully doing real and necessary work would be the panacea for most of the world's ills. I've always been certain of this.

Just before we disbanded, Maya waved two papers Daigan had passed to her and announced that we had almost enough money to fund a movie-quality commercial promoting the Party's presidential campaign. "We'll be making that TV spot pretty soon, people, so time to start losing weight if you want to be in the movies!" she said. (Fine, I thought, everyone aspires to be a star—except Dan Hachek.) Pancho asked Maya where the ad would likely be televised, and she said she hoped we could air it in all the major markets in Nevada, Oregon, Washington, Idaho, and Utah. She wanted to hit some stations in California, too.

On my way out the door I noticed Harry standing on the side as though he was intending to talk to Maya. Pancho waited for him nearby. Jimmy sat by the opposite wall, looking on. Normally Harry and Pancho and I would have walked outside to our cars together; this time since nobody immediately came forth, I ambled off and left. What I didn't know was that Harry and Pancho would remain inside with Maya at least five minutes longer.

CHAPTER 43

FAITH

We prayed to Cybele to aid our supply ships and keep us strong until they arrive; conditions for us are hard. Now I wrap myself in my lion-skin mantle—a gift from my king—and wish for the comforts of mead or barley beer. Agamemnon, cloaked also in fur, seats himself on the earth beside me. Our camp stool remains unused.

Agamemnon says, "Remember before our journey to the far north country for the brown metal for our bronze—I think I told you of the old Crete sailor who advised me before we set out."

We had been sent by our fathers to sail and trade, also to work the mines, and thus to become men sooner. We thought we were men before we left; we truly became men by the time we returned. (From that journey I learned I would never again willfully set out to trade afar, and I learned of many other things alongside my shipmate and future king.) I answer to Agamemnon that he told me often of what he now speaks.

Says Agamemnon, "If we have faith in everything we set out to do, we are heroes even if we die in the attempt. Yes, I remember telling you this but did I tell you something else the old sailor said to me: He said we must be willing to die in our expeditions or they are not worth undertaking."

I remind him that when we were youths we spoke of this often during our journey to the north, and then on the dangerous return journey to our nostoi *(so richly earned by us!). Thus we learned we could not choose to die or not to die. Gods—and storms and disease and pirates—would always do that for us.

"Ah, that is so true," says Agamemnon, "and this truth holds our saving belief."

He falls silent and gazes into the night, as I do. Then we stare at our tiny fire. Soon I think to ask, "Sir, what belief saves us?"

Agamemnon answers, "We are of the gods. You yourself say this often. The gods will not abandon us nor will they refuse us, for we strive to please and serve them—as we serve ourselves. I rely on this belief. Thus we must keep our faith in all we do."

With this he knows I agree. I have only to nod.

Soon we must find wine and make a better place to sleep. First I rise to look once more upon our lines of chariot horses.

Agamemnon's voice comes to me from a stride back. I think he counsels himself as he declares: "We must stay to our course. Generations to come will call us heroes. I know this to be true."

I will not speak nor will I nod but simply look to the stars on the horizon. Reputation among men yet unborn is not grace, is not gold. If our lot today is not important, nothing is. This I do know to be true. But to voice this now would be senseless.

(* *Nostoi* = return of the heroes)

*　　*　　*

Julie was more than curious about our latest strategy meeting and pending TV ad, so when I got home from Carson City that evening I told her all that I knew to say. When she asked where the Party stood on dealing with Islamic extremism I answered that we wanted the U. S. to be smart; we've got the best counter-terrorism apparatus imaginable. It's actually *layered,* which means lots of redundancies and far too expensive. Probably we'd better streamline it.

"I don't want us to be seduced by fear," I said. We, Julie and I, understood that I posed a cross-purpose with the prevailing mentality of our government, maybe most of the country.

Then Julie asked whether we had found a Vice-Presidential candidate and I told her about Jay's discovery and my telephone conversation with Savannah Sheikaday.

"*Interesting,*" said Julie (exactly as Maya often responded). She then recommended that I invite Savannah to our next meeting; if Savannah would attend, everyone might benefit. To which I commented, "*Interesting.*"

The next day neither of us had to be anyplace in particular (a blessed event!), so I took the time to unload on Julie my story about "Slovenes in the Alps." Doing that seemed strongly relevant to our—that is, *my*—endeavors.

When I concluded Julie said, "Your perspective might be skewed. From now on, I want you to consider this: your reform party isn't just trying to conserve and reform, et cetera. You're also trying to help save the planet, you know, before it's too late. *Gaia* must thank you. And people, y' know, have to *live* here! Those are two distinct ends in themselves; right? They're intrinsically good. Make sure you compute that, and don't forget the old 'ripple effect.'"

I was glad to hear Julie's thoughts about my perspective. Plainly, some things *really are* a "big [bleepin'] deal."

*   *   *

Apropos of apparently nothing, the second quarter dropped through and Julie looked up from the sink to pose her fifty-cent question: "I'm sure you know, I never got my answer."

Turned out that she was referring to her request of a long time before that I disclose what I'd like to see as my epitaph. How would I like to be remembered on Earth? At the moment we were preparing ratatouille and salmon, gratifying stuff requiring intensive work that allowed us mental space.

I thought I could never give her a true answer. (I *had* told her I would think about this, so I actually had, with almost no success.) Briefly I temporized. Finally I said: "Well, I've done my best. That's gotta count for something. Let's just say, 'Dan Hachek—He did his damnedest (with loads of help).' —Sounds right to me."

"And—" said Julie.

For three seconds I found myself trying to reconstruct an interchange I'd had with—*yes*, Agamemnon. Now it proved to be useful.

I said, "If people would say, or think, I have cultivated an aesthetic sensibility and that I truly care about others *and* the Earth, now that would be really cool. Especially were it true!"

"Unpack that for me."

I reconstructed my reasoning before I said, "If I've actually *demonstrated* those gifts I just mentioned, I can be a marker for the world. We are of the gods, you might say. Those qualities I mentioned *must be* divine. If *I've* got 'em, *everyone* has 'em. That's a useful point for the world to hear."

Beat. Julie said: "Okay. So . . . . . What of it? Where does that take us?"

Unvolitionally I flashed on a poolside scene in the movie *The Graduate*. "Beats me," I said. (Pause, a shrug.) To my credit I quickly added, "So *be* divine. Do what you're supposed to."

"Dan Hachek's 'Book of Revelations,'" Julie commented, her tone neutral but respectful.

"Well, I'm not a prophet or a preacher or a prophet's kin. My phone connection to the *Source* of the Cosmos—seems like it hasn't worked since about 1949. And I *can't read* His or Her handwriting! But I'm as qualified as any man to be your next god-king or spiritual redeemer."

I thought that was all I had to say. But after a moment, not quite. "Thus I make a proclamation: I declare that we take a vacation *this week*! [Beat.] Would y' pass the olive oil."

I turned from my task to behold the most endearing smile on Earth. Immediately we started planning where on Lake Tahoe we would go, given we could only snatch away a few days.

TOUGHEN UP

"Hey, you fool," I said into Harrison's voice mail, "Maya tells me you and she had some hard words at her office last week, after I left. I'm really hoping that isn't true. We *need her*, man. Do you get my drift?"

Actually I knew about what I spoke from a source besides Maya. I'd met Pancho at Party headquarters the day after Julie and I had returned from Lake Tahoe, and he told me what Maya soon confirmed: after our last meeting Hal told her, in no uncertain terms, that he didn't like the role she'd been assuming in the campaign (which, according to Maya, he didn't really comprehend). The ensuing personality clash escalated because Jimmy joined in.

Harry's way of dealing with people was to speak his mind and not mince words, and his choice of words was rarely the best. The upshot was Maya and Jimmy getting offended and

Harry turning bellicose. I knew I had to defuse the conflict before it would fester even worse.

But I was behind the power curve. When Hal responded to my message about our needing Maya in my campaign he started with a riposte: "*You* might need her, man, but that doesn't mean *we* do."

"Oh, yes, we do," I countered. "She's invaluable, I'd say irreplaceable."

"No one's '*irreplaceable*,'" Harry said, to which I silently concurred.

"Well, we can't have you jumping all over one of our most valuable assets, if you'd excuse the term. [Beat.] She wouldn't stomp on *you*, even if she had the chance."

He sought to quarrel with that. Then he said, "She's the one who started everything by constantly trying to order me around." I was about to tell him this was lame when he added, "That queen—I mean that *queer*—doesn't exactly help to keep things rational." A sharp vocable of disgust from Harry's end.

I refrained from requesting details. I could only reiterate that we—the Party, and getting out the Party's message—*needed* Maya, who often relied on Jimmy. And that was understatement. I tried not to be too subtle.

Conversely, two days later, after I'd returned from speaking in Eugene, Oregon, I detected Wilson stretching to be subtle with the message he'd left in my voice mail. He was calling, he said, to confirm the time and place of our follow-up strategy meeting, with the "probably superfluous hope that the altercation Mickey said he'd overheard after last week's meeting wasn't severe." His message concluded with the enjoinder that "an enterprise such as ours requires e*sprit de corps* as well as unity."

I thought, oh, great! Then I recalled Kip once having remarked that we couldn't "afford to have divisive personalities in the Party at this stage of its formation." So now we had this deepening rift between, of all people, Maya and my brother . . . while I still grappled with problems regarding my own integrity, or lack of it.

*   *   *

"It's possible that this job-corps, peace-corps thing doesn't really fit in the program coherently. It's kind of an incongruity." —This was Kip speaking.

"It does kind of clutter things up. If we're going to do maximal good we have to deliver a short, impactful set of related points. We can't wave around a little flag with an extraneous, albeit important, message. Our method of communicating has to be just the opposite of that." —This was Wilson speaking, with whom people voiced concurrence.

I caught myself flashing on a brief visit Ira made to Party headquarters about five months before when he insisted I elide from the Party platform all "distracters" regardless of how worthy each might be as a cause. All right, I acknowledged that, but people shouldn't stomp on my baby with log-roller boots.

This was during our follow-up strategy meeting at Julie's and my house. All the cadre were there, plus Julie (somehow to my relief) and a few key volunteers. Trevor Butts wasn't present, but a stranger, a good-looking, fiftyish black fellow, was. I'd heard mention of his being "an associate of Mr. Butts"; Maya had referred to him as a "media guru."

The stranger was constantly poring over papers, with Maya handing him others. Occasionally she also passed something to Hal or Pancho, which either accepted cursorily. Before we had taken up business Julie and I gave everyone a bowl of shelled peanuts and a bowl of snack crackers. Our living room-dining room was redolent of coffee, for which all were grateful because we had to cover a lot of ground quickly.

My pet proposal, my personal centerpiece, fared badly for maybe all the right reasons: we had to keep the Party "on message" and "right now the U.S. can't afford a box of popcorn if we regard the national debt rationally" [Wilson's words].

Still, I argued that I *knew* I had the long-range solution to so many problems all over the world—provided it were executed properly. Tackling unemployment with widespread job training, say, in India or Indonesia or Africa or the Mideast would go a long way toward eliminating critical world problems and forestalling new ones.

I let it be known that I had long harbored this vision, which is one reason I'd formed the Conservative-Reform Party. (If necessary I could play my trump card.) I appended that we need a much-better-trained workforce at home because high-tech people—and most people sitting at desks—won't get the daily work done that's required for a nation's high-level survival. "I mean, today, how many tool-and-die makers do we have left in this country?"

But even my claim that a national-international job-training program would cost "chump change" compared to, say, the price of the U.S. embassy in Baghdad went the way of morning dew. Fact: the federal budget was in deep red. Fact: the U. S. needed to rebuild basic infrastructure all over the land, even while transforming our economy to a climate-safe one. Another fact: federal policies must at least *start* relieving crippling college-student debt. All this is barely to mention the need to shore up Medicare funding.

Maybe I should have pulled rank. Ultimately I capitulated to consensus; my team got the best of me. Does that dramatize a lesson? I'll never know.

Quite a few major points got short shrift as we focused on proposing concrete steps, such as formation of a Green-Energy Fund, that our country should take—and would have to take—to lead the world in averting environmental disaster, even though ours was not the Green Party and none of us could claim to supplant Al Gore. In short, as someone declared, "The technologies for doing the job *aren't* `out there'; they're *here* as we speak. Now we've gotta *use 'em everywhere*." After the Paris Climate Summit in late 2015, we mostly agreed that the next step for the U. S. would be to implement ancillary-*bilateral* agreements, like the one President Obama cut with China, on deploying key technologies to arrest carbon and methane emissions.

I was proud of the way we hammered out the major points in our party platform. We got on a roll and stuck with it until we were done, giving Julie and our guest "media guru" reason to be impressed.

How about water-resource conservation? We can't get eso-teric just yet; maybe next year. Can we propound a single-payer "universal" health-care program? Well, it subsumes elegant sim-plicity. If it were implemented it would save lives and surely save corporate and local-government and household budgets. ("Those are reasons to felonize such a plan!"—Kip Whitbread's words.) But that's not for us to propose. How about more HIV research—better protection, a cure? Nope, our plate is too full right now. At this juncture, dear Julia, only a nominal mem-ber of the Party and not a voting principal in this meeting, became so appalled she spoke out to the contrary, to no avail. Happily, since we had considered how the U. S. should deal with terrorism in our last meeting, we only touched on the subject this time. ("We've got to keep our *mojo workin'*!" was how someone capped the discussion.)

During all this I noticed that our technology expert, Hal, appeared detached if not bored. Twice I spotted Maya glance at him askance, not with hostility but with plain displeasure. What else had developed between them I couldn't possibly know. I just knew the situation was unwholesome.

After about three hours, Maya saw fit to conclude our meeting with a multiple announcement: We now had the money and we already had a contract (with Paragon) to pro-duce a "fairly elaborate" promotional spot for television. And this evening in our midst we had the person who would script the production—the silent, intense stranger toward whom she motioned, Isaiah Ogden.

Mr. Ogden did a little wave and flashed a dazzling smile across 180 degrees. Then he arose to proffer, in melodiously macho tones, a few remarks about how he enjoyed attending this meeting and undertaking "the challenge of dramatizing" our party's "point of view." With another smile he added he'd "get right on it." Only then did I find the prospect of making another TV ad vaguely pleasing.

Later, at home alone with Julie, after we'd touched on my defeated proposal that the U.S. establish a network of "occupation-training stations" around the world, I decided I had some explaining to do. At last I told Julie about the unhealthy situation intumescing between Harry and Maya, with Jimmy also involved.

"How are you going to handle that?" she asked.

"I really don't know." Again in my mind's ear I heard Kip's words about our party not being able to afford divisiveness. So I added, "—yet."

Then I told her about my position in the Party probably having been weakened in the minds of key members—and how a hammer hovered over me in the shadows—because of my association with "Cassius Pantera," even though it seemed permissible for Maya to accept a huge "loan" and bona-fide PAC from an especially well-known scuzball in Las Vegas. To all this Julie had little response.

So I bounded onto a different subject, I said: "Aside from intentional stupidity and greed, *by far* most of the problems we face in this country—and the world—devolve on one thing: *energy.* If it's not energy to generate power, it's to drive swarms of vehicles or run factories. Ultimate product? *Carbon.* You might say the besetting problems of the world come down to stupidity and greed, energy and carbon. —And too many people having too many kids."

Plainly, Julie found this set of topics unappealing. To me that was infelicitous because, as I had often mentioned, my greatest fears were my greatest enemies—mass indifference and endemic despair. Cancer? At least some forms of cancer can be cured.

They seek to harry us with quick attacks at our weak points. Often they waste Achaean life and do damage to our fortification or ships, then they run. They strike us at different times, in different ways.

Early today two lines of mounted archers charged us from across the plain to aid a swarm of infantry striking us behind our trench at the tip of our flank, having come at us from cover to the east. Almost without resistance—until Achilles did arrive—they took lives and brought down part of our bulwark, perhaps as preparation for later assault. Then their infantry vanished back down embankments into morning mist. Their archers turned and rode off to Hittite fortifications, then to an open gate.

We give chase to the archers; this they expected. But this time our plan is different. My o-kas turn off and race across the plain all the way around to their north wall. There we clear the way for our horsemen to charge their gate, with the plan to pull up short and turn back before taking casualties, but causing damage and disrupting their commerce. Then we will take no flight, only a swift and orderly retreat. But our speed this morning thrills even me—and it causes surprise to all.

The north gate is yet open as our riders charge toward it, and for the first time we Achaians behold the very streets and palaces of Troy. Rather than stop short, our marauders enter the open gateway and the first riders go down from a hail of arrows. Others cannot pass and pull back. I direct Theron to drive at the opening; the rest of my chariots will follow. My intent is to see if we can hold a position before the gate and keep it open until more Danaoi arrive to storm inside.

When Theron makes our turn I see Thracian horsemen approaching our right flank at a steady pace. They are not many. But more come at us from our left. Daring Hittite tribesmen, some mounted, some on foot, try to block our horsemen from retreat, a futile gesture that only slows our riders.

I wave the order for chariot retreat, for I know Trojan horsemen and chariots will set upon us soon. My plan relied on reserve o-kas coming forward to strengthen our numbers—but my signal turns them back. Crude Thracian riders make no attempt to engage us. They appear content only to group before the gate. For this I feel grateful as we drive away.

Today even the gods of the Trojans and Hittites must be pleased by Achaean heroism and fighting skill. Yet this day Ilios was again spared. Our hope is to gain strength while they weaken. Our story must not be otherwise.

*   *   *

CHAPTER 45

TRACTION

The morning after our last strategy meeting my first stop was our Safeway where I could find good bagels and a Starbucks stand. Since I was in a supermarket I thought I'd pick up some cheese and flowers as well, and that's why Mickey and I spotted each other in the dairy section.

Probably I knew or was acquainted with about half the shoppers in the store that morning. Reno sprawls all over the Truckee Meadows, but in some ways it reminded me of small-city Austin, Texas, in the 1960's and 70's, with cosmic people seemingly springing from the earth (or coming in from California) but a lot of rednecking going on.

Mickey and I paused from our errands to trade a few words about last night's meeting, and Mickey cut glances in different directions before he said, "You'll never guess whom I just had a pleasant tête-à-tête with, so I'm gonna have to tell you: Isaiah Ogden. Does the name ring a bell?"

Of course it did but I had to be reminded: the fellow who's going to write the script and supervise "Maya's big production" (Mickey's words).

"He's probably still around here somewhere," said Mickey, looking around again, then he remarked, "Your brother's not exactly PC [meaning *politically correct*], so now would be a really good time to get him to modify his language."

"How do you know Harry's not PC?"

"Anyone can tell by some of the words he uses."

"Regarding, say, Maya and Jimmy?"

"Regarding Maya and Jimmy. True enough."

We parted and I got my cheese and flowers and made my way to the Starbucks stand where I approached the back of a medium-sized African-American man in a suit, whom of course I would know.

"Hello, Mister Ogden," I said.

He turned all the way around and said, "The name's Isaiah, buddy. —How're y' doin', Dan?" (Out beamed that killer smile.) He must have been surprised at being recognized in a town where he didn't reside, especially from behind.

We shook hands and he told me that he had decided to stay in town, rather than head back to the East Bay, so he could scout locations for our "promo shoot." As though he were confiding something he added, "Any kind of art is integrated. Form *is* content, content equals form. Setting is part of the form, so I won't know *what* I'm going to write until I know the setting."

"Makes sense to me," I said. "I'm glad you're here."

We talked about commercial art for a moment before we ordered our coffee concoctions, which took a few minutes of preparation. This gave us time to revisit key Party issues before we sipped (and burned our tongues) together while leaning on a counter. When I asked Isaiah if he envisioned any broad outlines for a script, he told me that he wanted to find an especially good natural setting in which to present me and thus Conservative-Reform's "point of view." Something would develop from there. I suggested a county park in the Washoe Valley and would have given him directions if he hadn't said he was already planning to go there. As sort of a post-script he remarked that our Party and campaign seemed to be "demographically challenged."

"How's that?" I said.

"From what I see, you don't have many black people in your bunch."

"We have some college students who are black doing volunteer work."

Isaiah emitted two ambiguous vocables. I added that maybe mature black adults were smart enough to avoid getting involved in a party and campaign that stood *me* for President. Had he ever thought of that?

"Well, I'm not getting paid to be necessarily smart," he said.

"You're smart enough to get paid a hell of a lot more than me."

Late afternoon of that same day at Party headquarters, which I still liked to refer to as "my office," Alyssa came in to inquire whether any new developments relevant to the Party might be reported in *The Reno Chronicle* (the alternative news-paper she had helped found); our meeting of last evening had produced substance but that was barely newsworthy. I told her that we'd probably be making a "big-time TV-promo shoot, maybe in the Washoe Valley," and that we needed volunteers to do all kinds of work.

Then Pancho came in to apply his technical skills to some computer problem we had and maybe score a free Coke and slice of cold pizza. He mentioned that he and Hal had been getting a lot of jobs lately, and that inspired me to see a window.

I said, "You and Hal have done a lot of work for the Party, all gratis. I'd be glad to pay you, if I could afford it, but I can't pay my own brother for volunteering. That wouldn't be exactly politic."

Pancho looked up from a computer at which he was seated and shrugged.

I said, "If you weren't so busy I'd ask Maya if she knew of projects that would actually pay both of you. She's probably got a lot of contacts."

"That's okay, Dan," said Pancho. "Harry and Maya don't get along very well. Best to just keep us clear of that lady."

"I might have to do that," I said, "but it really shouldn't involve *you*."

"Well, I guess it does," said Pancho.

"Listen, Panchito. I owe you a lot. The Party owes you. We—you and I—have got to keep our eye on the common good. —Remember? In the process we've gotta try to save Mama Earth from total disaster. Naturally I still want to do any favors I can for your family. —Right? Right! I'm thinking globally, I'm thinking locally, I'm thinking *pais*, I'm thinking family. We can't jeopardize any of these."

Frankie "Panchito" Lopez regarded me levelly for a long second. "I hear you, Dan," he said and bent back to his task.

Later dear Alyssa said to me quietly, "Thinking globally *and* locally—*and* trying to work for the common good, et cetera—that's got to be some kind of strain, huh?"

"It is if you don't weaken," I responded.

My point took most of a second to trigger a smile.

*   *   *

After Alyssa and Pancho and other volunteers left for the evening I sat on the edge of my desk, can of lukewarm diet cola in hand, and thought—heck, I really could make a beneficial impact on people; I just had to get enough of the right kind of exposure.

I hoped to avoid paying a lot of "bills" for my efforts because there were big ones pending. (Phantasms of "Cassius Pantera" and Jeremy Rakes passed through my conscious, as did a glimpse of Ira; I didn't know if I could afford what these might cost.) I was already paying plenty: a vision of Julie—and the sound of her soft voice—arose in my soul. I should have been *with her* at this very moment. Seemed like I was sticking out my chin at considerable expense.

The telephone rang next to my ass. Maya calling. She had just been talking to Daigan, also to someone at the Paragon Agency, and she sounded excited. Then came an audible moment of confusion as she interrupted herself: Someone from *The Wild Bunch Brothel* had telephoned her and mentioned my name and expressed regret for being unable to attend our last meeting at . . .—but that just didn't compute! Just forget it.

Then Maya told me (happily) that now we had the money as well as the stratagems to put me and the Party on the general-election ballot in maybe six states here in the West. Of course that would take a lot of work. And if we generated more cells in other parts of the U.S., the Party's cachet could become truly national.

"And you're not even a serious contender!" said Maya. "But if we get you on some ballots, the major parties will *have to* listen to you. *Minor* parties'll take their cues. You'll be making your impact."

"Our campaign is a work of art, designed and built with sheer genius," I responded. "Who could deny this?"

Maya demurred that my brother might. Hal's ideas and modus operandi were different from hers, she advised me. "He should face the fact that generating effective publicity on a large scale just isn't his profession."

I chose not to disagree. Silently I noted that Maya avoided any mention of the grating personality conflict between her and Hal. So she was good at keeping her work on a "professional" level, and I had to appreciate that even knowing her ultimate motive was to make money.

Her closing gambit: "I hope you don't mind traveling." —Which by then I sure did (and still would).

After Maya and I rang off I went home to Julie. En route I conjured up visions of Tahoe City where she and I had spent a few glorious days recently. A kind of weariness at the core of my mind told me I was already ripe for another break.

CHAPTER 46

TREMBLORS

We stand upon a tiny rise of land and gaze across the Plain of Troia in wonder. For certain we had felt the earth shake—hard—for a very short time. Did they feel it in Ilios as well? They must have. What ruin did it cause? Perhaps none, but if the shaking had been longer they would have known damage.

Gods jolted our ground in the Argolid, but neither Agamemnon nor I recall when last it happened. He tells me of great damage wreaked upon Mycenae and Tiryns when his father was a young man. "That is one reason we redesigned the walls of our citadels and, over time, rebuilt them," says Agamemnon. "They must defend against enemy attack, also withstand strong earth shaking."

We gaze again at Troy and have the same thought. Agamemnon bids me voice it: "Walls of Ilios are unlike those of Mycenae, and the towers will come down if shaken hard. This could happen soon, for trembling today perhaps foretells of stronger movements *to come. We should be ready when that happens. It might be to our great fortune."*

Agamemnon needs barely to nod. Within his helmet (we both wear our helmets here) his eyes show him thoughtful. For a moment he peers at Troy, then to me.

"I think I know how to use well our Thracian brothers in there," says the king.

"Sir?" He knows my confusion. At Troy men of Thrace ride for Priam.

"We must turn some to become our allies. Surely we have things they want."

Our helmets dip toward each other. We need not guess what those things are.

*   *   *

"Harry, I've got some news that affects you. Call me ASAP, please."

This message I left in Hal's voice mail after I had telephoned him and received no answer. When he returned my call, maybe twelve minutes later, he was likely prepared for some kind of shaking.

As soon as I answered I said: "I've given this deep thought and I've talked to key people—*not* including Maya or Kestrel—and the consensus [I was bending the truth, not lying] is that we can't afford any kind of divisiveness in the Party, not at *this* stage."

I intuited he could see what was coming, which made this less difficult: I told him there was no longer a place for him in our (not *my*) campaign.

Harry's tone of voice sounded vaguely amused.

"What—you're firing me from the campaign?" he said.

"Yup. Don't tell Mom."

"Sheeze! What about the Party? You can't run me out of the Party, can you?"

"Hell, no. I wouldn't if I could. But you're a de facto officer; remember? I'm gonna appoint someone to replace you on a permanent basis." (I didn't know who.)

"You're gonna have to tend your Twitter account."

"I'll make do with Facebook, maybe Tumblr."

Otherwise by the end of our conversation this affair was bloodless. Harry understood what I was doing. It gave him relief because he was busy. But who would be my Web *Meister*? That would be someone who came highly recommended by Wilson; I thought his first name was Jordan. He'd need Harry's help to initiate working alongside Paragon.

"Not much of a problem," said Harry. "What about the favor you promised Frankie?"

"I'm working on it now," I said. And for the most part, that was that. So the campaign really had developed a life of its own. Proof: my brother and Pancho and I would not be pals until this was over; we were in different orbits now. The *Cause* had so determined.

Maybe I was trying to embrace more than my psyche and brain could handle. For all I could tell, my neighbor Bully might have gone back to Texas. Discussions with Kip or Mickey I found too demanding again. At some point I realized I hadn't returned their phone calls, nor did I plan to contact them soon.

I hoped I wouldn't meet them at the supermarket or downtown. Should I contact Savannah again? Now *that* seemed an interesting prospect, but she was difficult to reach except maybe by Email. Besides, I didn't know what to tell her.

By contrast, Daigan knew precisely what to tell *me*: "We need to get more money, Dan. We're down to almost zip."

"Last time we talked," I said into the telephone (taking comfort from talking directly to someone through my old-fashioned phone), "you said we were pretty flush."

"We've had to pay Paragon; we still owe 'em something for expenses setting up the TV shoot, like paying Isaiah. We've gotta pay the PC's [political consultants] in San Francisco; they're involved in promoting the TV spot. [Beat.] You know, once the ad is shot, it'll cost money to air. We'll have to buy time on local stations."

It occurred to me that our party's expedition to gain high profile, including my campaign for President, didn't have a manager we could point to. Ergo it wasn't actually managed. Proof: Daigan advising me that I'd probably have to cover "maybe all" my travel expenses to speaking engagements Maya had set up in such neighboring places as Atlanta and Dallas.

"Looks like I won't be traveling as much as we thought," I said. "Believe it or not, Daigan, I'm actually on a personal budget."

"Well, we can only do what we can do," said Daigan. "Maya usually tries to get the other guys to pay your way. I'll stay on her for that."

"Has Maya been paid?"

"Up until lately, yes. Some of it she pays to Kestrel, I think."

"At least she's not working for free, like some people I know."

"One of these days I'll send the Party *my* bill," said Daigan. "So far—hah! I got Jimmy to cover the tip at lunch last week."

A bright spot was Daigan's averring that our campaign coffer probably would not get entirely emptied as long as he kept the lid on runaway expenditures and didn't get blind-sided, say, by high P-C fees. Moreover our new Web *Meister* would likely be effective at getting us donations. I made a mental note to contact Daigan maybe once a week for a reality check.

An hour or so later I got the proverbial wet-blanket treatment. Hal Emailed me, then asked me on the phone whether I'd seen a TV spot attacking an "independent, so-called `conservative' candidate" for U.S. President. Although I and the Party were never named, the point of reference in the ad was obvious. Just to be sure, it showed silhouette shots of someone who almost resembled me, exaggerating my gestures, ranting before digitally extrapolated audiences. Intercut was stock footage of landscapes, legal tender, the Pentagon, and fleet-footed Mexicans, with key points punctuated by the sound track.

During the thirty-second spot, one hears a macho, sardonic voice-over declare: "This alleged `conservative,' a small-business owner in Nevada, stands for downgrading our national security. He, with his new political party, proposes *drastic cuts* in defense spending. Just ask him! But what this candidate *really* wants is illegal immigration to go unchecked—so businessmen, like him, can prosper from cheap, undocumented labor.

"This alleged `conservative' proposes open borders to the north *and to the south*. That's right. He wants totally open borders! If you want proof, *ask him*. If he says that is not his position, do not believe him! You want to know his *real* intention. And while you're at it, ask him where he stands on the issue of legalizing drug use. You'll be shocked by his answer—if he'll be honest with you."

Bold subtitles repeat the operative words heard in the voice-over. Its point is crystal clear: the guy belongs at Guantanamo Bay.

Harry told me someone alerted him to it so he searched for it and caught it twice, both times preceding local news on two channels. Dr. Jay said he was transfixed by it when he woke up in front of his television about three o'clock one morning. Other people, such as volunteers at party headquarters and store clerks, told me they'd seen it. Ostensibly the ad was hung on the 'Net, too. I looked for it, of course, but had to catch it piecemeal on TV.

But somehow I had to defend against it, with vigor. We couldn't learn who was responsible for it. The product was supplied by "AmericaFirst," some kind of front. It was paid for as a public-service announcement by Money Order sent from a bogus address. When I called the local station managers and demanded they pull it they said they would, so I decided to ignore the damned thing. Then Jimmy reported having seen part of it on a Sacramento channel; Maya said people in Vegas mentioned seeing it there. She and Jimmy (and Harry) urged me to do something about it, so I had to let myself get diverted by the damned thing. Since I did, I tried to make this an opportunity for getting extra traction for my candidacy and the Party. But that was mostly wishful thinking.

We couldn't afford to make countering ads, and I didn't want to call attention to the slander, so I wrote letters to newspaper editors all around the state in which I deplored "character smears" and "intentional distortions of a political party's positions." I made a point of using the words "half-truths," "lies," and "slanderous." (Newspapers in major cities in adjacent states also got a letter from me.) I said much the same in my blogs but added "mud-slinging" and "slinging" *other* stuff. Then I phoned my attractive contacts at the local TV stations and asked them to interview me about the topic of "dishonest political activity," which two of them did so at least I got a little publicity. This sad enterprise, so gainfully productive, would gladden the heart of any cynic.

CHAPTER 47

COSTLIES

During one azure morning Julie asked me, "How goes the 'boutique campaign,' Abe? Or is it Thomas or Teddy?"

"Aahr-r, 'tis a noble cause we serve, my dear. *Es geht mit mir* okay."

"Well, as a doctor and HMO slave, I can say it's necessary . . . from various angles."

"It is, it is," I said and toddled for my coffee mug.

Julie was prepping for work at the hospital. When she'd come home I'd be gone. For me, marching orders: Back to Boise. Or was it Provo? Small wonder that I couldn't keep track of little things, such as the words I'd vented in public or how much money we (I in particular) had bled on my trips.

Our "noble Cause" ostensibly excused all that. But at home I was letting things go undone, which meant Julie had to do them—if she had time. And I still had visions of trying to play my fiddle and of physically rebuilding myself, and they were becoming ever more remote.

A half-hour before Julie would leave—to begin our going separate ways for the day—I took radical action by pulling on enough clothes so I could take a walk outdoors. The plan was to be back in less than fifteen minutes by walking up our street to capture a clear view of things, which is what I did.

My vantage point about two blocks away is better than most, and it grants a wide vista of the Truckee Meadows. Often this prospect helped me clarify issues. Clarity I sought now although it required two things of me: receptivity to inspiration and deploying imagination. Those are no mean endeavors of an early morning.

So I gazed upon all I could see in our little corner of the Great Basin and beheld many square miles of neighborhoods (liberally studded with green treetops even in high desert) sprawled in the bowl formed by ribs of arid mountains. Always I felt aware of our fresh little Truckee River slipping through the Meadows. As I expected, a realization recurred to me: Everything I beheld is good, except when it's corrupted by individual acts of greed or stupidity.

Of course I had known this. I just wanted the clarity afforded me in fresh air so I could reaffirm something: my noble quest, our "noble Cause," was *apart from* being noble; it was necessary. I had to pursue it to my limits.

Just the fact that Julie and Jay live on Planet Earth always crystallized my resolve. But the prospect of not seeing Julie's face at the beginning or end of any day, and some days having to forgo feeling her hair on my cheek (a taste of pure heaven) with her dear breasts nudging my arm—bolstered a conviction I would carry even now: serving some Great Cause makes contracting a serious case of bronchitis a comparative pleasure.

*   *   *

Evidently a fellow named Charlie Applewhite had been trying to reach me for more than a day; I hadn't been aware of that until he succeeded over the phone. And evidently Mr. Applewhite was not used to exercising his patience.

"I'll get right to the point," he said. "I know something about you and your party and your prexy candidacy. [He actually said this.] I'd like to start a PAC on your behalf." Heartbeat of a pause to let me catch up. "It's not out of the goodness of my heart. I'd like you to stand behind my organization occasionally. Also I need tax write-offs."

"Fine," I said. "What *is* your 'organization,' sir?" (I would have liked to say more but I was plainly dealing with a Yankee.)

"The Coalition for Soil-Resources Conservation. Ever heard of it?"

"I can't say I have."

"There; you've got my point."

"And your point is . . . to get exposure?"

"The right kind of exposure. You with me?"

"I'm sure I will be once I learn more."

"All right—two hundred thou'. It can buy a lot of bagels."

"Maybe I didn't hear right," I said, "it sounded like you mentioned a large sum. I've got to learn about your organization. Like, what does it do?"

"You heard right, and does it make any difference?"

"Of course it does."

"I'll send one of my people over from Frisco. He can explain it to you."

"Can't we meet for lunch or get together at Party headquarters? You might as well see what you're getting."

"No thanks. You're there; I'm here. I've got two days; then I'll be in my office, mid-town Manhattan."

"Ah. If you don't mind my asking, where is `here'?"

"Bermuda. One of my people will contact you; I forget which one. Tomorrow."

I would have said more but the connection was gone.

Sure enough: within twenty-two hours at Party headquarters I was sitting vis-à-vis one Dustin Coker, recently arrived from San Francisco on assignment from Charlie Applewhite of NYC. Dustin, a well-dressed, pleasant-looking California white guy in his thirties, took the initiative as soon as he got seated:

"Normally I would fly in, but I love the drive here. Guess that means when I drive back I'll have to stop at Tahoe. —Too bad, huh?— Good thing I've got reservations."

"Oh, yeah. Does your coalition operate here in Nevada?"

"Well, it's not really a `coalition' per se; it's more like an amalgam of operations, each one having a distinct function. But we all go in the same direction, which is to purchase and utilize and sell blocks of raw land."

My antennae were quivering, hackles beginning to rise, nasal membranes twitchy. The figure 200,000—as in dollars— nagging my conscious like a distant air-raid siren.

Dustin continued: "The south of Nevada is too arid; here in the north we're being blocked by a few ranchers, especially a Cassius Pantera. Ever hear of him? Seems like he and some others have an iron grip on any land we'd have to acquire."

By now I knew why my antennas were quivering. And I was right: Dustin's fairly candid answers to the few questions I asked disclosed that *Soil-Resources Conservation* meant acquiring water rights, usually through land purchases, to sell to power utilities; it also meant evacuating old mines (of all kinds) that still held mineral potential. Yes, it sold land for new coal-burning power plants, and, yes, repeat-mining operations did cause toxic waste, particularly acute in ground water. Some "*Conservation*" land acquisitions were used for shopping strips and gas stations—which the "Coalition" also arranged to happen as a kind of sideline.

"I'll bet Charlie Applewhite's corporation [I decided to use the accurate word] has got title to a lot of acres," I said.

"Oh, ga-*zillions*. Charlie is really big in the Rust Belt, although he's got a lot of acreage here in the West. Uh, that's not really his name yet, although it will be pretty soon; he's making a legal change. His name is still Ravi Uppal. Very interesting guy. His father's from India via Iran; his mother's a waitress—well, not anymore!"

And what did this "interesting guy" want of me and the Conservative-Reform Party? —I thought I'd pose this question pro forma. Otherwise our meeting was over as far as I was concerned.

Well, I was told, there would be no formal *quid pro quo* agreement between the Party and the PAC. When appropriate, the Party—or its spokesperson, Candidate Hachek—would endorse or recommend Coalition actions or proposed actions. I'd be sort of a "character reference." Demands on the Party—or me—would be "few, but vital," Dustin said. "There's always big money involved; it's called trust funding. Investors must be paid, so we're always ready to pull out all the stops."

I decided to ask the obvious: "Wouldn't the connection between our party here [I waved my arms and looked around the office] and Applewhite's `Coalition' be sort of, uhm, *deleterious* to the Party's reputation, the Party *image?*"

I was told "Likely not a problem." Indeed, the head of the PAC would be . . . *Ravi Uppal*, not Charlie Applewhite. Said Dustin, "Mr.Uppal likes to utilize an array of devices to maintain the Coalition's *interspace*, if you get my meaning."

"Oh, I do. But why would that be so?" (As if I didn't know.)

"People don't want their association with Coalition operations to be known. Still, we do require good public relations— that's why *character references* get handsome rewards."

I had to admire the fellow's candor.

"What if I renege and can't back something the Coalition is trying to do?" I asked.

"That would be your choice. It might be unfortunate."

"Oh. Well, there's no sense in entertaining this further," I said. "Why would I recommend, why would I endorse, practices that are basically . . . evil?"

"It depends on whose eye is beholding, if you get my meaning. Keep in mind that our `Coalition' is not exactly benighted. Mr. Uppal—Mr. Applewhite—loathes unnecessary destruction, so our operations try to avoid it. Also bear in mind that if the Coalition didn't do what we're doing, there'd always be someone who would, like maybe a firm based in China or the Netherlands. Right now—as I speak—we're competing for some turf in Ohio with an outfit from the Emirates."

There was nothing for me to say. Dustin said his coda: "Bear in mind—joining us doesn't just get you money for making TV ads and traveling around. Effective corporate support means contacts, networking, influence to get things done outside your pale."

I stood; he stood and we shook hands. I bid him good luck and good bye.

Before Dustin Coker turned to leave he fetched three business cards from his sport jacket and laid them on the desk before me. Two bore information for contacting his boss in Manhattan; the third was his.

"Now don't be a stranger," he said with a smile. Then: "Off to Tahoe!"

The three little cards somehow remained on my desktop for a few hours. Eventually I picked them up and, instead of trashing them, slipped them into the upper desk drawer.

Jimmy was calling me (it sounded like from inside a helicopter) on Maya's behalf regarding campaign minutiae. In passing he brought up Daigan's assertion that we needed "maybe a couple-hundred thousand yet" to pay for and to air the "infomercial" Maya was intending to put on television. (She had in mind placing it on several, and potentially many,

many stations.) When we'd finished Jimmy's business I asked whether he knew anything about a Charlie Applewhite.

"The name rings a bell," he said. "Any connection to Ravi Uppal?"

"He *is* Ravi Uppal."

"Oh. How do you know?"

I responded that I'd been approached by one of "Applewhite's" representatives without saying for what. Jimmy didn't ask. He simply said, "Ravi Uppal's bunch is notorious for buying and essentially destroying land. They do it everywhere."

I muttered something like "Oh." Jimmy added, "Uppal—or Applewhite—is a New York real-estate mogul. His corporation operates under various covers. It's important to recognize it, you know, and if possible contain it. Dealing with him or his bunch is equivalent to having sex with Satan's old lady."

"Well, one of his minions left me his business cards."

"Burn 'em!"

Then Jimmy and I told each other (in effect) to keep soldiering on; adieu. I decided this was a good time to clear my mind; sometimes a person *must* meditate. I would have done that immediately but troubling memories intervened.

Always our horsemen are outnumbered. Today they will depend on my chariots to protect their retreat after they attack the east gate. Agamemnon orders attack there, for commerce of all kinds enters and leaves Ilios freely to the east. Trojans and their allies must learn to fear us at all points, he reminds us. For us to weaken them, and then to overcome their defenses, they must be denied points of constant strength.

We know the truth in what he says. Our strengths are not constant; we can yet be overcome. I have proof of this, for all my squadrons need new axles; repairs we make do not last long. We have no more replacement wheels, and new ones do not arrive as I and the king have ordered. Harness parts look worn; they cannot hold up much longer. We have been losing plating, and it is precious. But we must try to show only strength.

Trojans and Hittites and their many allies here are determined and clever. We can barely block them from their bay. On the water, I have heard, we cannot stop them most days, and some days they block Achaean shipping. Yet we must continue to press them. The key is to keep attacking.

Away from all the others Agamemnon says to me: "Will we return one day to Mycenae—our heads held high? Even I must wonder."

My answer: "Nostoi will be ours. We know this. I have believed this always."

"Thank you for that," says my king. "I must not imagine Achaean defeat."

A thought strikes me and I say it: "Sometimes I think even you fear to fail."

"Oh-ho! That is something worth fearing! No wise man can do otherwise. And my fear is broad beyond understanding, for we—for the good of all Hellas, even of Thebes—dare not fail. Is that fearsome enough?"

"Sir, even the gods must shrink."

*   *   *

CHAPTER 48

FORTUNES OF WAR

"My 'scepter' is this," said Maya. (She'd use terms like that to remind us she'd been Ivy League and therefore knew stuff undreamt of in our philosophy.) "We shoot for the moon. We can generate impact *and* rebut those moronic attack ads. We do this by putting our little mini-movie on people's TV sets *in tandem with* our Web campaign. Jordan here will generate the cyber dimension. Folks at Paragon can figure out how to accentuate our combined effort."

"We don't have enough money left to make the ad, let alone get it aired," Daigan said. Be aware, we've had way too many expenses."

"Well, we can tap the PAC that Dan doesn't like," said Maya. "If we have to, we'll borrow a couple hundred thou'; the PAC can repay it. That's what I mean by shoot for the moon."

"Sounds like 'let The Devil take the hindmost,'" Wilson interposed.

"Well, not exactly. We use prudence. Dan said he's gotten us access to a large helicopter, complete with pilot. We use that for transporting our movie crew to location. The location's free. Actually it's a county park so maybe it'll cost us for a permit. Jimmy here is using his leverage to get us a base price from a TV-ad company out of Berkeley; that's our movie crew—what, about five personnel. Then we get everyone to pitch in. We've got dozens of volunteer cast members."

I said, "Can't we wait until we've got more money? There's no rush, is there?"

"Well, yes and no," Maya responded. "Lately money hasn't exactly been forthcoming. America's the richest country on Earth, but people are in debt. We've got to *induce* them to pass some of their dollars our way."

"Starting today I'll hit 'em with different parts of your message," our new Web *Meister* Jordan Bean said looking my way. "Plus, I'll show 'em various—let's say flattering—photos of you, like your brother did."

Nobody allowed or added anything. A man's voice spoke up:

"We've got cells working all over the state, also in big cities in nearby states, like Washington—where people are kind of, you know, *aware* of certain realities . . . . We'll put out the word: Everyone, new members, old members, non-members: please invest three dollars toward planetary and national survival. [Beat.] Cells usually come through." —Said by one of our lead volunteers, a thin university-affiliated activist called Brick. Before this, I'd never met a person with that name.

"Atta-way!" Jimmy gushed. He was the person we credited with the idea of starting "cells."

For the short and intermediate terms, our campaign excluded a real plan. Although we hadn't set a date for the "mini-movie" shoot, it would evolve partly determined by weather forecasts. I asked Isaiah Ogden if he had written the scenario for our "infomercial," and he replied that it was almost "wrapped." (Later I learned that it would be actually "wrapped" only when we'd shoot it; in fact it was being finalized by committee, which happened not to include me.) Happily for everyone, we had a telegenic, charismatic face to foist on a deserving public.

Twice during our late-afternoon meeting at Party head-quarters someone asked me how I liked the idea of *"starring"* on TV. And I had to be honest:

"I think I'd rather be 'waterboarding,'" I answered both times. "It's a lot quicker." Which was true. Probably I should have taken off a couple days for a serenity break.

I knew I couldn't do that. After everyone left the office I sat propped up in my cushioned-old chair behind my desk and simply stared at pictures on the wall for several minutes. Soon I found myself recalling the preceding morning when Julie was getting ready to leave for her work.

As I strode into our bedroom, she looked up to smile at me even though she was busy. (She never just smiled: she beamed joy and spirit beyond anything we can identify on Earth.) For a moment before passing through I stopped to gaze upon the most wondrous being in all creation and—yes, it was invisible but I could feel it: her ineffable grace enshrouding me as would a gossamer cocoon. This was her gift to me every day.

Dwelling on this made me recall Julie's statement (repeated occasionally) that, despite everyone's best efforts throughout millennia to confuse themselves, "*love is recognizing*—and *appreciating*—the other's characteristics or essence. It's essentially intellectual." (She got this from her undergraduate days, but it holds up well in both our experience.) Between us we agreed that "all the rest of the stuff is reinforcement, window dressing" [Julie's words]. That said, she and I had become experts in "all the rest of the stuff" because it made life better.

As I had so many times before, I wondered whether those qualities in Julie (or in anybody *like* her, such as my hero Dr. Jay) might exist for some mysterious purpose beyond us. —To put it differently, what are those qualities for?— And the answer is self-evident: Who *cares*? They are absolutely (mysteriously) precious onto themselves. You know what I mean. They're *not inherent to* this physical planet, or this galaxy—or any galaxy.

These matters I would raise whenever I could because they helped keep me whole.

Six barbaric riders—soon followed by three more—entered our encampment from the east, weapons and shields down, each with a raised open hand. By joining us behind our trench and bulwarks (and the brush we use for defensive cover) their movements are hidden from Ilios.

They speak crude Helladic; we wonder if they can understand us. They called for our king, and soon Agamemnon came forward to address them. But first I set an entire o-ka to stand near them, my chariot closest. Another o-ka with a squadron of horsemen arrive in their view. They see my weapons undrawn but I wear my bronze shield. They look long at my helmet.

Two days before, a party of Thracian marauders came within easy sight of Achaean supply ships waiting to be unloaded. Astride their horses they stopped to behold Cretan women, Corinthian women, also many island women amid our cargo. Before they rode off one of our captains, under orders from Agamemnon, called out to them to join us, saying we have plenty of gold and women, also our barley beer is good. "We know they have beer and women," Agamemnon told me later, "but nothing as good as ours. And they will always seek gold."

Now he talks to them and I draw closer to see the gold they wear, the gold in their weapons. They have some that is beautiful, and Agamemnon offers them more and shows it to them. In return they must do his bidding. They listen and their eyes stray to his helmet. I hear them talk rudely to the King of Men. One who often speaks for his comrades demands Agamemnon's (or my) helmet as his reward for Greek victory. Their price is high but accepted.

*   *   *

One day soon after, when a fearsome shock had passed I stood without my helmet atop our earthen fortification for a better view of Ilios. Agamemnon had done likewise but leapt down into our defensive trench and came up on the other side. In his glorious bronze helmet he turned to see me and waved for me to join him on the edge of unprotected plain. This I did with ill grace, for a charioteer to go afoot unarmed—and unhelmeted—on enemy soil—is to choose madness with nakedness.

Peering at Troy we leave the edge of our trench and stride quickly to a plot of unleveled earth. Just as we tread onto higher ground I see it clearly: some thing, a piece of building, falls from the west tower to land near their front wall. Troy is beginning to come down.

"Ah, hah!" says Agamemnon. "We must get ready. You see what is happening."

"We are ready as much as we can be. Today we shall call to readiness our Thracian allies, few as they are."

The helmeted head nods twice. Then silence tells me of thought. In vain I look to see more of Troy falling. Soon words come from the man I accompany here.

"We are Helladic," says Agamemnon, "even `Achaean' does not define us right. We are Greeks. That by itself is enough to make a man's life worthy to live." He pauses, and I am struck by sadness I feel coursing in his voice.

This man's courage is monumental and his heart is almost as large. His temper, also sometimes monumental, is never allowed to cloud his judgment in matters of arms. I think he can read as well as I, and I believe he understands men well; he surely knows to govern in ways that attain his goals. But like his father and my father and the king of Ilios (and me), he lacks mastery in learning why things happen as they do.

"But now I fear," says Agamemnon, "all of earth shudders often in our homeland. Yet shaking within Mycenae we cannot see or feel. Until . . . the cause for it kills us."

"Sir?" I say, for his meaning escapes me.

"Reports I hear tell of treachery at home. They say it awaits my return."

"Treachery? Treachery by whom?" I demand to know this.

I see the helmet barely turn—to right, to left, then tilt downwards. No words come, and we turn back to cross our trench and return in silence.

*　　*　　*

CHAPTER 49

SEDUCEMENT

Jay came by our house to visit briefly and tell his mother and me about some of his misfortunes in practicing medicine. His points of travail were real enough; yet most of his career lay ahead. I sympathized, I empathized. Then I said I had to pack some items and my papers and laptop computer for a trip to Santa Cruz (I was pretty sure) to speak at a dinner I didn't wish to attend, then go on to one of those cities sprawled in the East Bay.

"I betcha I'll put on a pound or two while I'm gone," I said to Jay and Julie. "Maybe I'll come back with some good zinfandel, or a delicious pinot [noir] none of us has ever heard of."

My point: rewards are where you find them; I'd accept what I could get.

Jay remarked that maybe I was starting to look "a bit soft."

I responded by patting my stomach then my butt, as though to assess them.

"I think the word is *fluffy*—just in certain spots," was my attempt at humor that Jay didn't appreciate although he smiled. As happened so often, I marveled at how easily one can fail at being funny, especially by using irony. So of course I tried again:

"I'm still not much of a target, though" I said, presenting Jay a lateral view of my physique. My wit did not impress Julie.

Happily, Julie and Jay turned to discussing their profession. I left the room to prepare and pack, which caused me a tentative sense of gratitude: Maybe everything I had done in all my decades of living had actually been prelude. Maybe now, in trying to roil political waters, I had found my life's real work. If this were true, I was the paradigm, I set the benchmark, for being a slow study.

*   *   *

When I got back from Northern California about two days later, I knew a decision had been working its way through my inner fabric. It felt creepy; sometimes it caused a kind of mental nausea to flare up and momentarily disable me. So the next morning, as early as I could get moving, I stopped at Starbucks and went to Party headquarters to act on it.

I was glad no one was there when I arrived so I could reflect on what I thought I'd have to do because it was part of "my work." *Undeniably* it was part of my work. No, I did not have to reflect.

"If you do something, you do it all the way; you don't *kvetch*," I audibly coached myself. Axiomatic: the Party's program *must be* broadcast. Therefore, I dare not hold back promoting it. If going full bore involved taking foolish risks, I would take foolish risks.

Hey, not so fast, I thought. Much of the Party's youthful support came from "Ecotopia." If anyone who believed in my campaign were to learn what I've been considering lately, I would have reason to slash my wrists. Did *I* want to give myself cause to slash my wrists? Of course not.

Suddenly it seemed so easy—don't *kvetch,* don't welch! Again, I did not have to reflect: *Go* full bore, take those really long chances.

"Let's just *hope!*"

I uttered this audibly to the mountains and sky outside the window.

Then I opened the top drawer of my desk to fetch three business cards pushed into the far corner. The first one bore the name Dustin Coker, who might not have been surprised to learn how near I came to phoning him.

Only out of curiosity, I would like to have seen what his boss, Ravi Uppal (Charlie Applewhite) *looked like.* (Was he a vegan, perhaps?) I doubted I'd want to meet him, except maybe to ask him some questions. I got off my chair to walk across a few yards of open floor to jam the little cards into the party's new shredder.

We tested their battle order this day and they tested ours. They are many but they come in many camps. We are like one and becoming strong. Agamemnon beholds their cooking smoke rising in all directions above the walls of Ilios. Unbidden, I walk to join him as he stands alone on a bulwark.

"Do you think they ever dreamed we could press them as we do?" I say heartily.

Agamemnon's answer catches me off guard.

"See what all my gold has brought me?" he says. At once I know contempt in his voice is not aimed at Troy. In a stately manner he removes his helmet and turns my way.

"At home," he says, "I face invasion from barbarians; Helladic soil seems desired by many. Now reports tell me I will face treachery at home—from within! We have no telling yet who is at the root.

"Perhaps I will reach old age. Short of death no amount of gold and power from the gods will halt that. Thus far my gold has lent me no wisdom or peace, nor will it. True, I possess some wisdom, but not from my riches. Peace—contentment—yea, these I have known . . . but they come to me here!"

A thickly muscled arm rises to show homage to Ilios looming above the Plain of Troia, beautiful in her colors of earth and massive in the last sunlight of the day.

"My contentment," says Agamemnon "lies here, in seeing the sun descend after a day well spent. Here we struggle to save our Helladic ways and please the gods—while we face disaster for the doing. No other actions can be so clearly right."

For a moment we stand in wonder at the truth in those words—for yes, we did come here, but also we were brought to this place thus to become part of us.

"On some days I myself reap contentment here," is all I can say.

*   *   *

CHAPTER 50

WORKING

For want of a better term, the "plot" of our pending television message would first entail me stepping out of a silver-gray hybrid car (rented by Paragon) wearing my midnight-blue pinstriped suit, a white Stetson, and nut-brown cowboy boots (the hat and boots having cost me plenty). Isaiah had recommended I finish my image with a white shirt and shiny-blue tie, so I did.

I would doff my hat, casually pitch it into the car through the open driver-side window, render my usual *namaste* to the camera, and turn to behold a gathering of a few dozen people seated at outdoor tables to whom I'd extend another *namaste*.

Right there, with no further movement or lapsed time, the camera would show me standing before a pine-studded, rocky embankment, where I would face outward to address families and groups of young people and distinctly senior people arrayed before me in a park setting. (Some of the groups of souls would be edited in digitally.) Upon my arrival they would all be picnicking and barbecuing and carrying on in the prescribed manner of the American middle class. The entire scene would appear immediate and real; movie techs could show me creating the Earth if they wanted.

My job: in twenty-two seconds articulate the major planks of the Conservative-Reform Party and say, "I want to be your President—to *get this done!*" Then I would add, "Conservative-Reform needs *you* to come forward!"

"So that's all I've got to do, huh?" I said to Isaiah.

"Well, not quite. Here's the text of your talk. See if you can improve the content, the coherence, and—especially—where to put emphasis. We'll run it by Trevor, then."

He handed me two sheets of printed lines, triple-spaced.

"Is that all?"

"Well, maybe not. Maya gave me this statement she'd like to hear woven into your talk. She wants to rebut that TV ad attacking you. It's libelous; it's really got her steamed. —But *without* rebutting it, y' know, not directly. See what you can do with this."

He handed me another sheet bearing the statement, "We must *stop allowing* components of the power industry to raid our state's water resources and degrade our beautiful environment." Handwritten a few spaces underneath this lay the directive: "Do NOT mention anything SAID in the attack ads. Don't acknowledge!"

"Well, I'll see what I can do," I said to Isaiah, and at the moment I resolved to tell the picnickers that Conservative Reform stood, foremost, for *protecting* this beautiful miseen-scene and all Earth's citizens. "We have to *conserve* what's good for everyone, starting with Mother Earth." I thought this sounded like a nifty start, and I told this to Isaiah.

"Okay, but be sure to time yourself," he said. "And *practice* your delivery! Remember, you're the star."

Just what I've always wanted, I thought, and I went home to recast my script, which should have been easy to do because in twenty-two seconds I couldn't say much.

*   *   *

Not quite correct. In the context of the script I had to sharply define the Party and our platform. Basically I tried to advocate immediate *collaboration* between government and free-market forces to utilize available technology to cut carbon emissions and develop renewable-energy resources. (The national goal of transitioning to a totally "green" economy seemed utterly reasonable to me. Might I have been misinformed? Or was I just weird?) Other main planks demanded smarter defense spending and implementing a plan for paying off the national debt ("under a reasonable formula we'd tackle later"). And terrorists must be rooted out like all criminals; they are *not* "warriors." I thought, sorry, we really have to deep-freeze "entitlements," veterans' benefits included, but I dare not say that (yet).

Somehow I had to simply leave out singular objectives that "Conservative Reform" would foster, such as flat income and business taxes and funding certain crucial initiatives. For sure America will have to establish a kind of "bank" to pay for building a new, safe electric-power grid (we actually need the bank to be operational right now), but on camera I wouldn't have time to even mention this. It occurred to me that I *might have* been willing to give up one of my favorite body parts if doing that would bring out the shovels sooner. I could think of even crazier things to say in public, none entirely facetious.

Obviously, writing this twisted my brain. During the course of an extended evening and night I consumed no less than four caplets of phosphatidyl serine (so-called "focus complex") to help me get it right. Reality, even mundane reality, poses hard problems for me.

* * *

My fun began the next week when I met Trent Glasscock, a lean, sunny-looking but wired young fellow who showed up in Carson with his assistant Josh and four "techs." Trent's crew and Isaiah and I got together in a vacant, drafty shop Maya provided (I hoped at no cost) off Main Street. Our intent I found hateful: rehearse enacting our "infomercial" script although it was yet to be finalized (pending input from Trevor, Trent, Maya and probably the gods).

This we did. And did. And did. And did. After a short coffee break, with Maya's help we drove to a waiting helicopter on the north edge of town and the film crew loaded themselves on while Isaiah and I told the pilot where to take them. The two of us drove the silver-gray Toyota Hybrid to the shooting location, about twenty minutes away in the Washoe Valley.

There a surprise met us: four or five earnest young strangers wanted to talk to us. These were press people alerted to the scene by Maya. (She must have thought publicity would be a good idea.) Were we planning to shoot our promotion piece today? No, we would shoot it tomorrow, a Saturday, right after lunch. (I had insisted on that last fact, or, I told Trent, I would not attend.) Today we would merely rehearse. The press were welcome to stay and watch if they wanted, I said (despite Trent's disapproval), if only because we were in a county park. Any attempts at security there would have been a joke.

The wind was a pain, the sun felt unseasonably hot. We worked out each "scene" meticulously. In the process we rehearsed, again and again and again. We had to get it right because this project was costing the Party dearly (surely more dearly than I was meant to know) and Paragon Agency's plan was to place videos of it not only on TV stations but also with college political organizations, even some libraries. A line of contact and donation information for my campaign would appear emblazoned on the end of the video and stamped on the plastic case.

Thank goodness Trent's crew had brought cans of chilled soda and bags of tortilla chips to the rehearsal. Before they packed up for the day they took a break under trees (newly flushing) next to the nineteenth-century mansion-turned-museum on the park grounds and invited Isaiah and me to join them, which we did, gratefully.

By then I thought everyone there, copter pilot included, knew my personality fairly well. After I took a few gulps of cola, perhaps the pall of silence that had dropped on this gathering made me feel that everyone expected me to say something singular—for them alone. Briefly I pondered this and found no reason to disappoint.

Abruptly I declared: "You all should know *The Secret of Life*—actually, the secret to living well—is to *look good.*" To a slight degree I believed this; keeping a poker face was easy for me.

I resumed: "That's really my specialty, I mean obviously. Given my age, though, looking good *at a distance* is what I do best."

I paused to make eye contact en masse, and everyone seemed to be anticipating something more, so I added: "You all probably know, I'm no more qualified to run for President of the United States than I am to run for county coyote-control officer, and I'm *not* qualified for *that.* All I've got to offer is brainpower and *cojones.* I admit it, so at least I'm not a fraud. [Beat.] I'll admit I wouldn't mind being a *successful fraud* if the pay were good enough."

Most of the gathering smiled upon me benevolently.

"That is all I have to say," I perorated. Immediately I thought that in my little dream on Earth at least I was exercising my nature. —By telling you this story, I might be doing that now.

As the film crew arose to strike what they called the set, Isaiah gave my shoulder a friendly tap. Here in the Washoe Valley beneath leafing trees under azure sky, all was good. Fifteen miles away, up in Reno, Julie awaited me at home. By following the subtle current that runs through my life, I had reached this destination, and it was right. Now I would be happy for you to say the same thing when you can.

CHAPTER 51

SETTING STAGES

That Friday evening at our home, Julie and I, with Jay and Petra (Jay's winsome beloved) contrived to mitigate the rigors we'd be facing the next day in the park. A movie shoot demands catered barbecue! Barbecued *what*? On such short order? We'll need ice chests for beer and soda. Et cetera. Et cetera.

Usually I avoided elective complications, but I had to go along with amenities that would help us produce a high-quality video that might (ultimately) affect many lives beneficially. Having good treats available to eat can actually buttress our effort to be idealistic and perform at our best. In the process we'll have enjoyed a little self-indulgence. My wisdom astounded even me.

When we finished working out details, seemingly on a whim I declared, "You always need faith in your personal design; after that, you'd better have an eye for consequences."

Somehow this fit right in the context of our doings, although I didn't know what prompted it. Maybe I said that for Jay's benefit. Later I was glad I had—maybe I still am.

First a slight blow that one can feel in a dream. Then another and another, becoming less slight. I rush to make fast Demon and Thunder, my lead horses, and for the moment my voice calms them.

Now, like the mightiest thunderbolt I had ever beheld at sea, the earth beneath us strikes everything. All the land shakes with power beyond any known to men. In my dread and surprise, a thought rises in me. I will know it to be true if I but live.

*

Amidst the ruin and rubble and screaming horses I still live. I hasten to grasp my weapons and shield. I find my helmet under my fallen tent and raise it on. Haste is necessary to make fortune of this moment, if the thought I had is true.

Soon we see the shaking earth has rent the north wall of Ilios; the wall still holds. Then we see what we hoped: part of the west wall fallen onto fortifications outside it. Some bulwarks and sturdy huts and sheds lay in ruins from which men and horses and other beasts struggle to rise as we approach. Their noises are pitiable; we give them no mind as we seek our first goal and find it:

The west gate of Troy is down. Soon they will raise it but it cannot be closed. Clans of Hittites with their Phrygian and Lydian allies mass to defend the opening; we know Trojan archers also wait atop the walls for our attack. By our speed and strength we mean to unsettle and awe Troy's allies. But now we hold back, and then we know to wait.

For we see our new Thracian brethren make quick entry to Troy. All are mounted—with Achaean riders among them but all wearing helmets and weapons from Thrace. Together they bring a line of pack horses and wagons of supplies for the royal Trojans and their helpers and households. They bring—from Mycenae—all manner of "supplies" Troy can never want.

This day Achaean action—inspired by Achaean cunning and gold—foretells the fate of Illios beginning deep in the night to come. Then the south gate of the city, upon sounding from a Mycenaean horn within, will welcome total strangers. Those will be massed archers of Sparta and the Argolid, and they will deploy their fearsome skills inside the walls of Illios. Happily for me, the role of my chariots must wait upon first daylight.

CHAPTER 52

CONSEQUENCES UNINTENDED

Ah, spring in the Truckee Meadows—on a Saturday at that. For a change, no wind to speak of, sky clear and deep azure. As Stone-Age men on bareback horses charging U.S. Army carbines might have said (and surely some did say)—a good day to die. But for me there was a job to do, and I had to do it well even though a detached, reasonable observer might have considered my enterprise a little absurd.

Basically my job was to deliver carefully scripted lines in front of cameras in a beautiful setting with a lot of people watching. Trent (and Jimmy, who was on the set) stressed that when I was on camera I had to project the relaxed personality of someone preternaturally confident and knowledgeable. This was the easiest part of my job, a fact that enhanced the absurdity.

Julie and I had arrived at the park about noon for a final run-through before shooting. Jay and Petra showed up, too, probably to ensure I stayed the course. (Actually they were there to help out.) Before we finished the rehearsal I saw Maya and Kip taking in the proceedings, looking pleased; also an attractive not-so-young woman I'd never seen before who appeared to be on good terms with Jay. As soon as he could, Jay introduced me to my "potential running-mate": Savannah Kim Whatever's-her name, and she and I finally met vis-à-vis. Isaiah and Trevor Butts were there of course, listening and looking anxious. The media had also showed up; they did their job with dispatch and left for more fruitful events, which was fine with us.

After the rehearsal, Julie and Jay and Petra and Savannah helped serve up the catered barbecue lunch to our film crew and Isaiah. They also invited our lead volunteers (who would have their hands full before long) to join in. I was too busy going over fine points with Trent and Josh and Isaiah to eat anything but a few tortilla chips and pickles, although I expected to get leftovers later. My deferring self-gratification turned out to be a notion dramatists would view as tragic irony, albeit low-level.

The actual shoot was scheduled for two o'clock although we hoped to start earlier. As the hour neared I noticed that a lot of people were arriving to watch, and I began to perceive something I thought strange: many onlookers, most of them men, carried long leather or canvas cases, as for rifles or fishing rods or ski poles. And they seemed to be placing themselves, even crowding, at points with an unobstructed line of vision to the spot where I'd be standing to address the folks picnicking.

One good-looking young fellow with thick black hair actually carried a viola case but caught my eye for another reason: he looked like a youthful version of Ira. He appeared to take pains to obscure himself from Maya's sight.

When I mentioned my surprise at the number of onlookers to Maya and Jay and Petra, someone sated my wonderment. In recent days I had been too busy to know that Maya and Jimmy had informed all the local media at least twice of our intention to shoot this ad. ("All these people here is totally cool!" Maya declared. "It's like a *folk gathering,* so good publicity.")

What we were poised to do, and where and when, had thus been common knowledge in the Truckee Meadows for about a week. Since Maya was usually right about things, I wasn't surprised to hear live clarinet-and-accordion music nearby enough for me to recognize a polka.

All of a sudden for a moment, for less than a moment, I heard strident notes of a totally different music—primitive, very foreign, familiar, ecstatically jubilant.

It passed too quickly for me to loosen even a twitch of smile. You might recall my saying, way back, that I never claimed to be especially well.

Our revelry cools quickly for we fought too long, too hard for joy to have strong hold on our psyches. Yes! Nostoi *will be ours when we make our sail. My first hope for all my seasons that follow is to live and work—and die—with no more need to be heroic. Merely to harbor this thought tastes of contentment.*

I see Agamemnon smile, thinly, as he and my fellow captains gaze over the plain to vanquished Troy—so worthy of disaster even with all her wealth and beauty. As if on signal we turn ourselves fully toward Mycenae, a three-day sail from here unless winds are good. For a little time we gaze in that direction, then wordlessly start to disband.

We have much work to cover before going to our ships. I am eager to set upon mine. But we stop to hear Agamemnon's voice tell us—in the same manner he uses to tally grain accounts or assess a spear point—"Soon we will learn of changes taking place in Hellas . . . in ways unwelcome to us." The tone changes when he adds, "I think, now, I almost wish not to leave here."

I ask, "What changes are those, sir?"

And he responds, "Changes that rise from within. Reports tell me pestilence strides upon our homeland as never before. It is every kind of false-heartedness—fueled by greed and fed by disregard—even hatred—for laws we value. Mycenae is not alone in this affliction. Hellenes now accept, even embrace, any treachery and all forms of greed—no matter the harm caused—as simply living true to our mean nature."

I hope he is wrong and I try to say so. My words I know carry thin comfort.

*　　*　　*

Just before we started filming (although cameras now are digital) Jay approached me and said, "Looks like things are pretty well under control, D."

He and Petra stood before me holding hands. Jay averred, "I've got to get Petra back. We've gotta *both* get back . . . or face The Law."

"The Law?"

"Of Unintended Consequences."

"Ah."

I wished they weren't leaving, and I would have liked to join them.

"Enjoy yourself with this, D. Don't do anything too outrageous," Jay added. I told him I'd try, and he and Petra went to gather up empty ice chests and say their good-bye to Julie.

A moment later, even as he finished wiping off his mouth and fingers, Trent Glasscock announced: "Let's get this road on the show, shall we!"

The crew of "techs" took up their positions; the "cast" overtly took up picnicking; Josh cleared onlooking kids from a wide swath of ground. Meanwhile I sauntered to the silver hybrid Isaiah had brought in to the setting and Julie removed herself to watch from a distance.

CHAPTER 53

ENTER THE TROJANS

Don't ask me how I know this. I just do. Take on faith as I tell you that—

Brett Blumenthal, lately without funds for Stanford, had started dating a taciturn, recently unattached anorectic-looking woman named Wren Topley, who had trouble keeping terrible secrets. Now a dutiful son, Brett had decided to reconcile with his disgraced father and intended to secretly make the first move, for which he had pawned his laptop and bought a shotgun.

An immigrants'-rights activist in the throes of premenstrual syndrome and effects of an overactive thyroid, Benita Juarez was smitten by Frankie Lopez and thoroughly vexed by her erroneous perception that I had failed to help out his kin.

Now, she had determined, was a good time to demonstrate her concern—and her marksmanship.

Three very patriotic VFW members had been reading my blogs and ascertained that I was anti-Pentagon, anti-unlimited Department of Defense spending, and therefore a certifiable enemy of the United States of America. They had chosen now to fight back.

Feeling pangs of guilt for liking George Clooney's and Bill Clinton's looks, declared-homophobe Maxwell Gaunt had learned of my association with Jimmy Kestrel, long considered a scourge of wholesome America. A lover of firearms, Max thought to redeem himself by showing Jimmy a bit of reality using a congenial method.

These people planned to act autonomously, without benefit of community or solidarity. Quite a few other people at the park were there for the same purpose as the parties just noted. But the others were members of a confederation, enjoying the strength inherent in a united front. A "front" united about what? That would be the desire to put someone away . . . forever. And guess who that was.

Not that I was perceived as dangerous. But what I *said* (or would say), they felt, was too hateful to abide. They didn't exactly *think* this. Thought plays no major role in their part of this event, except in determining the right ammo for the job and the best getaway route.

I would never have surmised that a fugitive Basque ETA member, or a Chechnyan jihadi (also a fugitive), or a militant

Irish Unionist (deeply Catholic), or a sharp-shooting Serbian nationalist might be living in northern Nevada and would read my pejorative remarks reported some time before in *The Reno Chronicle*, but they were and they did. And, yes, they were in the park with me on this fine Saturday afternoon.

As fortune would have it (and fortune *will* have it), the jihadi had recently hooked up with a Black-Muslim Al-Qaeda wannabe who was offended by me *and* the Party because somewhere I'd said publicly that Muslims shouldn't kill each other; moreover no Conservative-Reform Party officer was black. Both these outliers had come to the park accompanied by a new buddy of theirs from Austin (Nevada), who happened to be an oversexed Primitive Baptist outraged by knowing that *this* trouble-making pagan was married to an accomplished, attractive woman and therefore *deserved* termination ASAP.

Granted, today no employee or officer or shareholder of any "big oil" company lurked anywhere near this scene of intensifying activity, even though on numerous occasions I had publicly indicted oil corporations for all sorts of malfeasance, and their people were alert to criticism and sensitive to adverse facts. But a pair of their "contractors" observed me now with great interest. These fellows were double-dipping by collaterally working for an unnamed mega-corporation based in Texas that was also sensitive (and alert) to factual public charges.

Somehow this lot had become allied with, were actually *in league* with—

a merry trio of vacationing Mideast jihadis that had partnered with a band of their spiritual brothers from the American

"Evangelical Right," all of whom must have thought I was anti-God, or worse;

some highly disgruntled truckers, two highly disgruntled airline employees, and three commercial sailors, likewise highly disgruntled by anti-carbon, anti-petroleum rhetoric;

girlfriends and wives of those disgruntled workers, all of whom didn't have enough to do on this beautiful Saturday so they were merely along;

a soldierly Libertarian who had determined that the best use of this weekend would be getting in target practice with a practical application;

and watching me keenly were a militant land-use rightist, a deranged environmentalist (also militant), and an angry vigilante from the U.S.-Mexico borderland.

Even among over seven billion people on Earth, is such a league of potential miscreants remotely possible? Of course it is. Those advanced products of evolution and redemption I've denoted had not only focused their wrath, they had coalesced their desires into a single goal. And they (and many of the wives and girlfriends) were armed for action and strategically deployed. Remarkably, every one of them turned out to be a poor shot. Happily, only one of them packed an AR-15. That was the guy who'd soon take off the top of a short tree nearby.

GRACE

Waiting patiently, Trent and his crew—along with that gang I have named—watched me get into the car and drive it to a marked spot where I stopped, put it in "park," and slid out to salute all humanity through the eye of the camera. I doffed my hat and pitched it into the open car window. Turf felt good under foot as I took a step and beheld happy souls arrayed before me. I tendered my customary *namaste*, took another step, and was startled to hear a loud, dreadful word:

"Cut!"

Everything stopped. Trent stepped into camera cynosure, his head shaking.

"That won't do it, Dan. You give 'em your little number *after* you reach the spot where you stop and address the folks. Try it again. [Beat.] We'll take it from the top; I don't like the way you walked. You gotta stride."

I said, "Of course" and got into the car, backed it up forty yards, then drove to the marked spot to begin the drill. Turf felt good under foot when I slid out of the vehicle . . . and somehow managed to knock my hat off. I tried to snatch it but it fell to the ground.

"Cut!"

"Yeah, yeah, yeah."

Back into the car, I put it in reverse for maybe thirty yards, then took it forward to the spot and slid out to salute all human beings in the world. Lovingly I took in the scene before me, lifted off my hat, and pitched it into the car. Damned if I didn't miss putting it through the open window. Ackh! It hit metal framing behind the door and dropped onto gravel and started flopping away. With total absence of dignity I bent and scrambled to retrieve it.

"*Cut*, goddammit."

I dusted off my hat and Trent called for a conference with me and the techs. Josh was dispatched to assuage the cast and keep the locus clear of kids. Trent and his crew briefly discussed the opening scene and reached a consensus that suddenly struck them as self-evident. They would modify the angle of my approach after I stepped from the car. First we should do a quick run-through to enable them to adjust equipment.

Fine. This we did. The techs went to work. Then they asked Trent to do another run-through, which we did. Before I got back into the car I heard one of the camera men and the sound person (Bubba and Missy, siblings from East Texas) suggest that Josh reposition a few "cast members" to lend better perspective.

Things like this didn't happen during rehearsals! I felt distinctly glad Jay had left. While they finalized procedures (once again), I thought myself wise to pay attention to Julie so she wouldn't think I was taking this affair too seriously—which I wasn't. And that would soon result in another act of "tragic irony."

When I strode to where Julie stood, I saw that she was regarding me attentively. As I fixed on her dear face and form, I was seized, so to speak, by true inspiration. (Very fortunately for me, during my lifetime I had been the recipient of *many* such seizures. I'd never regretted acting on them, and so I would act now.) I stood next to Julie, shoulder touching shoulder; I took her hand and revealed what I felt.

I said: "Being with you is the most precious gift I could ever imagine. I can't imagine *anything* remotely close to this."

She responded as I knew she would, and I was utterly grateful for having been moved to say what I had said. To affirm that I'm "grateful" *now* would be epical understatement.

CHAPTER 54

NOSTOI

Trent Glasscock announced: "Let the magic begin!" And again we performed the drill, and again—well past mid-point—we heard the dreaded word: "Cut!"

But this time it was because of some kids acting stupid on camera. Otherwise the "take" had gone smoothly. A firm feeling arose in me: our next take would be perfect. I fully expected that Trent would call it "a wrap."

Indeed, as we played our scenario again I felt some pride in performing the first segment precisely and with pleasure. My manner was supposed to appear relaxed, and it actually was. Still enjoying that feel of turf under my feet, I had strode to the spot before a wooded embankment that was my backdrop for addressing the picnickers and—just as I opened my mouth to speak, before I got a word out—I heard loud, untoward popping noises, like strings of different-sized firecrackers going off at the same time but intermingled with *thuds* and really hard pops. Instantaneously a little gray bird on the ground in front of me appeared to explode as a soda can flew and tree branches fell.

And, yes, take this also on faith: I realized that those advanced products of evolution and redemption that I had revealed a little ways back (the entire gang) were shooting *at me*. Bullets snapped, whistled. And I knew they had all missed. I almost featured me saluting them with the back of my middle finger.

In that same instant a ricocheted bullet tore right through me. It spun me around and dropped me like a duffel of laundry. At first I knew what had happened and where I was (next to a graveled path). Then I went blank, maybe for only a short time. I came conscious from pain as someone tried to stanch the bleeding. Again all memory vanished.

*

I look into shimmering faces of medical personnel—earnest young men and women hovering over me. Soon I learn that the bullet had ripped through my spleen and other vital parts. One of the technicians reports this into a radio. Part of my gut hurts like an ice pick is passing though it but only when I am moved. Does time pass? I overhear the technician's voice, "Blood loss critical." They place me face down, a position I hate.

Pain recedes, my mind roves. It causes me to see the black-ink etching of Don Quixote on the cover of a book I owned when I was a boy. *Ah,* of course. But my running for President and striving to advance our reform cause was *necessary*. This I am happy to know. New faces swim before me: Jay and Maya and Jimmy and Pancho, many others; they can be mostly proud of my efforts.

Yet I wish I had not taken myself seriously. I wish Jay and Harry were beside me now. I would give anything to be at my desk back in Party headquarters. Other wishes recur like mercury: that I hadn't made stupid mistakes in the campaign, and that everyone who is motivated by fanaticism or fear or greed would instead have a complete life . . . .

Julie is miraculously with me. I felt her take my hand; now she holds it between hers, an act that always puts me in satori. For this I thank the *Source* of all being, the presence of which I begin to perceive everywhere about me.

I try to ask Julie to smile. I want to see her face. But nothing works right.

Agamemnon regards me intently and I know he means to speak. We have just raised off our helmets. In the hard light by the sea I think my face glistens like his, our hair matted, damp.

"We are of the gods," he declares. "You yourself say this; remember? You have lived—and done—as they design you. Now you need only thankfulness—to all the cosmos—for your days well given."

I nod for his benefit. Agreement with him is not required; this much we understand. Yet I say, "True. I have faith in my design. Thus in my destiny."

"You do accept such a gift?" he says, drawing me out.

"With gratitude unreserved," I respond. Thus I thank the cosmos for my life.

His turn to nod. He says heartily: "That is such great comfort—faith in simple truth! All other faith is senseless; it goes the way of smoke."

"Other faith is *meant to be* senseless." Now, somehow, I know this is true.

Julie says something to soothe me. I can only respond tersely. Then I hear myself say: "My desire also is sure. I wish us to be home in Golden Mycenae."

Words that are not Julie's reach me: "Ah! Our heads held high, our backs erect. As would Apollo declare the will of Zeus."

Yes. Hearing this heartens me and I think to say so.

From a small rise of earth I cradle my gorgeous helmet as I gaze a final time at the remains of Troy and ponder why such a state—late of great wealth and beauty—would harbor boundless greed and willingness to cause harm. I ponder as well those same curses arising in Golden Mycenae, my true home for all time. And I know that cannot be possible.

Then I am gone.

Join with me when you can.

O, GOLDEN MYCENAE

lighting my days into
even these silver ages
sweet sweet powerful living
each day new cause for
lifting all our psyches
above beloved Argos
to gaze from Mount Elias with
fondness beyond our language

O, Golden Mycenae
will me back to holy soil
if only for this moment